Also by Karin Gillespie

Bet Your Bottom Dollar:
A Bottom Dollar Girls Novel

A Dollar Short

THE BOTTOM DOLLAR GIRLS GO HOLLYWOOD

KARIN GILLESPIE

Simon & Schuster

New York   London   Toronto   Sydney

SIMON & SCHUSTER
Rockefeller Center
1230 Avenue of the Americas
New York, NY 10020

SIMON & SCHUSTER and colophon are registereåd trademarks
of Simon & Schuster, Inc.

For information regarding special discounts for bulk purchases,
please contact Simon & Schuster Special Sales at 1-800-456-6798
or business@simonandschuster.com

Designed by Jeanette Olender
Manufactured in the United States of America

10 9 8 7 6 5 4 3 2 1

Library of Congress Cataloging-in-Publication Data
Gillespie, Karin.
A dollar short : a bottom dollar girls novel / Karin Gillespie.
p. cm.
1. Married women—Fiction.   2. Motion picture actors and actresses—Fiction.
3. Women sales personnel—Fiction.   4. Department stores—Fiction.
5. Female friendship—Fiction.   6. Runaway husbands—Fiction.
7. South Carolina—Fiction.
I. Title.
PS3607.I438D65   2005   813'.6—dc22   2004058629

ISBN-13: 978-0-7432-5011-5
ISBN-10:   0-7432-5011-7

To my dear friend and encourager

Nancy Clements

A Dollar Short

Menstruation, menopause, mental breakdown. Ever notice how all women's problems begin with men?

Comment overheard under the hair dryers at Dazzling Do's

CHAPTER ONE

It isn't every day a movie star steals your husband. Chiffon Butrell certainly wasn't expecting such a major upheaval in her life on that nippy Tuesday in January. Instead, she was grappling with more trivial aggravations, such as hunting down a pencil for her eight-year-old daughter, Emily.

Her oldest child stood near the front door, fully dressed, her light brown hair gathered up into a neat ponytail. Wearing a mask of quiet stoicism, she kept glancing at her Hello Kitty wristwatch.

Chiffon, her blond hair snarled into rats from sleep, rummaged through the junk drawer of a battered desk. "You'd think that somewhere in all this mess there'd be one lousy . . . Ick!" She snatched back her hand as it touched something sticky.

With her thumb and index finger, she picked up the offending object, a Hulk action figure, covered head to toe with peanut butter.

"Dewitt, what *is* this?" she asked her five-year-old son, who was slicing the air with a series of karate chops.

"It's a spearmint," he said, continuing to deliver blows to an invisible assailant.

"What?" Chiffon said, bewildered.

"An experiment," Emily said matter-of-factly. She was a frequent translator for her younger brother. "He likes watching *Bill Nye, the Science Guy.* We'd better go. The bus will be here any minute."

"I just can't believe— Wait a second." Chiffon picked up her pocketbook from the floor and scrabbled inside. "Aha!" she said, handing Emily a pencil she'd fished from the bottom. "Here we go, baby."

Her daughter examined it with large gray eyes. "Mama, this is an eyeliner pencil."

"It won't do in a pinch?"

"I'm taking a standardized test today. I need two sharpened No. 2 pencils."

Chiffon vaguely remembered signing an official-looking letter from Emily's school about an upcoming test. And Emily, being a responsible child, had almost certainly mentioned that her pencil supply was running low. Unfortunately, Chiffon had completely forgotten about both.

"Don't worry, Mama," Emily said in an even voice. "My teacher will probably have some spare pencils. Come on, Dewitt, let's go."

Emily opened the front door, letting in a gust of frigid air. Chiffon shivered and gripped together the lapels of her skimpy leopard-print robe. The local morning TV show had said it was 28 degrees outside, uncommonly chilly for Cayboo Creek, South Carolina, even in winter.

"Stay warm!" Chiffon hollered after the pair. They waved at her with bare hands already pink from the cold as they crossed the frozen lawn, which looked like it was covered with a layer of powdered sugar.

"Shoot," Chiffon said to herself as she sprinted barefoot across the freezing wooden floor. "I should've made them wear mittens." Trouble was, when she'd looked earlier, she hadn't been able to find a pair anywhere in the house. Yesterday there'd been a light snow, and the kids had had to wear their daddy's athletic socks on their hands to make snowballs.

"Gotta go to Goodies and get some mittens," she said to herself, adding to a mental list of errands she needed to accomplish today. Tuesday was her day off from her waitress job at the Wagon Wheel steak restaurant.

Gabby, her six-month-old daughter, who up until now had been amusing herself with a plastic spoon, screwed up her face and let out a cranky cry.

"Hey, kiddo," Chiffon said, scooping up the baby from her walker. "Yeesh. Your diaper's sopping."

On her way to the nursery from the living room, she banged her hip against the corner of her husband Lonnie's pool table. "Dang it," she said with a grimace, knowing a vivid yellow-blue bruise would soon blossom there. She didn't know how many women would put up with a deluxe-size pool table smack dab in their living room, but she guessed the number was few.

She changed Gabby's diaper and outfitted her in flannel footie pajamas and a knit stocking cap. Then she dressed herself in a black turtleneck, jeans, and a fleece-lined denim jacket. Taking it from the hook by the door, she clapped Lonnie's plaid, ear-flapped hunting hat over her head. Before she started her day, she wanted hot coffee, along with a dose of chitchat, and she knew exactly where to get it.

With the baby in her arms, Chiffon slammed the front door behind her and made her way to her elderly Pontiac Firebird parked in the drive. As she strapped Gabby into her car seat, she noticed her eyes looked as glassy as blue marbles. Her daughter's vacant look and the fine thread of drool on her lips meant she was moments from naptime.

Chiffon cranked the car's engine, which wheezed in protest, and backed out of her gravel driveway lined with halved tires, wedged in the ground and painted white. Her purple one-story house stuck out in the neighborhood like a peacock in a flock of wrens. Its garish color and its location, directly in front of an ABC Package Shop, were the reasons she and Lonnie had been able to afford it.

She traveled down Main Street, watching red-cheeked passersby struggle against the sting of the icy wind. Unlike many boarded-up and abandoned small Southern towns, downtown Cayboo Creek bustled with a collection of thriving businesses. Boomer from the butcher shop stood on a stepladder taking down the letters from his outdated portable sign that read JANUARY IS HEAD CHEESE MONTH. Reeky Flynn, bundled up in a bulky ski jacket and wool mittens, fumbled with her keys to open the Book Nook. When she passed the storefront for Dazzling Do's, Chiffon touched a hand to her unruly blond curls. She was way overdue for a cut.

Parking outside the Bottom Dollar Emporium, she slung her sleeping daughter over her shoulder and strode toward the entrance. The pansies out front, potted in gleaming copper washtubs, had wilted faces, stunned by the polar temperatures. The row of white rocking chairs on the porch, often occupied by the town elders in balmier weather, creaked in the bracing breeze.

Chiffon pushed opened the door and immediately heard the querulous voice of Attalee Gaines, the soda jerk, coming from the soda fountain in back.

"What a lot of twaddle!" Attalee said. Chiffon guessed she was addressing the owner of the Bottom Dollar Emporium, Mavis Loomis.

Chiffon threaded past several wooden barrels, heaped high with bulk candy from another age. Every time her children came into the Bottom Dollar Emporium, their eyes glazed over as they tried to take in the vast hodgepodge of sweets. Voluptuous wax lips brushed up against Teaberry gum and lengths of licorice pipes. Burlap bags bulging with Gold Nugget bubblegum were nestled among Charleston Chews, Chick-O-Sticks, and a tangle of Slo Pokes.

If the barrels of treats failed to tempt customers, the line of glass jars crammed with Swedish red fish, anise squares, and peppermint sticks would definitely set mouths to watering.

Chiffon gazed greedily at a jar packed tight with gummy bears, imagining them beating their fruit-flavored fists against the glass, pleading, "Let me out!"

With a swift motion, Chiffon shook a menagerie of bears into the metal scoop of the candy scale, poured her purchase into a small white paper bag, and scribbled the amount on a chit sheet, which she stuck by the register.

Weaving her way to the back of the store, she paused at a display of sourwood honey jars and courtin' candles (used long ago by fathers to let their daughters' beaus know when their dates were over). The Bottom Dollar Emporium was chockablock with all manner of items from a bygone era. Button-flap union suits, pine-tar soap, and galvanized watering cans could all be found among the cluttered aisles of the store.

Stiff floorboards groaned beneath her feet as Chiffon headed toward the rich fragrance of roasted coffee beans, which curled from the break area to her eager nostrils. She parked her gum in an old brass spittoon attached to the wall and poured steaming coffee into a heavy chipped mug with her name on it. The toasty cup warmed her hands, which were raw from the cold. She saw Mavis and Attalee fussing over some kind of contraption lying on the soda fountain.

"What have you got there?" she asked the two women as she settled the baby into her carrier.

"A Diaper Houdini," Attalee said, pointing a yellowed fingernail at the box on the fountain. She wore her soda-jerk uniform, and her crisp white cap sat on her head at a crooked angle.

"Diaper Genie," Mavis corrected.

Attalee brushed a gray sausage curl from her wrinkled face

with the back of her hand. She was well into her eighties but still sported the fussy hairdo of a seven-year-old girl.

"Heck," she said in a voice like sandpaper over wood. "A real Diaper Genie would change the young 'un *and* wipe its bottom."

Mavis scratched her head in bewilderment. She was a plump woman with short, wiry salt-and-pepper hair and bemused brown eyes.

"As it is, we're not real sure what it does," Mavis said.

"That must be your baby-shower gift for Elizabeth," Chiffon said. Elizabeth used to be a clerk at the Bottom Dollar Emporium, and she and Chiffon had gotten to be best chums over the years.

Chiffon picked up the Diaper Genie box. "These things are all the rage. You can stuff about thirty diapers inside, and the Diaper Genie will twist them up into a cone with no stinky smell."

"That's all?" Attalee said, looking dispirited, as if she'd expected something more miraculous.

"Don't worry. Elizabeth will love it."

As Chiffon dropped into a heart-backed chair and propped her elbows on a small table, her eyes fell on the baby-word scramble Attalee had been working on as a part of the shower games.

"'Drool,' 'spit-up,' 'colic,' and 'stinky,'" Chiffon said, picking up the paper from the table and reading from it. "Shoot, Attalee. Couldn't you come up with some sweeter baby words for the scramble? You'll put a scare into Elizabeth."

Attalee straightened her cap in the mirror behind the soda

fountain. "Raising young 'uns is dirty work. Don't see no need to prettify it."

Chiffon nibbled on her thumbnail, trying to come up with some nicer baby words to add to Attalee's list. But with an infant in the house, the first thing that came to mind was the mounting pile of spit-up rags she'd gone through while Gabby fought off a bug. Attalee was right; there was nothing glamorous about raising kids. And with Lonnie gone for the last few days, it'd been doubly hard.

"When's your man going to quit hobnobbing with movie stars and get on back to Cayboo Creek?" Attalee asked, as if she'd been reading Chiffon's mind.

"His plane leaves California Sunday morning," Chiffon said.

A few months ago Chiffon had entered the Be-a-Movie-Star contest at Showtime Video Store. She'd long forgotten her impulsive entry when a company representative called and said she was the grand-prize winner of two round-trip tickets to Los Angeles and the opportunity to appear as an extra in a movie starring Janie-Lynn Lauren.

Lonnie and Chiffon had squealed like a couple of game-show contestants when they'd found out the news. He ran to the liquor store and picked up a box of Almaden white zinfandel, and they toasted each other with plastic cups. Chiffon tossed out her dinner of charred Tuna Helper—burnt in her excitement over the news—and Lonnie took the whole family out for chicken-fried-steak night at the Chat 'N' Chew.

Chiffon, who'd spent most of her thirty-six years in Cayboo Creek, was going to Hollywood! She'd get to visit a real movie set and maybe even meet America's most famous female movie star, Janie-Lynn Lauren.

Two weeks before their trip, she'd made arrangements for the kids to stay with Mavis and had driven across the Savannah River to the Kmart in Augusta, Georgia, and bought a brand-new coordinating outfit from the Kathy Ireland line.

Two packed suitcases had stood by the front door, ready to go, a full week before their departure date. Chiffon fretted over the contents of her bags for three days, packing and repacking, hating the look of her frayed panties and scuffed shoes—wishing she had the cash to buy all new things. Lonnie pitched a fit over her Kmart purchase, saying it was criminal to spend sixty-two dollars for just one outfit. He was used to Chiffon digging out dollar-fifty slacks and shirts from the bins at the Methodist Church thrift shop, and didn't have a clue about the high cost of clothes.

Two days before they were set to leave, her best friend, Elizabeth, dropped by the house with a pink-and-white-striped Victoria's Secret box and a playful grin on her face.

"I figured this trip could be a second honeymoon for you and Lonnie," she said with a wink as Chiffon unearthed a wispy white nightie from the layers of scented tissue.

Chiffon appreciated her friend's gesture, although she couldn't imagine wearing such a virginal-looking nightie to bed without Lonnie laughing her right out of the room. When it came to lingerie, Chiffon's tastes tended toward animal prints, peekaboo cutouts, or fire-engine red panty-and-bra sets.

Besides, she and Lonnie had never needed any extra help in the bedroom. That area of their marriage was rock solid, even after three kids, a near bankruptcy, and her ten-pound—okay, maybe it was more like twenty-pound—weight gain since their wedding day ten years ago. Chiffon looked forward to having her husband all to herself in a hotel room without any interruptions from kids.

Unfortunately, on the night before they were to leave, Gabby woke at two in the morning, squalling. Chiffon knew immediately that her baby's cry sounded peculiar, and sure enough, when she reached into the crib, her daughter's forehead was hot as blue blazes.

Chiffon rummaged in the medicine cabinet for the baby thermometer and took Gabby's temperature. When the thermometer registered 104 degrees, she shrieked loud enough to startle Lonnie out of bed.

Long story short, the next morning Chiffon did not get on the plane to California in her Kathy Ireland sherbet top with matching flower-print capri pants. Instead, she spent the better part of her day in a grungy sweatsuit, slumped in a hard plastic chair on the pediatric floor, waiting for the doctors to tell her what was wrong with her baby.

Despite Gabby's illness, Chiffon insisted that Lonnie fly to California without her.

"Babies are all the time getting high fevers. Most times it's nothing," she said to Lonnie, fighting back tears of disappointment. "No sense in both of us missing out."

Lonnie hemmed and hawed for about ten seconds, and then grabbed the tickets from Chiffon's purse, saying, "Okay, darling. If that's the way you want it."

By the time Chiffon imagined her husband on the plane, tearing open his foil bag of peanuts and leaning back in his seat to watch the in-flight movie, Gabby's fever had broken. The doctor couldn't find anything wrong, and Chiffon's one-and-only opportunity to see Hollywood had gone straight down the drain.

"Lonnie's living it up," Chiffon said as she popped a red gummy bear into her mouth. "He's already visited Knott's Berry Farm and the Gene Autry Museum. He got to see the Colt firearm display and ate lunch at the Golden Spur restaurant."

"Has he rubbed elbows with any movie stars?" Attalee asked eagerly.

"He'll be an extra on the Janie-Lynn Lauren movie for the next few days; no telling who he might run into," Chiffon said. "But I've read that extras aren't supposed to fraternize with the movie stars. Once an extra got fired on the spot just for eye-balling Sylvester Stallone."

"I bet you wish you were with him," mused Mavis.

"I don't know. I hear California has some god-awful smog," Chiffon replied.

Since Lonnie had left, she'd been trying to conceal her disappointment over missing out on the Hollywood trip. Who cared about palm trees and a bunch of plastic movie stars? And did it really matter that she'd been on only one lousy vacation in her entire life? She and Lonnie had driven to Gatlinburg, Tennessee, for their honeymoon. Once there, she'd seen only the inside of their mountain cabin with the heart-shaped Jacuzzi and knotty-pine walls, completely missing out on some of the area's most famous attractions, like Ripley's Believe It or Not! and Hillbilly Golf.

Chiffon bit into her quivering lower lip. "Lonnie's promised to take lots of pictures and bring home a bunch of those tiny bottles of shampoo and hand lotion from the hotel," she said with a brave smile. "And yesterday Dewitt lost his first baby tooth. If I'd been in California, I would have missed out on being the tooth fairy."

The bell over the front door jingled, and Birdie Murdock marched in carrying an armful of baby bottles.

"I thought we could fill these with Jordan almonds," Birdie said, wearing a pair of navy pumps that reverberated on the floor planks. "They'll make delightful party favors."

"That'll be cute," Mavis said, relieving her of some of the bottles. She glanced at Birdie's navy-and-white-checked suit and saw a red press ribbon pinned to the lapel. Birdie was publisher and reporter for the *Cayboo Creek Crier.*

"Looks like you've just come from covering a story," Mavis said. "Anything interesting going on in town?"

"The principal of Cayboo Creek Elementary had to climb up on the roof of the school because her students read over four hundred books in one month," Birdie said.

"Brrrr," Chiffon said with a mock shiver. "It must have been like the North Pole up there."

"Indeed it was. I'm completely windblown from taking her photograph," Birdie said, removing her basin hat with the matching checked ribbon around the rim and smoothing her silver coiffure. "There was some real concern for the roof shingles. Esther Holmes is a woman of considerable girth."

"Plus, she's fat as a suckling pig," Attalee remarked.

Birdie ignored Attalee's comment and sat across from Chiffon. "I was reminded of your sister, Chenille. When she was in the fourth grade, she held the record for most books read in a month by a single student. What a studious child she was! Have you spoken with her lately?"

"It's been a while. Chenille keeps busy with her teaching job in Bible Grove," Chiffon said, refilling her coffee cup. "But she'll come home for the occasional holiday."

"I haven't seen her in years," Birdie said. "Isn't Bible Grove only about two hours away?"

Chiffon smiled thinly. Truth was, her sister, Chenille, was a weird bird. She wore prissy blouses buttoned to her chin and shoes with large buckles or bows. And she continuously fussed over that little dog of hers, dressing him up in outfits that matched her own, brushing his teeth with a miniature toothbrush. It just wasn't natural.

The sisters hadn't been close as children (Chenille with her nose in a book; Chiffon out and about with a tribe of friends), and they were even more distant as adults.

Chiffon glanced at a clock on the wall. *Where'd the morning go?*

"I better be on my way," she said, picking up the carrier in which her daughter dozed. "See you all tonight?"

The ladies had promised to help Chiffon prepare for Elizabeth's shower tomorrow. She'd agreed to host the party, since she wasn't going to be in California.

"We'll be there," Mavis said, with a good-bye wave.

. . .

That evening Birdie stood on a kitchen stool, hanging pink and blue streamers from the living room ceiling. Chiffon filled baby bottles with pastel almonds from a large plastic bag, while Attalee and Mavis sat across from her at the kitchen table, putting the finishing touches on corsages fashioned from paci-fiers.

As usual, Chiffon had to pee, but she wanted to fill one last bottle before she went to the bathroom. Ever since she'd given birth to Gabby, her bladder had been all out of whack. Now drinking a half a can of Diet Pepsi would make her fidget in her seat. As she crossed one leg over the other to delay nature for a spell, Attalee looked up from her work and snapped her fingers.

"I plumb forgot. I saw a commercial today for that TV show, *Hollywood Hijinks*. They said Janie-Lynn Lauren was going to be on tonight."

"Really?" Chiffon said. "What time does it start?"

"Seven o'clock," Attalee said.

Birdie climbed down from the stool and glanced at her wristwatch. "It's a minute till right now."

Chiffon picked up the remote from the lamp table and aimed it at the television. "Let's take a break for a minute," she said. "Maybe she'll talk about her new movie."

The women abandoned their projects and gathered around the television.

"Up next, a *Hollywood Hijinks* first," announced Godiva Jones, the host, wearing a slinky silver dress and diamond chan-delier earrings. "Superstar Janie-Lynn Lauren snuggles with a mystery man outside an L.A. watering hole. *Hollywood Hijinks* has exclusive footage of the torrid twosome."

"That Janie-Lynn is skin and bones," Birdie tsked as the show went to a commercial. "Why, a good strong squall could carry her away."

"I read she takes three bites of her food at meals and then

dumps salt all over it so she won't eat any more," Chiffon said.

"She's thin as a cake of lye soap after a week's washing," At-talee said. Her trick eye jumped behind the lens of her glasses. "A woman needs some meat on her frame."

Chiffon patted her middle, which was still plenty fleshy after the baby's birth. Her mother had given her a Belly Buster for her birthday last month, but the gadget hadn't shrunk her tummy one whit.

"Onlookers gawked when Janie-Lynn Lauren fraternized with a new fellow at Joseph's, an L.A. nightspot," Godiva chirped after the break. "But the cozy couple only had eyes for each other. Rumor has it that Lauren's latest lad is an extra on the set of her new movie, *The Mail Order Bride*."

Chiffon's stomach twisted at the word "extra," and she scooted to the edge of her chair.

The footage of Janie-Lynn Lauren and her new boyfriend was dark and grainy. All Chiffon could discern was a shadowy, masculine figure smooching with the actress. Then, as the camera panned in for a tighter shot, she made out a familiar profile. A pair of copper-colored eyes sprang open, and her husband, Lonnie, stared directly into the camera, a hangdog look on his face.

Time stood still as Chiffon gaped at the TV from her spot on the La-Z-Boy. Then a wet warmth, spreading from her bottom to the back of her thighs, jolted her out of her daze. It took a couple of seconds to realize she'd peed her britches.

It takes forty-six muscles to
smile, but only four to flip
someone the bird.

Graffiti in the men's room at the Tuff Luck Tavern

CHAPTER TWO

At 10:10 the next morning, Chiffon pushed sixty in the Firebird. She was late to work, and her car rattled as she swerved off Mule Pen Road and lurched into the parking lot of the Wagon Wheel. When she hit the brakes, she patted her passenger seat, looking for the button she was supposed to pin on her uniform that said, "Howdy Pardner! Would You Like to Try a Piece of Pecan Pie?" but couldn't find it. Leaning across the front seat, Chiffon shoved aside a stack of SpongeBob SquarePants coloring books and a tangle of Betty Spaghetty dolls in the back, hoping to unearth the foolish-looking button.

Two weeks ago, the owners of the Wagon Wheel had hired a

new manager named Wilbur Peets. Ever since he'd arrived, he'd made it his business to fuss at Chiffon for every piddling thing. Yesterday he'd blessed her out because she didn't suggestive-sell Hank Bryson on the Wagon Wheel's new Flowering Onion appetizer.

She'd tried to explain to Wilbur that, number one, Hank had been coming in the Wagon Wheel for going on ten years and always ordered the same dish: the Cowpoke chopped steak combo with a pineapple ring on the side. And number two, she happened to know that Hank had been keeping a close eye on his cholesterol count ever since he had a shunt put in his artery two years ago. The Flowering Onion crawled with fat and cholesterol, and to Chiffon, offering it to Hank would be like slipping a pack of Marlboros to a middle-school student.

"You're a waitress, not a doctor," Wilbur said, rolling his eyes. He enjoyed putting her in her place, unlike Roy, her former manager, who called Chiffon his "secret weapon" and claimed that losing her would be worse for business than a mad-cow scare.

But a month ago Roy was offered a job managing three Applebees over in Augusta, and the Wagon Wheel owners brought in Wilbur with his hotsy-totsy degree in hospitality from Georgia State University and his uppity attitude.

Chiffon gave up on looking for her button and slammed the car door shut. She stormed across the parking lot, fuming.

If Wilbur says anything to me, just one darn thing. She simply couldn't handle it. Not after seeing the stunned faces of her friends as they feebly tried to convince her that maybe they'd seen someone who just looked like Lonnie with Janie-Lynn Lauren. Not after staying up all night dialing and redialing

Lonnie's hotel room until her finger throbbed, only to hear the drone of the phone ringing in her ear. Not after eating all the sweets in the house, which included a pint of freezer-burnt Neapolitan ice cream, a bag of semisweet chocolate chips, two capfuls of cherry cough syrup, and a thick layer of pecan dust at the bottom of an empty bag of Sandie Swirl cookies. Then waking up in the morning with her face plastered to the pillow, feeling like a stewed witch. Finally, the ultimate humiliation, finding a package of Depends on her doorstep as she left for work this morning. Attached was a note from Attalee.

"From one gal with a bad bladder to another. This is our little secret."

Chiffon barreled though the door of the Wagon Wheel. Her platinum-blond hair sprang out from her hair net in frantic corkscrews (the wearing of the hated headwear was another one of Wilbur's dopey new policies), and her chin jutted from her face like a half-cocked shotgun.

Just let him say one single solitary thing. I'll tell him what's what.

She spotted Wilbur standing by the cash register, clipboard in hand. As soon as he noticed her, he tapped his wristwatch and frowned. Then his gaze scanned her from head to toe, searching for something out of place. It alighted on the empty space on her blouse where her button was supposed to be.

His lips, thin and colorless as rubber bands, twitched with displeasure.

"Mrs. Butrell, not only are you ten minutes late, but you're also out of uniform." He scribbled on his clipboard. "I'm documenting this incident in your employee file."

You can set it on fire for all I care, Chiffon thought, and before she could stop herself, she stuck out her middle finger.

"While you're writing, Mr. Peet, put this in your dang file."

Wilbur's whole body squirmed with a mixture of indignation and shock. Before he opened his mouth to speak, Chiffon turned around and flounced out of the restaurant. When she was safely inside her car, she shook with laughter for a full ten minutes.

As liberating as it had been to flip off Wilbur, it had also been incredibly stupid, she thought as she wiped the tears of laughter from her eyes with a corner of her uniform. Not only had she quit a job she'd held for ten years, but, in the heat of the moment, she'd clean forgotten that she'd counted on today's tips to buy a bag of diapers and other necessities from the grocery store. There was only a dollar or two in her purse, and Lonnie had the Visa card. Their checking account was tapped out, and before he'd left, Lonnie had taken the hundred bucks or so they'd socked away and cashed it in for some traveler's checks.

Fiddlesticks! She was going to have to ask her mother for a few bucks, just until Lonnie dragged his sorry behind back to Cayboo Creek and cashed his paycheck from the NutraSweet plant in Augusta. (And Chiffon had no doubt he'd be back. This wasn't the first time Lonnie had gotten loose from his leash, and she guessed it wouldn't be the last.) She slammed the car into gear and screeched out of the parking lot.

Her mother, Wanda, lived a couple of miles away in a modular home in a development called Whispering Pines. The emphasis was on the word "modular." Wanda would frostily correct anyone who called her spanking-new manufactured home, with its garden tub and cathedral ceilings, a "mobile home" or, God forbid, a "trailer."

Chiffon parked next to Wanda's pink Buick Regal, which she'd earned as a top-selling Mary Kay consultant. Her mother had also earned an all-expenses-paid tour of Europe that kicked off in a few days.

Chiffon knocked on the door and it swung open immediately. Wanda stood in the white-carpeted foyer, wearing the red Mary Kay jacket that she'd gotten when she made sales director six months before. Now she was hell-bent on earning Mary Kay's most prestigious award, the diamond bumblebee pin.

"Chiffon Amber Butrell," Wanda said. "I've been calling you all morning long. I just rang the Wagon Wheel and the manager said that you were no longer an employee there. What mess have you gotten into now?"

A phone ring interrupted her interrogation, and Wanda clipped down the hallway to answer it.

With a furtive glance at her mother, who was now gabbing on the phone, Chiffon zipped into the kitchen and flung open the pantry door where she knew Wanda hid a gold foil box of Godiva chocolate. She located the stash and simultaneously stuffed her mouth with an Amaretto truffle and a milk chocolate raspberry starfish.

"What do you think you're doing?" her mother squawked.

Wanda was directly behind her. Chiffon nearly choked on the candies.

"Wilbur ish imposhible," she mumbled as an explanation, her mouth stuffed with chocolate. Liquid raspberry trickled down her cheek and was immediately lapped up by her tongue.

"Give me those chocolates, Chiffon Amber," Wanda said. Her voice had the eerie calm of a SWAT team leader negotiating the release of a hostage. "They have eight grams of fat *each*. Hand them over."

Chiffon reluctantly surrendered the plundered chocolate box to Wanda, who placed it on the highest shelf of the pantry and shut the door behind her.

Looking at her mama was like looking into a ragged version of Chiffon's own future. Wanda's long faded blond hair was pinned up on her head. The once-strong jawline had disappeared into the folds of her neck, and despite the liberal use of Mary Kay's Triple Action Eye Enhancer, the skin around her washed-out blue eyes looked like it had been trounced on by a whole flock of crows.

"I've been trying to get in touch with you, because I received the strangest phone call this morning," Wanda said. "Effie Stykes was watching television last night and she could have sworn she saw Lonnie kissing that movie star Janie-Lynn Lauren."

Chiffon had naively hoped that nobody, except she and her friends, had seen the show last night. The last thing she needed was a repeat of last year's fiasco, when the whole town knew that Lonnie had been sleeping around with Jonelle Jasper. As the affair became public, Chiffon could sense folks' eyes pressing into her back when she marketed at the Winn-Dixie or pushed her kids on the swings at the playground near the creek. She could hear the muffled whispers following her everywhere she went.

Poor, pitiful Chiffon! Her husband's running around on her again. Why, I remember when she had the world by the tail. We expected such grand things from her. I wonder what happened?

No, she definitely didn't want a repeat of that humiliation. And if the town's tongues wagged when Lonnie had an affair with a local woman, imagine the brouhaha if people found out he was salting his beans with a real, live movie star.

"Effie must be taking a nip at suppertime, Mama," Chiffon said with a snort. "What in the world would a movie star like Janie-Lynn Lauren want with my man Lonnie?"

"I've no idea. I don't even know what *you* want with him," Wanda snapped. "But everyone knows Lonnie is as faithful as an alley cat."

She eyed her daughter, who was nibbling on a lock of her hair. Chiffon chewed her hair so often it was a wonder she didn't cough up hairballs.

Wanda picked up her leather clutch bag from the counter. "How much do you need?" she asked brusquely.

"Who said I needed money?" Chiffon said.

"You didn't work today, and it's the end of the month. And why else would you visit me in the middle of the day?" Wanda plucked a crisp bill from her wallet. "Will fifty dollars tide you over, or do you need more?"

Chiffon took the cash and stuffed it in the pocket of her brown polyester uniform, bracing herself for the inevitable lecture. Fifty bucks was a heap of change, so it was bound to be a doozy. Wanda didn't disappoint.

First she harped about Chiffon and Lonnie's financial situation, living from paycheck to paycheck and spreading themselves thin every month. Then she questioned Chiffon's tolerance of her husband's wandering eye, wondering why she'd married such a hound dog in the first place, throwing away her chance to be "somebody." Wanda had been over this road so many times, Chiffon knew every pothole and dip. It was now white noise to her ears.

"Where are my grandbabies?" Wanda said, her voice finally taxed from her tirade.

"Gabby's at Wee World. Dewitt and Emily are at school. You know that, Mama," Chiffon said. She jingled her keys in her pocket, desperate for escape.

Wanda wrinkled her nose. "Those child-care places with cutesy names are always the worst. What was that last place you'd enrolled Gabby? The one with an outbreak of hoof-and-mouth disease? It had a cutesy name, too."

"It's called Little Cherub Child Care," Chiffon said wearily. "And it was hand, mouth, and foot disease, Mama. Not hoof-and-mouth."

Chiffon had taken Gabby out of Little Cherub because they'd raised their rates to seventy-five dollars a week for an infant. Wee World only wanted fifty-five.

"What does it matter, Chiffon? Those places are petri dishes for infections. Every time I see those youngsters of yours, their noses are running like faucets."

"Yeah, well—"

"And I guess you're not going to tell me what happened at work."

Obviously Wanda was winding up for another go-round. The first sermon had just been a warm-up.

"Not that it was much of a job anyway," she continued. "Maybe now you'll consider coming aboard with Mary Kay. I'll even pay for your starter kit. With your nice looks, you'll attract all kinds of customers. Of course it'd help if you lost some of those extra pounds you've been lugging around."

"Mama," she protested with one foot edging into the hallway. If Wanda started on her weight, Chiffon would be here clear into next month.

"Are you using that overnight cream I gave you? Your complexion looks like it's going to hell in a handbasket."

"Gotta go, Mama," Chiffon said, dashing out of the kitchen before her mother had a chance to attack the condition of her hair, nails, or God knows what else.

She slowed her pace when she came to a wall in Wanda's hallway, displaying photographs from Chiffon's beauty-queen days. Chiffon had held so many titles as a young woman, she couldn't keep track. Most of them didn't amount to beans: Yam Queen, Miss Cayboo Creek, Pine Straw Princess, Miss Catfish Stomp of 1989. Her biggest accomplishment had been first runner-up to Miss South Carolina. There was a framed shot of Chiffon tearfully hugging the newly crowned Miss South Carolina, Eurlene Struthers. In the picture, she looked happy for Eurlene, when in reality Chiffon wanted to punch her in the stomach.

The title should have gone to Chiffon, but Eurlene gained the sympathy vote of the judges because she had a facial tic. During the interview portion of the pageant, Eurlene rambled on about her "struggles" with her tic, trying to make herself appear as brave and afflicted as Helen Keller. In reality, all the tic did was cause her mouth to twitch a little at each side. As a result, Eurlene walked away with the crown, even though her ankles were thick as fence posts.

The one award that Chiffon had truly been proud of was absent from Wanda's wall of fame. During her senior year in high school, Chiffon had won the blue ribbon at the Cayboo Creek fair for photography. But since photography took time away from the pageant circuit, Wanda pooh-poohed it, and Chiffon eventually gave it up.

"You gotta make your mark on this world, girls."

She could hear her mother's voice in her ears. After Chiffon's daddy had left the family when she was four and Chenille was eight, Wanda poured all her energy into her two daughters, driving them toward success.

"Second place is just a nice way of saying 'loser,'" she'd constantly remind them, and both Chiffon and Chenille responded with tireless efforts to please her. Chenille had been named valedictorian in high school, and Chiffon had worn more tiaras than the queen of England, but after years of trying to please their mother, the two sisters fizzled out. There were no more photos or awards to hang on the hall of fame. Newspaper articles on the girls' achievements yellowed in Wanda's scrapbook.

"It ain't like I didn't try, Mama," Chiffon whispered as she walked out of the house to her car. After high school, Chiffon discovered the hard way that a Yam Queen title or even first runner-up to Miss South Carolina didn't amount to much. She hadn't concentrated on her studies in high school, so she wasn't able to get into college. After graduation, she'd drifted around, collecting more obscure beauty titles and trying to find fashion work, but she was too short and curvy to be a model. Finally she got married, had babies, and went to work as a waitress.

She took one last look at the photos on the wall and sighed. Making her mark on this world was like trying to scratch a diamond with a toothpick. It just wasn't going happen.

Metaphors be with you.

Poster hanging in Chenille Grace's English composition classroom

CHAPTER THREE

Chenille watched from her classroom window as Mrs. Schmatt waddled to her pickup truck for a cigarette break. Once she was certain the woman was out of sight, Chenille scurried to the blackboard to correct all of the spelling errors her teaching assistant had made while writing down instructions for the sixth-period grammar and composition class.

Mrs. Schmatt was Chenille's brand-new "para-facilitator," a show-offish word for someone who was supposed to help out with grading papers and other routine classroom duties. The term certainly didn't seem to fit Mrs. Schmatt, who, with her frizzy, bleached-out hair and Day-Glo spandex pants, looked more like a female wrestler.

Chenille had been assigned a para-facilitator ever since she'd started teaching remedial English at Bible Grove High School. Her classes were large and she taught second-year freshmen, so she was entitled to extra help.

For the past ten years her assistant (Chenille's tongue tripped over the word "para-facilitator") had been Mrs. Birchfield, a lovely, grandmotherly woman whom Chenille had grown to adore. Every Monday morning Mrs. Birchfield brought a loaf of homemade Amish friendship bread to share with Chenille. She also carried a big appliqué bag brimming with multicolored skeins of yarns for the afghans she knitted between classroom duties. How soothing it was for Chenille to hear the steady click of knitting needles during classes! And how jarring it was to have such a reassuring sound replaced by the ceaseless smacking of Mrs. Schmatt's lips chewing her gum!

Oh, it was a dreadful day when her assistant retired. Just before her departure, Mrs. Birchfield pressed the faded recipe for the friendship bread in Chenille's hand, saying, "This has been in my family for generations. You're the first person I've ever given it to."

The gesture made Chenille cry, even though she knew she'd never bake the bread herself. The kitchen in her condominium was the size of a broom closet, and she didn't even own a bread pan, but never mind, she was overwhelmed by Mrs. Birchfield's heartfelt gift. She'd scarcely had a week to mourn her beloved assistant's departure when Mrs. Schmatt appeared on the scene.

One morning Chenille entered her classroom and saw a wide lime-green rear end poking out of her supply closet.

"May I help you?" Chenille asked.

The woman turned to face her and revealed a front side more alarming than her caboose. Vivid blue shadow ringed eyes the size of caraway seeds. Heavy orange-tinted foundation settled into the pockmarked terrain of her face. Hair the color and texture of yellow Easter grass sprang from her scalp.

"Your supply closet is a pigsty," the stranger declared.

The woman's voice sounded like a fork being chewed up in a garbage disposal. For a moment Chenille thought she might have wandered into the wrong classroom.

"I'm Mrs. Schmatt, your new para-facilitator, and I don't do bulletin boards," she said.

. . .

Mrs. Schmatt arrived at the start of the semester just as Chenille was getting a brand-new group of students in her classes. Chenille always held out hope that the incoming batch of adolescents would be more well-mannered and motivated than their predecessors, and the first couple of days of winter semester fulfilled that promise. Her new students raised their hands for questions and listened attentively as Chenille discussed instances of allegory in *The Pilgrim's Progress*.

But by the third day, the whiffs of anarchy began with a ripple of fidgeting and whispering spreading across the classroom, and by the fourth day, the ripple had swelled into a roar and Chenille could scarcely be heard over the din. After the dismissal of a particularly boisterous class, Mrs. Schmatt eyed Chenille from her roost behind her desk.

"You gonna let them kids walk all over you every day?" she asked.

Chenille blushed. Despite much shushing and finger-wagging on her part, classroom discipline had never been her strong point.

"I ask them to be quiet, but they don't listen," she said with a resigned shrug.

Mrs. Schmatt sighed. Chenille had noticed the woman sighed a lot, and she took each exhale of Mrs. Schmatt's breath personally. The sighs seemed to say, "Why did they assign me to such an idiotic teacher?"

When Mrs. Schmatt wasn't sighing, she was questioning Chenille's way of doing things, from the color of chalk she used on the board (yellow is easier on the students' eyes than white, she claimed) to the haphazard way Chenille handed out papers.

During these confrontations, Chenille longed for Mrs. Birchfield, who had praised her at every turn.

"That gerund presentation was compelling, my dear," she'd coo, or "I think the Bard himself would have been delighted with your keen analysis of *Macbeth*."

Sometimes she'd applaud after a truly inspired lesson, causing Chenille to blush. When the students were disruptive, she never questioned Chenille's leadership abilities, but blamed the children instead, saying, "Those young people must have been raised by orangutans."

But now, instead of a beaming and benevolent Mrs. Birchfield, Chenille was stuck with a squat-bodied Mrs. Schmatt glaring at her with barely disguised contempt from the top of her *Dell Horoscope* magazine.

Day after day, Mrs. Schmatt continued to rattle her. Chenille made it a strict policy to leave work matters behind at the end of the school day, but sometimes while watching *Law and Order,* her dog, Walter, on her lap, instead of concentrating on what was going on in the Special Victims Unit, she'd think of ways to placate Mrs. Schmatt.

Maybe if I got her a little gift of some sort. Chenille wasn't sure what type of present a person of Mrs. Schmatt's ilk might appreciate. A set of fuzzy dice? A black-light portrait of Elvis? On the other hand, Mrs. Schmatt might regard her kindness as a sign of weakness and redouble her bullying behaviors. It was probably safest to do nothing at all, Chenille decided, hoping Mrs. Schmatt would blow over like a bad odor. Or maybe she'd catch some lengthy but essentially harmless illness like mononucleosis and have to stay out for the rest of the school year. Chenille could only hope.

One afternoon during an especially rambunctious sixth-period class, someone, Chenille wasn't sure who (but she suspected the foul-mouthed Steven McPhee), was throwing wads of paper at her back while she wrote vocabulary words on the board. The class thought it was hysterical that she was unable to catch the offender, and Mrs. Schmatt, who could easily have kept an eye on the class while Chenille was stationed at the chalkboard, didn't bother looking up from her magazine.

By the time Chenille had written the entire list of words on the board, there were at least ten balls of paper at her feet. She was near tears. Mrs. Schmatt wasn't helping, and in fact seemed oblivious to what was going on.

"You can look up those words in the dictionary now," Chenille said to her class in a huffy voice, not caring if they did the work or not. She sat and stared down at her desktop calendar, willing herself not to cry. When the bell mercifully rang and students dashed out the door, Chenille glowered at Mrs. Schmatt, who was licking her fingers as she turned the pages of her magazine.

"Mrs. Schmatt," Chenille said in a chagrined tone. "Why did you allow students to throw paper at me while I was at the board? Did it ever occur to you that I could have used your assistance during this class?"

Mrs. Schmatt glanced up. "No," she said curtly, her eyes returning to her reading material.

Chenille stared at Mrs. Schmatt with openmouthed surprise. She was accustomed to insubordination from the students, but she'd never before experienced it in an adult. Didn't Mrs. Schmatt care about her job? Didn't she know that Chenille could report her to the principal?

Mrs. Schmatt glanced up once again, defiance tugging her mouth into a grin. Chenille immediately understood the message contained in the woman's self-satisfied smile. Mrs. Schmatt was betting she wouldn't say a single word to the principal. She'd learned that Chenille would rather endure Chinese water torture than become involved in a face-off.

"Excuse me. I have to run off some worksheets," Chenille said, her eyes cast to the floor. She intended to sequester herself in a bathroom stall in the teachers' lounge with a handful of Kleenex.

Mrs. Schmatt heaved herself up and put her hands on her ample hips. "All you have to do is ask," she said in her ragged voice. "But since you're such a control freak, I was afraid to get in the middle of things."

"Control freak?" Chenille stammered. "I'm not a—"

"Insisting on using white chalk instead of yellow even though I told you yellow is better. Never listening to a single one of my ideas. I've made at least a half a dozen suggestions. You haven't used a one."

"Suggestions?" Chenille swallowed nervously. "I didn't seem them as suggestions. I saw them more as . . ."

Mrs. Schmatt studied her from beneath her bush of bangs.

"Attacks," Chenille said softly. "On the way I run my classroom."

Mrs. Schmatt's eyes widened, as if she was genuinely shocked by Chenille's statement. "Ms. Grace, I'm the para-facilitator; you're the teacher. It's not my place to be telling you what to do in your classroom. If you see my friendly suggestions as attacks, I'll just keep my mouth shut from here on out."

"Mrs. Schmatt, you're misunderstanding me. I want to hear your ideas. I just—" Chenille lowered her voice to a near whisper. "It's the way you present them. You're so . . . gruff."

Mrs. Schmatt tensed. "So now it's my personality you don't like. Just who is attacking who around here?"

"I'm not attacking you," Chenille said helplessly. "I'm not like that. Why, my last para-faciliator, Mrs. Birchfield, thought I was a lovely person."

"Yeah. Birchie told me all about you," Mrs. Schmatt said with a smirk.

"Birchie?"

"That's Birchfield's nickname at the central office. I ran into her when she was filling out her retirement paperwork. She said I'd get along fine with you, just as long as I kept my mouth shut and did everything you said. Boy, did she have you nailed!"

"Mrs. Birchfield talked about me? Behind my back?" Chenille said, flabbergasted. "I don't believe you."

Mrs. Schmatt clapped her hands over her ears. "Don't yell at me. I may be just a para-facilitator, but I don't have to take this kind of abuse."

"I'm not yelling."

Chenille couldn't get the image out of her mind. Mrs. Schmatt and Mrs. Birchfield (Birchie, indeed!), thick as thieves in the central office, comparing notes and cackling over her failings as an educator.

It couldn't be true. Why, surely Mrs. Birchfield, with her Peter Pan collars and hand-knitted sweaters, would be appalled by the spandex-clad visage that was Mrs. Schmatt. Still, there was that fine line of hierarchy between teacher and para-facilitator. Maybe Mrs. Birchfield had resented Chenille's authority over her. Maybe all those afghans she knitted were actually a way to channel her bitterness. Chenille racked her brain, trying to remember a time when she might have inadvertently squelched Mrs. Birchfield's spirit, but she couldn't recall a single unpleasant incident in their entire ten-year history.

Chenille shook her head in bewilderment. "I had no idea she felt that way. When it came time to do the bulletin boards, I always let her choose the theme."

"Look, Ms. Grace, I wouldn't get all broke up about Birchie. I'd just appreciate it if you wouldn't take your anger at her out on me."

"I'm not angry," Chenille said in a clipped tone.

"You could have fooled me."

Chenille had always considered herself a pleasant person,

easy to get along with, but maybe she'd been kidding herself. Was it possible that she had the personality of a despot and Mrs. Schmatt was just the first person to call her on it?

She wrung her hands. "I'm sorry, Mrs. Schmatt, if I've been too overbearing. Certainly, I will welcome any of your suggestions."

"I'd like to help out some more. Sometimes I feel like this big useless lump," Mrs. Schmatt said with a sad little frown.

Chenille felt an unexpected tug of sympathy for this poor hulk of a woman. Was Mrs. Schmatt's bearish behavior just an act to cover up her needy, sensitive side?

"I'm sorry. I didn't know," Chenille said, genuine contriteness shining in her eyes.

Mrs. Birchfield had always been so content with her knitting—or so she'd led Chenille to believe—that Chenille had never imagined that Mrs. Schmatt might feel unproductive.

"Please feel free to do whatever you'd like to help out," Chenille said.

"Even when it comes to telling them kids what to do?" Mrs. Schmatt asked with a zealous little smile.

"Whatever you think is necessary," Chenille said.

They were words she would soon regret.

. . .

Since their talk, Chenille had tried to involve Mrs. Schmatt in more classroom routines. Her assistant was now responsible for writing all the lessons on the board as part of her regular duties. Unfortunately, she was a terrible speller.

Chenille peeked out of her classroom window once more to make sure Mrs. Schmatt wasn't coming back, and when she didn't see her, she picked up a piece of chalk and changed "asigment" to "assignment." Considering their fragile relationship, she didn't want to embarrass the woman by correcting her spelling mistakes outright.

The bell rang, and Chenille stood outside her classroom waiting for her sixth-period students to file in. She tried to behave as if every school day was fresh and new, unmarred by any unpleasant history, though her heart couldn't help but sink as the teenagers tramped in the room, bringing their laughter, hoots, and general mayhem into her classroom. Mrs. Schmatt also strolled in, smelling like Chernobyl from smoking Kools in the cab of her pickup truck. Chenille nodded congenially and then shut the door of the classroom as the tardy bell rang.

A journal topic was up on the board, and students knew they were supposed to begin writing as soon as they sat down in their seats. Trouble was, nobody was sitting. Two boys by the pencil sharpener were making obscene undulating movements with their hips, to the delight of a bevy of girls. Three young men were huddled around a computer, surfing the Internet. Nothing educational, she'd wager. Web pages like thuglife.com or hotgirls.net kept appearing in her history cache. The rest of the class milled about the room in a stupor, like patients on a mental ward.

"We need to sit down, young people, and we need to work on our journals," Chenille said with a clap of her hands. Her announcement had as much impact as a sneeze during a tsunami.

"Young people, please," she continued. "If you'll just listen—"

"SHUT YOUR TRAPS AND SIT DOWN!" Mrs.

Schmatt bellowed from her desk, waving a yardstick in a menacing manner.

Stunned students hurried to their seats like fiddler crabs scuttling to burrows. Chenille stared at Mrs. Schmatt in horror.

"I don't want to hear another peep out of you smart-mouthed kids," Mrs. Schmatt wheezed, whacking the yardstick against the side of her desk. "You can go ahead and teach now, Ms. Grace."

"Yes. Well." Chenille glanced at Mrs. Schmatt, who gave her a nod of encouragement. "Please remain quiet and start your assignment."

She was so shaken it was all she could do to monitor her students' work lesson. Mrs. Schmatt had undermined her authority and had behaved in a grossly unprofessional manner. No matter how much she dreaded it, Chenille would be forced to confront her assistant after class to prevent any further outbursts.

The classroom remained quiet for five minutes, and then a couple of giggles erupted in the last row. Steven McPhee was up to his usual nonsense. He waved an imaginary yardstick and puffed up his cheeks in a chillingly accurate imitation of Mrs. Schmatt.

"Steven—" Chenille began.

Mrs. Schmatt shot up from her seat. "Let me handle this, Ms. Grace." She stalked over to Steven's seat and hovered over him. "You got a problem with me, boy?"

Steven glanced helplessly in Chenille's direction. "What's wrong with her, Ms. Grace? Tell her to leave me alone."

"Mrs. Schmatt—" Chenille began.

The large woman continued to loom over Steven. "I'm tired

of listening to your yammering. If I hear one more word out of you, I'll have your hide."

After delivering her threat, she plodded back to her desk and tore open a bag of cheese curls. Chenille felt woozy, as if she'd just gotten off the Tilt-a-Whirl ride at the fair. Whatever tenuous hold she'd had over her classroom was slipping from her fingers and into Mrs. Schmatt's oversize palms.

Chenille collected the journals and began a lesson on dependent clauses. She stuttered in front of the class while Mrs. Schmatt, seemingly oblivious to the upset she'd caused, contentedly sucked cheese dust from her thumb and forefinger. *Forty-five minutes until the bell rings*, Chenille thought as she sagged against the chalkboard. Then she'd have to stand up to Mrs. Schmatt.

More tittering came from the back row. Chenille ignored the noise and raised her voice a notch. "The difference between an independent clause and a dependent clause is that the independent clause—"

"What's that racket back there?" demanded Mrs. Schmatt.

"What's that racket back there?" came Steve's sassy reply.

"An independent clause can stand on its—"

"I warned you, boy," Mrs. Schmatt said. She pulled open her drawer and waved a shiny object in front of her face. It took Chenille a couple of seconds to realize she was holding a machete.

"Mrs. Schmatt. My God! What are you doing?" Chenille gasped.

Mrs. Schmatt ignored her and lumbered over to Steven, slicing the air with her machete.

"No! Stop!" Chenille pleaded. She was rooted to her spot

by the chalkboard and could only watch in horror as Mrs. Schmatt swung her arm back.

Steven's mouth fell open and the girls sitting around him scattered like pigeons. Everyone's eyes watched the blade of the machete as it slowly swooshed through the air. Just before it could cut into the soft, pale skin of Steven's throat, Chenille let out one last feeble shriek. Then she crumpled to the floor in a dead faint.

"I Miss You Only on Days That End in Y"

Selection C-8 on the Chat 'N' Chew jukebox

CHAPTER FOUR

The last thing Chiffon felt like doing that evening was hosting a baby shower, but she couldn't let Elizabeth down. After all, it was her best friend's first pregnancy, and Elizabeth had gushed over every aspect of it, from her swelling belly to the blurry black-and-white sonogram pictures she flashed at every opportunity. Last night she'd called Chiffon and spent thirty minutes fretting over her choice of maternity dresses for the shower. She'd be heartbroken if it was canceled.

While Mavis ran out to the grocery store for some last-minute items, Chiffon mixed green sherbet with ginger ale into a cut-glass punch bowl on her kitchen table. Stirring the punch, she picked up the phone and dialed Lonnie's hotel room again. As usual, there wasn't any answer.

"Darn it!" Chiffon said, slamming down the receiver. The noise startled the baby, who had been snoozing in her carrier on the kitchen floor. Gabby whimpered, and Chiffon popped a bottle in her mouth.

As she turned her attention back to the punch, she wondered for the zillionth time if she could have been mistaken about seeing Lonnie on *Hollywood Hijinks.* Maybe it *was* someone who just looked like Lonnie. Had Chiffon automatically jumped to conclusions because of her husband's low-down past? When she'd questioned Birdie, Attalee, and Mavis, they all said the image on the TV screen had been too fuzzy to say for certain. But if it hadn't been Lonnie, why wasn't he in his room last night?

"Mama. Can I eat one of these little cakes?" Her daughter Emily had come into the kitchen and was poking a finger into the pale pink frosting of one of the petits fours that Mavis had gotten from the bakery.

"Just one," Chiffon said. "And I want you to keep Dewitt busy while the ladies are here. Y'all can play a game of Old Maid or Chinese checkers in your room while Mama is having her party."

"When's Daddy coming home?" Emily asked.

"Sunday afternoon. We'll drive over to the airport in Augusta and see him zoom in on one of those big jets," Chiffon said.

Once Lonnie arrived at the terminal and she saw his face, she would know for certain if he'd strayed. That man couldn't hide anything from her.

Gabby dropped her bottle, her head lolling back as if she'd

drunk too much wine. Chiffon picked her up to check her diaper. In her arms, the baby felt soft and heavy as a mesh bag full of ripe peaches. As she lay Gabby back down in the carrier, someone knocked on the kitchen door.

"Come in!" Chiffon hollered, and Mavis stuck her head inside.

"Hey, Mavis," Chiffon said, taking a brown bag of groceries from her.

Mavis stood in Chiffon's kitchen, stamping her rubber boots on the straw mat just inside the door. She smiled at Emily, who waved and scooted to her bedroom in stocking feet.

"Birdie's laid up with a bad cold, so she won't be coming," Mavis said as she picked through the bags. "I hope I didn't forget anything."

"I'm sure you got it all covered."

Mavis pulled a box of Sociable crackers from her shopping bag. "Saw Maynard yesterday afternoon. Said you weren't out at the Wagon Wheel anymore."

Pretending she hadn't heard Mavis, Chiffon arranged sprigs of parsley around a platter of cold cuts. She wasn't in the mood to discuss the scene she'd made at the restaurant.

"I could always use someone at the Bottom Dollar," Mavis said, measuring her voice as carefully as a pharmacist doles out sleeping pills. "That is, if you're interested."

"I appreciate it, Mavis, but I talked with Jewel at the Chat 'N' Chew today. One of her waitresses quit, and she said she could use me on the weekday lunch shift."

Mavis's brow bunched with concern. She obviously had more questions buzzing between her ears, but she wasn't a busybody, so she held her tongue.

The door opened and Elizabeth burst in, pink-cheeked and swollen as a plum.

"I know I'm early, but I couldn't wait another second," she said, unfurling a plaid scarf from her neck. "Timothy shooed me out the door. He was tired of all my pacing." She came inside and stood at the threshold of the living room. "Oh my goodness, Chiffon. It looks so festive in here!"

Chiffon surveyed the room that she and the other women had decorated with streamers and balloons. In the middle of it all was Lonnie's blasted pool table. Chiffon had covered it with a white crepe paper tablecloth and set the refreshments on top of it. The pastel finery looked out of place against the dark wood paneling and the camouflage-print curtains.

"Thanks, Elizabeth. I gave it my best shot," Chiffon said, taking her friend's coat and scarf.

Her remaining guests trickled in. Mavis pinned a pacifier corsage on Reeky Flynn, who clutched together her wool sweater as she came through the door. A few minutes later Gracie Tobias, Elizabeth's grandmother, swept in wearing a mink pillbox hat with a cape to match.

"My goodness, Chiffon! Your house is painted such an unusual color," she said as she slipped out of her cape. "What would you call that? Magenta?"

It was actually Mulberry Bush. At least that's what the dried-out paint cans in the shed out back said on the labels.

"I'm constantly after Lonnie to take a paintbrush to this place," Chiffon muttered. "I tell him purple is for grape juice and dinosaurs, not houses. But I still haven't been able to get his butt out on a scaffold."

Mrs. Tobias gave her fur cape a little good-bye pat before

she surrendered it to Chiffon. "Well, it certainly makes your home easy to find," she said with a smile.

Attalee arrived, toting a coconut cake in a Tupperware tub, and the ladies gathered in the living room. Chiffon had covered the couch with a quilt to disguise the splits in the vinyl and all the stains from Lonnie's dogs and the kids. She'd also prettified some borrowed folding chairs with pink ribbons, but despite her best efforts, the room still looked dark and masculine.

Not that Elizabeth cared. She oohed and ahhed as if the ginger-ale punch was Dom Pérignon and the cocktail weenies were caviar.

Chiffon tried to remember if she'd been half as excited as Elizabeth when she was pregnant with her first baby. She recalled fierce cravings for banana Icees and cream cheese sandwiches. And she'd diligently rubbed olive oil on her belly every night before bed, because she'd heard it prevented stretch marks. Not so with her last baby. She'd let the thin yellow lines have full run of her birth-battered body.

"Timothy's been a treasure," Elizabeth said with color so high she looked almost feverish. "I can't tell you how many times he's gone out in the middle of the night for pistachio ice cream."

When Chiffon was pregnant and had a yen for a banana Icee during the wee hours of the morning, it was she, not Lonnie, who slipped into some shoes and drove to the all-night Quick Curb.

"Have you thought about getting a doula, Elizabeth?" Reeky asked, blinking through her granny glasses. She was pale, with long, straight hair that hung in her face like a dun-colored curtain.

"A *whosa*?" Attalee asked.

"Doula," Elizabeth said, patting Attalee's scrawny wrist. "A doula is someone who helps the mother during labor. Almost like a handmaiden."

"If you're considering using one, I know a lovely woman in Augusta," Reeky said. "She specializes in labor with aromatherapy, and she also has a birthing ball."

Attalee tugged at the lace collar of her dress. "I don't mean to be scaring you none, Elizabeth, but when that young 'un tears you in two like a wishbone, you ain't going to be in the mood for no ball game."

"A birthing ball isn't to play with, Attalee," Reeky said with a sigh. She owned the Book Nook and Novelties shop on Main Street and was always up on the latest trends. "It's an oversize ball that helps the mother find a comfortable position while she's in labor."

Attalee thrust out her chin. "I don't cotton to these new-fangled ways of having a baby. Women should have their young 'uns the way God intended them to. Flat on their backs and doped up on ether."

"Oh, Attalee, things have changed so much since we were girls!" Mrs. Tobias said with a practiced flick of her wrist. "There used to be a certain decorum associated with labor. Now it's a sideshow. Why, just a few days ago, I read about a woman who gave birth while parachuting out of an airplane."

"I read that, too, Mrs. Tobias," Mavis said, unconsciously rubbing the faint fluff of hair just above her upper lip. "It was in the Sunday supplement of the newspaper. And not to contradict you, but as I recall, the woman said her *wedding vows* while jumping out of a parachute. She gave birth underwater."

"Scandalous!" Mrs. Tobias said with a shudder.

"Water births aren't as oddball as you might imagine," Reeky said. "When I lived in Columbia, I knew several women who gave birth that way."

"Well, *Columbia*," Mrs. Tobias said. Her nostrils flared in distaste. "One might expect such shenanigans in a university town."

Reeky receded into her turtleneck and jutted out her lower lip. Before she could say anything in response, Chiffon plunked a bowl on the coffee table. "Time to play a game."

The afternoon wore on as the ladies tried to retrieve diaper pins from a bowl of rice while blindfolded. Attalee had surprisingly nimble fingers and fished out the most diaper pins. Following the diaper pin game, the party guests cut off lengths of yarn to guess the circumference of Elizabeth's belly. (Reeky was closest and won a bud vase filled with baby's breath.) After several activities, the women sat in a semicircle in Chiffon's living room, balancing paper plates filled with cookies and cake on their knees.

"There's enough sweets left over to feed an army," Mrs. Tobias said. "I imagine Chiffon's children will have a field day."

Mavis sat in Lonnie's La-Z-Boy and nibbled on a ginger snap. "I have a suggestion, Chiffon," she said. "Why not take these leftovers to the Senior Center? All they ever get are cookies from the bargain bin. I know the older folks would appreciate a special treat."

"Maybe I'll just do that," Chiffon said in a small voice. Considering she was down to her last dollar, she'd been hoping to keep the leftovers for herself.

Elizabeth looked up from her plate. "I didn't know you were involved with the Senior Center, Mavis."

"I stop in now and then," Mavis said. "Birdie's on the board of directors out there, and she tells me that the center is really hurting for funds. We're going to have a community meeting to see if we can't come up with some kind of fundraising plan."

"You can count on me being at that meeting. Matter of fact, I wouldn't mind hosting it," Elizabeth said with a nod. "How about you, Chiffon? Would you like to be involved?"

"Sounds okay to me," Chiffon said distractedly.

"I'd like to be included as well," Mrs. Tobias said, a sugar cookie poised between her thumb and forefinger.

A grin spilled over Mavis's face. "That'd be sweet of you, Mrs. Tobias. Particularly since you don't even live in Cayboo Creek."

"Well, I'm just a few miles down the road in Augusta," Mrs. Tobias said. "And I visit Elizabeth and Timothy so often I've begun to feel a part of the community. I'd adore helping out the seniors."

· · ·

Shortly afterward, the shower broke up. Everyone went home except Elizabeth, who helped Chiffon tidy up.

"Tomorrow is my last day of work until after the baby's born," Elizabeth said, running a dish towel over a serving platter. Elizabeth was marketing director for Hollingsworth Paper Cups in Augusta, a company owned by her husband's family.

"I just hope I won't go stir-crazy for the last month of my pregnancy," she added. "I'm not used to being a lady of leisure."

"You could always help Timothy out at the bait shop," Chiffon said with a chuckle.

"Shoot. I can't tell a cricket from a red wiggler. Nor do I care to." Elizabeth eased herself into a chair at the kitchen table and rested her hands on the crest of her belly. "Besides, the boys who hang out at the store don't want to buy bait from a woman. You know how they are."

Darn straight she knew. Chiffon was married to one of them "boys." At the thought of Lonnie, she grimaced.

"Chiffon. Is there anything wrong? You don't seem like yourself today."

She met Elizabeth's concerned eyes. Part of her urgently wanted to share her troubles with her friend. But she hesitated to discuss the seedier side of her marriage with Elizabeth. The two couples often had supper together, and Timothy and Lonnie were fishing buddies. As far as Elizabeth knew, everything was hunky-dory in the Butrell household, and Chiffon wanted to keep it that way. Besides, what would Elizabeth think if she knew that Chiffon couldn't even keep her man in line?

"I'm just PMS-ing," Chiffon answered. She rubbed her pelvic area as if it ached. "Lonnie says I'm surly as a grizzly bear when 'Auntie Flo' comes to call."

"It's been so long since I've had a period, I hardly remember what it's like," Elizabeth said with a laugh.

"It's something I'd just as soon forget," Chiffon said with a derisive laugh.

The mood at the table changed, and Elizabeth described the furniture she'd picked out for the nursery. Chiffon was grateful Elizabeth had accepted her explanation and didn't ask any more questions. Had she probed just a bit more, Chiffon didn't know if she could hold back her worries about Lonnie.

. . .

Sunday morning Emily helped Chiffon get the two younger children dressed and strapped into the car for the drive to the airport.

Clouds floated lazily against a blinding blue backdrop, fluffy and fresh, as if they'd tumbled out of the clothes dryer. Chiffon filled her lungs with the chilled air and noted the way the bare trees scribbled their shadows on the front of the house. She was unexpectedly cheerful. Even if Lonnie was guilty of laying his pipe with Janie-Lynn, her man was coming home.

Not that she'd let on how much she missed him, because if he'd cheated again, there'd be a price to pay. For starters, he'd owe her a steak dinner, and not the overdone shoe leather they served at the Wagon Wheel: She wanted to eat in a restaurant with cloth napkins, fresh flowers, and a wandering violinist.

But a fancy dinner would be just the beginning. If Lonnie had been fraternizing with a movie star, he'd have to spend some serious time around the house with his tool kit. Maybe she could get him to fix the loose shutters or install the garbage disposal they'd bought six months ago. When she'd caught him cheating with Jonelle Jasper last year, she'd made him weather-strip all the doors and the windows. But fooling around with a movie star was a much more heinous crime. Heck, if he'd really been shaking the grate with Janie-Lynn Lauren, Chiffon might even get him to add on a Florida room.

She whistled as she crossed Tobacco Road and turned off to the Augusta Regional Airport. In the backseat, Emily read *Bob the Builder* to Dewitt in a singsong voice. Gabby napped in her car seat, her peaceful face striped with bars of sunlight.

Chiffon tried to put herself in Lonnie's shoes. Suppose she'd been the one to go to Hollywood instead of Lonnie and one of her favorite movie stars, like Ben Affleck, had propositioned her. Try as she might, she just couldn't see herself cozying up to a strange man, no matter how handsome he was or what fancy automobile he tooled around in. Chiffon was a one-man woman. Had been since the day she'd first laid eyes on Lonnie Butrell when he transferred to Cayboo Creek High School in his senior year.

Every female in the class had been smitten on sight by Lonnie, who was so handsome he could make a girl's eyes burn. His chestnut hair hung over a pair of alert copper-colored eyes, glinting with a secretive sort of amusement. His face was all sharp angles, broken only by a soft curved bottom lip that Chiffon had longed to touch with the tip of her finger. At the time, Chiffon had been dating the quarterback of the football team, Findley Barnett, a brutish fireplug of a fellow. All thoughts of fidelity to Findley fled her mind when Lonnie, sleek as an otter, ambled down the hallways of Cayboo Creek High School, his eyes flickering on the girls who lined the hallways like a row of spring flowers. When he saw Chiffon standing by her locker, eyeing him coyly over the top of her business math textbook, his face split into a heartbreaking grin. Chiffon felt like a beanbag in which every bean had shifted.

Truth be known, she was still under Lonnie's spell, making her much too quick to forgive his failings. Every time she intended to be tough on him, she weakened at his touch.

Chiffon turned on the road leading up to the airport as a jet rumbled overhead.

"I bet that's Daddy's plane. What do you think, Dewitt?" she said.

"Is Daddy driving the plane, Mama?" Dewitt asked. Her

five-year-old son was a carbon copy of his daddy, right down to the dimples.

"No, honey bun. The pilot's driving," Chiffon said as she parked in front of the terminal. "But when we get out of the car, if you wave real hard, maybe Daddy will see you through the window."

Emily and Dewitt tumbled out of the car yelling "Daddy!" and waving furiously at the incoming plane while Chiffon lifted Gabby out of her car seat and positioned her on her shoulder.

As they walked through the terminal, Chiffon recalled Lonnie's scent, a mingling of chicory, Big Red chewing gum, and musk aftershave. She thought about his eyes, the right one a darker copper color than the left, and how his pupils would darken as he gazed wickedly at her beneath a fringe of eyelashes when he was in the mood for love. Most of all, she thought about his hands, callused on the palms but soft on the fingertips, and how they'd expertly read her body as if it were covered in Braille instead of goose bumps. She was practically weak from pining for her man. They'd never been apart this long before.

They stopped in the airport ladies' room, where Chiffon slicked down tufts of Dewitt's hair with tap water and wiped a dab of drool from Gabby's chin. Then she glanced at her own reflection in the row of mirrors above the sinks.

For most of her life, the looking glass had been Chiffon's best friend. No matter what else went wrong, gazing at her attractive face in the mirror could nearly always cheer her. But for the last few years, her lifelong buddy had turned on her.

Now she automatically sucked in her cheeks, lifted her chin, and tightened her belly muscles before she dared a peek at herself. Even then, she was often bothered by the wrinkles and puffiness she saw reflected back at her.

Today was one of those rare instances when she was pleased by what she saw in the mirror. Her teal scarf complemented her eyes, and her hair looked as bouncy and full as a Breck girl's. A naughty little curl to her lip completed the pretty picture. And though her present-day body wouldn't pass muster in a swimsuit competition, her roomy black slacks and loose turtleneck covered up the worst of her sins.

Licking her full bottom lip, she thought, *You still got it, Chiffon Amber Butrell.*

. . .

She and the children arrived just as passengers from the plane were entering the baggage terminal. Groups of soldiers from Fort Gordon trotted past, and Chiffon noticed an acne-scarred recruit looking her up and down with approval. She ignored his attentions and kept her eyes riveted to the flow of people, her heart skittering in her chest like a frightened squirrel.

"Will Daddy bring us presents?" Emily asked.

"Maybe," Chiffon said, only half listening. A few minutes went by and the rush of passengers had slowed. Only a few stragglers wandered into the terminal: a man with an oversize package and a woman trying to corral two overexcited toddlers. It would be just like Lonnie to be the last passenger off the plane; he had the internal clock of a sloth. She continued to stare hopefully at the gate even after the flight attendants, in their navy blue outfits, exited, followed by a pilot and a co-pilot. Both looked barely old enough to commandeer ten-speeds, much less a plane.

"Mama, where's Daddy?" Dewitt whined. His palm was sweaty as he grasped her hand. Chiffon didn't answer; she kept looking, searching the baggage terminal, certain that at any minute Lonnie would appear.

My reality check just
bounced.

CHAPTER FIVE

Chenille sat in the principal's office, counting the miniature football helmets displayed on a shelf above the desk. Sport pennants and pictures of football teams covered the entire back wall, and a jockstrap, autographed by last season's starting quarterback, hung from the doorknob.

Mr. Brock was an ex-coach turned administrator, more interested in rushing records than in SAT scores. Normally Chenille would have frowned on a principal with such dubious priorities as an educator, but Mr. Brock was tall and muscular, with a rumbling baritone voice that made her heart careen every time it came over the P.A. system. With his flashing white teeth and golden hair, he reminded Chenille of the Brawny paper towel man. It was no accident that she'd dressed for their meeting in her nicest plaid dress with the flounced skirt and a nosegay of flowers at the collar.

The man himself entered the office, startling Chenille, who'd leaned forward in her chair to examine the family portrait on the corner of his desk. His children were also big, blond, and Nordic, like the progeny of a lumberjack.

"I'm sorry to make you wait, Ms. Grace," Mr. Brock said, taking a seat behind his desk.

"Not at all, Mr. Brock," Chenille said, approving his starched white shirt and light blue necktie, which matched his eyes. Too many male educators wore those silly novelty neckties. How a male teacher expected to garner respect from young people while wearing Three Stooges neckwear was a mystery to her.

Mr. Brock formed a steeple with his fingers and rested his chiseled chin on top. "That was some incident in your classroom the other day."

"Gracious, yes," Chenille said, smoothing her skirt.

"I'm glad you're feeling better. And that you were released from the hospital so quickly," he said.

"Much better," Chenille said, averting her eyes in shame. She regretted her one-night hospital stay after the scene with Mrs. Schmatt, thinking it made her look unprofessional and just a tad bit hysterical. "The doctors insisted I stay one night for observation and only because I fainted. I put up a fight about it, believe you me," Chenille said with an anxious chuckle.

Mr. Brock nodded and flashed a boyish smile, as if he understood completely. Thus far, their meeting was going swimmingly. It was a shame she and Mr. Brock didn't have more opportunities for one-on-one interaction.

"We're very lucky Mrs. Schmatt's machete was merely a plastic toy," Mr. Brock said. "Steven was physically unharmed. Mrs. Schmatt claims she was just trying to scare the youngster."

"She accomplished that," Chenille replied. "The machete looked so real!"

Glancing down at his desk, Mr. Brock picked up a doll-sized rake and began scratching it across a box of sand. He had one of those miniature Zen gardens, an executive toy intended to relieve stress. The office was quiet except for the *scritch, scritch* of the rake. After a few moments, Mr. Brock set it down and looked up at Chenille with a sheepish expression on his face.

"Steven's parents are making a big stink about this whole thing. I'm afraid they're blaming the teacher in charge."

"But *I'm* the teacher in charge," Chenille said slowly. Their lovely tête-à-tête was taking an ugly turn.

"I'm afraid so."

"Steven's parents are blaming *me*?" Chenille asked.

"Yes," Mr. Brock said. "Since Mrs. Schmatt was under your supervision, they consider you culpable. And they were influenced by Mrs. Schmatt's version of the episode."

Chenille gripped the arms of her chair. "Mrs. Schmatt's version?"

Mr. Brock swallowed, his voice a husky whisper. "Mrs. Schmatt claims she had your full approval to intimidate Steven."

"She *what*?" Chenille reared back in her chair as if she'd taken a hit from a shotgun.

"She said that you instructed her to use whatever means necessary to subdue your students."

Chenille clutched at the nosegay of cloth flowers at her throat and began to hiccup. Whenever she got really upset, her diaphragm would spasm and throw her into a vicious spell of hiccups.

"I may have . . . *hic* . . . suggested that she . . . *hic* . . . aid in the discipline of students, but I assumed she would stay within the parameters of . . . *hic* . . . professionalism as authorized . . . *hic* . . . by Bible Grove High School's Educator's Code of . . . *hic* . . . of Ethics."

"There, there, Ms. Grace. No need to get upset. Steven's parents aren't asking for your resignation."

"They're not?" Chenille said, although that possibility hadn't even crossed her mind.

"Not at all. They do, however, request that you be transferred from Bible Grove High. And seeing how Steven's uncle is on the school board, I've agreed to honor their wishes."

"Transferred? But I—"

"I took the liberty of calling personnel to see what openings were available in the county." He picked up a folder and peered inside. "The middle school in Dry Gulch has an industrial arts opening, and there's also an elementary Spanish position."

"Industrial arts? You don't mean shop class?"

"That's an outmoded term, but yes, I do mean shop." He took another glance at the folder. "Oh, wait a minute. The industrial arts position is only half-day. You probably want full-time. How's your Spanish?"

"Feliz navidad?"

"Good enough."

. . .

Chenille kept a shaky hold on her composure until she reached the parking lot. A torrent of tears gushed from her eyes as soon as she swung open the door of her Dodge Neon. What was she going to do? She couldn't *speak* Spanish, much less teach it. And Dry Gulch! She may as well have been banished to a gulag. Horror stories circulated about the teaching conditions there. Rat-ridden portable classrooms. Mimeograph machines always on the fritz. Textbooks last updated during the Eisenhower administration. She withdrew a Kleenex from the travel pack she kept in her console and blew her nose. Teaching was the one thing that gave her an identity. What would she do without it?

Chenille hadn't set out to be a career woman. Gracious, no! Despite excellent grades and much encouragement from her instructors, she always had her heart set on being a wife and mother. Maybe she would volunteer as a Brownie troop leader or a Pink Lady at the hospital, but she'd never anticipated a forty-hour workweek.

But attracting a suitable fellow—much less converting him into a husband—had proved troublesome. Although she wasn't as stunning as her sister, Chiffon, Chenille was hardly a hag. Her clothes were spotless; she meticulously coordinated her shoes with her pocketbooks, and she regularly sucked on Tic Tacs to maintain a fresh mouth. Nor had she withered away at home, hoping a man would materialize from the woodwork. During her twenties and early thirties, she'd been an active member of her singles Sunday school class and faithfully attended the monthly mixers at the VFW hall. But despite her diligent efforts, she had very few dates.

A few years ago, she'd stopped attending activities for singles. She'd blamed it on Walter, her Norwich terrier, who'd turned both diabetic and arthritic in his advancing years and required lots of care. But truthfully, Chenille had lost heart. An avid reader of romance novels, she'd always expected a tall stranger to sweep into her life and transform it. But now that she was a forty-year-old single woman, her girlhood dream of meeting and marrying Mr. Right seemed as out of reach as discovering an oil field in her backyard.

So, instead of marking time, waiting for a broad-chested Jake, Chase, or Dirk to happen along, she'd immersed herself in her career. She volunteered for all the school committees and handed in detailed and annotated lesson plans. She tirelessly and cheerfully accepted extra bus duty, and last Christmas she'd hand-decorated 250 cupcakes for the Junior-Senior Holiday Fling.

And now it was over. She was alone in this world with just her dog and his cartload of medical supplies. She envisioned herself and a flea-bitten Walter standing on a street corner, with a cardboard sign: WILL WORK FOR FOOD AND INSULIN.

Dipping into her Kleenex box for more tissues, she was startled by a knock on her passenger-side window. She dabbed at her eyes and rolled down the car window to speak with Winston Tobin, the school's public safety officer.

"Hello, Winston. How are you?" She faked a sneeze. "My goodness, my allergies are acting up today."

Chenille often exchanged pleasantries with Officer Tobin as he patrolled the halls of the high school. He was a short, jovial man (married, of course) with watery gray eyes and a neck the width of a tree trunk. He often recapped his Saturday-night bowling games with her during class changes.

"Ms. Grace, Mr. Brock tells me you're no longer on staff at Bible Grove High School. Would you kindly surrender your parking validation and identification badge?"

"Of course, Winston," Chenille said, unpinning her ID badge from her blouse. "But what's the rush? I still have to come back and pack up my room."

"No, Ms. Grace. Mr. Brock is having your personal items boxed up and sent to you via UPS. Steven's parents asked that you be denied further access to the school campus in order to prevent any further assaults."

"Great ghosts!" Chenille protested. "*I'm* no danger to Steven."

"I'm sorry, Miss Grace," Winston said, swallowing uncomfortably. "You need to leave now. Please don't return to Bible Grove High School for any reason, or I'll have to have you removed from the premises."

Men are like pantyhose. They run when you need them.

Graffiti in the ladies' room at the Tuff Luck Tavern

CHAPTER SIX

When Lonnie didn't get off the plane, Chiffon threw a hissy fit right there in the terminal. She harangued the reservation people, accusing them of misplacing her husband, as if he were a garment bag instead of a six-foot man with a mind of his own.

After repeated demands of "Where's my husband?" all three kids were bawling and the agent behind the airline counter had threatened to call security. Chiffon had no choice but to load her brood into the car and drive back to Cayboo Creek. Once home, she hustled the children inside and seized the phone, punching in the number of Lonnie's hotel room. Noticing the blinking light of her answering machine, she stopped dialing and listened to the message.

A familiar voice spoke on the recording.

"Hello, Chiffon? Chiffon Butrell? You don't know me, but my name is Janie-Lynn Lauren. I'm a film actress and I'm calling on the behalf of your husband, Lonnie. He won't be coming home today. Or the next day. In fact, he has no idea when or *if* he'll return. Good-bye for now."

Chiffon listened to the message at least five times, and with each play she got more frantic. Her first instinct was to toss a few diapers and clothes in a bag, scoop up the kids, and tear off to California to retrieve her husband. That idea lost steam when she checked her pocketbook and found she had just $23.17 left over from the money her mama had given her. With that kind of cash she'd only get as far as Alabama. Her second instinct was to head over to the Dairy Queen and suck down two or three Pecan Mudslides. She followed her third instinct, which was to call her friends for support. This burden was too heavy to carry all by herself.

Moments later, Mavis arrived at Chiffon's house carrying a Tupperware dish filled with homemade pimento cheese spread.

"There's nothing like pimento cheese to cheer a body," Mavis said, placing the container on the kitchen counter.

"Thanks for coming, Mavis," Chiffon said. "Attalee said she'd be here directly. I need some strong shoulders to cry on."

"That's what these shoulders are for, Chiffon," Mavis said, drawing her into an embrace.

Chiffon felt comforted by the older woman's arms around her. She'd known Mavis since she was a child, but it was only in the last few years that she'd begun to think of her as a surrogate mama.

"Pull your head out of the oven, girl," Attalee said, bursting through Chiffon's back door. "Attalee's here, break out the beer!"

Chiffon lifted her head from Mavis's shoulder and smiled weakly at her guest. "I guess the party's begun," she said.

"I don't know what ails you," Attalee said as she sorted through a cloth satchel that hung from her arm. "But here's something to help you forget your troubles." She withdrew a *Playgirl* magazine, saying, "Nothing like a little beefcake to chase away the blues."

Mavis picked up the magazine and glanced inside. "Oh my," she said, dropping it as if it were on fire.

"It's been a while, ain't it?" Attalee said with a sly grin. "They're making them bigger than I remember."

Attalee dropped into a chair and looked up at Chiffon. "So what's plaguing you? Put it on the front porch." She glanced at the back door. "Or are you waiting for Elizabeth to get here so you can kill three birds with one slingshot?"

Chiffon toed the linoleum with her tennis shoe. "I didn't call Elizabeth. I don't want to upset her right now, considering her delicate condition."

Mavis patted her arm. "That's real thoughtful of you, Chiffon, but knowing Elizabeth as I do, she'd want to be here for you. Baby on the way or not."

Chiffon nodded. "I know, but I just didn't think—"

The kitchen door opened and Elizabeth rushed in, holding a magazine to her swollen belly. Her bottom lip trembled as she spoke. "Oh, Chiffon. Sweetie! Why didn't you tell me?" She glanced at the magazine in her hand. "I'm so sorry."

"Sorry about what?" Chiffon asked. "Why are you so upset? What's in your hand?"

Elizabeth paled. "I thought you knew. I'd guessed you were keeping it to yourself." In her distress, she dropped the *People* magazine she was holding. It landed faceup, so everyone in Chiffon's kitchen could see the cover.

"Christ on a crutch!" Chiffon gasped as she picked up the magazine. "Where'd you get this?"

"At the Winn-Dixie," Elizabeth squeaked. "This photo is on the cover of every celebrity magazine in the grocery store— *US, In Touch*, even *The National Enquirer*."

The cover story was titled "Janie-Lynn's Latest Dish," but it was the accompanying photo that told the tale. There was a head shot of a man, cheek-to-cheek with Janie-Lynn Lauren. They were both grinning stupidly, like a pair of chimpanzees. This time there was no mistaking it. The man on the cover was her husband, Lonnie.

Attalee gaped at the photograph. "Well, I never . . . That boy should have his hide hung on a fence."

Chiffon wasn't listening. She was too busy rifling through her pocketbook for her car keys. "Okay, this is what we're going to do. Before anyone in town sees this, we're going to drive down to the Winn-Dixie and buy every single copy of this magazine. Then we'll get some lighter fluid and have a big old bonfire."

Just then the phone rang.

"What?" Chiffon barked into the receiver.

"Chiffon, I'm sorry to bother you, but this is Reeky. Listen, I just got in this week's shipment of magazines and I couldn't believe what I saw on the cover. Does Lonnie have a twin brother?"

"Please don't sell any of those magazines, Reeky. I'll be right down to take them off your hands," Chiffon said, hanging up the phone. It rang again at once.

"Chiffon? This is Effie Stykes. I was getting my hair done at the Dazzling Do's, and I nearly choked on my Tab when I saw who was on the cover of *The Globe* this week."

Chiffon slammed down the phone. "We need to run by Dazzling Do's and to all the other places in Cayboo Creek with magazines in the waiting room. Let's split up so we can cover the whole area."

The phone rang again. This time Mavis gently pushed past Chiffon and picked it up.

"Yes, Luna. No, it's Mavis. Chiffon knows all about Lonnie. You say they interrupted your TV program just to announce it? What kind of show gets interrupted by Hollywood gossip?" Mavis nodded in understanding as she listened. "Ah. I see. Carmen Electra, *E! True Hollywood Story*."

Mavis ended the conversation with Luna and then turned down the ringer on Chiffon's phone. "Chiffon, I think you should let your machine pick up for a little while. Until things die down."

"Okay," Chiffon said, nervously rubbing her hands together. "Here's our strategy. Mavis, you take the area north of Mule

Pen Road. I'll take Chickasaw Drive and Main. Attalee and Elizabeth, you cover Highway One."

Mavis touched Chiffon's shoulder. "Why don't you just sit down for a spell? I'll make some coffee."

"But I need to stop this before it gets out of hand," Chiffon insisted.

Mavis shook her head. "It's too late, dearie. Buying up all the magazines in this county isn't going to change that."

Chiffon flung herself into the ladder-back chair at the kitchen table, her body heaving with sobs. "How could he do this to me? Again! Doesn't he care about the kids or me? Doesn't he love us?"

Mavis patted her back. "Oh, Chiffon, who knows what gets into men these days!"

"Old Granddad whiskey used to get into my man, Burl," Attalee said. "When he was tippling, he'd make a play for anything in a skirt. Or a kilt, for that matter. Once he was so soused, he tried to chase down the bagpipe player during the Memorial Day parade."

"Attalee," Mavis said. "I don't think—"

"I do miss Burl," Attalee said with a sniff. "Struck down by a bread truck in his prime. He was just eighty-five. Still had all his teeth in his upper jaw."

"Attalee, that's enough," Mavis said. "It's Chiffon who needs our help right now."

"I feel so all alone in this world," Chiffon moaned.

Attalee, who'd recovered from her moment of self-pity, draped a scrawny arm around Chiffon's neck. "You ain't alone, girl. Not by a long shot. You got me, Mavis, and Elizabeth here. We can't take away the pain, but we sure can badmouth that boy all over town."

"And we can be here for you anytime you need us," Mavis said, squeezing Chiffon's hand.

Elizabeth pressed her cheek against Chiffon's. "That's a promise."

If you're not living on the
edge, you're taking up too
much space.

Bumper sticker on Chiffon Butrell's Firebird

CHAPTER SEVEN

Chiffon's children sat in front of the TV set watching a screen full of static.

"I can almost make out SpongeBob," Emily said. "If I squint real hard."

"I can't see anything!" Dewitt whined. He flung his toy truck to the ground. "Why is it always snowing on TV?"

It was snowing on television because Lonnie had forgotten to pay the bill for the satellite dish. Chiffon wondered what other bills he might have neglected before he left.

Struggling to pull a pair of pantyhose over her hips, she said,

"Y'all don't need to be watching TV right now anyway. Start getting ready for school. I can't be late today."

Chiffon was working the lunch shift at the Chat 'N' Chew, frantically hoping to pick up some decent tips. She was running on gas fumes in her car, Dewitt's tennis shoes were full of holes, and the only food in the pantry was a bag of slow-cooking grits. She didn't even want to think about the stack of bills that had arrived in her mailbox on Saturday, three of which had been stamped "past due." Earlier this morning she'd called the NutraSweet plant to see if she could pick up Lonnie's check, but the payroll clerk told her it had already been forwarded to California.

As Chiffon rummaged through her closet for her soft-soled waitress shoes, she felt a tug on her T-shirt. When she turned around, Emily stood behind her.

"Mama, Gabby's crying, and Dewitt spilled the orange juice," she announced.

"Why did you let him pour it? You know he's too little," Chiffon asked. She didn't wait for an answer, but instead rushed to the nursery to retrieve Gabby.

Once she'd hefted fifteen pounds of wet, squirming baby on her shoulder, she dispatched Emily to clean up Dewitt's mess and help him dress. Then she sat on the couch to feed her youngest daughter. While Gabby nursed, Chiffon inventoried the living room for items she could sell for a little extra cash. The pool table could gladly go, as could all of Lonnie's guns, but most of the room's furnishings were so dilapidated they wouldn't raise ten dollars at a tag sale.

As she burped Gabby, someone knocked on the front door. Pushing apart the curtains, Chiffon saw Wanda standing on her front porch, wearing her Mary Kay jacket and impatiently tapping a two-toned gold pump on Chiffon's doormat.

"Hey, Mama," Chiffon said, opening the door.

Wanda ignored her and muscled her way into the living room, slapping a copy of *People* magazine on the coffee table.

"Chiffon Amber, if this isn't the absolute limit! I guess you weren't content to air your dirty drawers in Cayboo Creek. Now everyone in the entire US of A has to know what a fool you've been."

"Mama, I really don't want—"

"Do you know who called me today?" Wanda's eyes bulged so much they looked like they might plop right out of their sockets.

Chiffon dragged a hand down her face. "I haven't the foggiest, Mama."

"Your aunt Minerva, all the way from Mud Lake, Idaho. She subscribes to *People* magazine, and she recognized Lonnie from her visit during Thanksgiving two years ago. Think of it, Chiffon! The decent, potato-eating people of Idaho have a front-row seat to your husband's debauchery."

Chiffon laid Gabby out on the couch to change her. "Mama, I'm sorry that Lonnie's tomcatting has caused you shame, but I didn't have anything to do with him being on the cover of *People*. Surely even you can see that."

Wanda sighed. "I don't need your lip, Chiffon, and I don't want to hear any excuses. Anyone with half a brain would have left that sorry specimen of a man years ago. This is too much for me to bear. I've been trying to prepare for my trip to Europe, and I'm as wrung out as a dish towel. Last night Chenille called with her awful news, and if that wasn't bad enough—"

"What's wrong with Chenille?" Chiffon asked.

"She lost her teaching job. Something to do with a machete. On top of everything, that broken-down dog of hers has developed eczema. She acts more upset about that mutt's skin problems than getting fired."

"Poor Chenille," Chiffon said, fastening the tabs of Gabby's diaper. "It's hard to imagine *her* getting fired."

"I don't know what's wrong with you girls," Wanda said, folding her arms over her chest. "I raised y'all to be something special, and yet both of you are scraping around at the bottom of the barrel. Last week when Effie Stykes told me her youngest just graduated from dental assistant school, I was pea green with envy. At least her daughter has some kind of future, even if it means rooting around in people's mouths all day long."

"I'm sorry I'm such a disappointment," Chiffon said quietly.

"Sorry isn't going put food in your children's mouths, is it, Chiffon? Now that your husband is AWOL, I suppose you'll be looking to me for handouts. I can help out some, but I can't keep throwing money in your direction. I've got my own expenses to consider."

"I don't need your handouts," Chiffon mumbled.

"Don't you sass me, Chiffon." Wanda opened her wallet, took out four twenty-dollar bills, and held them out to her daughter. "That's all I can spare right now."

Chiffon wished she could turn her back on her mama's money, but her maternal instincts were stronger than her pride. She took the cash and tucked it into her bra.

"To think of all the money I wasted on your charm lessons!" Wanda said, the door thwacking behind her.

After her mother left, Chiffon picked up the *People* magazine she'd brought over and pitched it across the room. She strode into the children's room and accidentally stomped on a LEGO piece.

"Dewitt, you need to keep your toys picked up or they're all going in the trash."

She lifted her foot and saw a stream of blood coursing from a cut. Both Gabby and Dewitt were wailing, and Emily was tossing clothes out of her chest of drawers, saying, "Mama, I can't find any clean panties."

Chiffon remembered the overflowing basket of dirty laundry in the trunk of her car. She'd meant to stop at the Laundromat on Sunday after she'd picked up Lonnie at the airport, but Sunday seemed like a million years ago. It had been one of the worst days of her life.

Today didn't look like it was going to be a heck of a lot better.

"Welcome to Dumpsville.

Population You"

Selection F-3 on the Tuff Luck Tavern jukebox

CHAPTER EIGHT

"Two chicks on a raft! Wreck 'em," Jewel Turner sang out to Mort Washington, the elderly black cook at the Chat 'N' Chew.

Jewel, the owner, had spent the morning showing Chiffon the ins and outs of working at the diner. And what a morning it had been! The Marquis de Sade couldn't have planned a more miserable few hours. As soon as Chiffon set foot into the diner, coffee cups stopped in mid-sip and mouths dropped open. Clearly there wasn't a soul in the Chat 'N' Chew who hadn't heard about Janie-Lynn Lauren and Lonnie.

Jewel, a curvy redhead with big brown eyes, ushered Chiffon into her office, saying, "Don't you mind them. You'll be the star attraction for about two minutes, and then they'll move on to who won last night's turkey shoot."

Chiffon wasn't so sure. This was the biggest thing to hit Cayboo Creek since DeEtta Jefferson had appeared on *The Price Is Right* and won the showcase featuring a Dodge Viper convertible. People in Cayboo Creek had been abuzz for weeks. Birdie Murdock did a three-part article on DeEtta's win in the *Cayboo Creek Crier*, and the Jaycees organized a parade in her honor.

"I'm so sorry, Chiffon," Jewel said. "Sounds like Lonnie has one too many mares in his barn. But I've been in your shoes, and I know how much it hurts."

"What do you mean?" Chiffon asked.

Jewel's brown eyes looked pained. "Let's just say I'm on a first-name basis with heartache. That's why I've sworn off men. Now my business keeps me busy."

Chiffon couldn't imagine a diner being any kind of substitute for a loving man. Jewel was in her thirties and as pretty as a bushel of strawberries. She shouldn't give up on finding a fellow so easily.

"Shoot, Jewel! No call to be all by your lonesome. I could introduce you to a few nice guys," Chiffon said.

"Nope," Jewel said with a smile. "Maybe someday. But right now I'm content being unattached."

Chiffon didn't believe a word coming out of Jewel's mouth. What woman didn't want the big, strong arms of a man wrapped around her? Why, it was the most natural thing in the world. Jewel had likely been brainwashed by the *Oprah* show, thinking a woman could be complete without a man.

Chiffon had no intentions of living without a mate. When Lonnie got over this latest episode, she'd take him back just as she had in the past. He'd pay, Lordy yes, he'd pay, but she couldn't turn out the father of her children. After all, every man has his flat side, and cheating happened to be Lonnie's. It humiliated her that everyone in town knew about his hanky-panky, but Chiffon would hold her head up high amid the gossip. It was her marriage, and she intended to do everything within her power to preserve it.

After Chiffon's talk with Jewel, things went from bad to worse. For starters, Chiffon wasn't familiar with the diner lingo at the Chat 'N' Chew and had a hard time catching on.

"Bossy in a bowl and a Coke. Hold the hail," Jewel called out to Mort, which, translated, meant an order of beef stew and a Coke with no ice.

"Mort's been a cook for over fifty years," Jewel explained. "He's the one who taught me diner talk. The customers like it. Gives them the feel of a real greasy spoon."

As far as Chiffon was concerned, the Chat 'N' Chew didn't needed diner lingo to make it seem like a greasy spoon; the chipped coffee mugs and the flypaper dangling from the ceiling did the job just fine. But Chiffon wanted to please her employer, so she tried to master the unfamiliar slang.

When a customer ordered two hamburgers with onions, no lettuce, Chiffon approached Mort. "Two cows. Make them sad. Mow the grass," she said tentatively.

"No, girlie," Mort said. "It's two cows, make 'em cry, and keep off the grass."

"Sorry," Chiffon said, trying to keep it all straight.

All day long she kept making mistakes and mixing up orders.

And her tips reflected her incompetence. By the time the lunch rush was over, she'd pocketed only $25. She used to make three times that at the Wagon Wheel.

When the diner finally emptied out, Chiffon relaxed at the lunch counter with a bowl of chicken soup and a slice of lemon meringue pie. Jewel stood at the cash register, checking her reflection in a pocket mirror.

"I hope your first day wasn't too rough," she said, combing her auburn bangs with her fingers. "I'm sure it won't take long to catch on."

Chiffon touched the thin roll of bills in the pocket of her uniform. If she didn't catch on soon, she and the kids would be eating a steady diet of ramen noodles.

The front bell jingled and Jewel closed her compact. "I'll get this one, Chiffon. You sit tight."

"No," Chiffon said, pushing aside the bowl of soup. "I'll see to it. I need the practice."

Chiffon wearily trudged to the back of the restaurant, where someone had taken a seat in a booth beneath a yellowed 1987 calendar. The customer's face was buried in the menu.

"How ya doing? Can I get you something to drink?" Chiffon asked.

"Diet Coke, three ice cubes, and a side of lemon," said a familiar female voice.

"What size Coke you want?" Chiffon asked.

The menu lowered two inches, and Chiffon found herself staring into the heavily made-up eyes of Jonelle Jasper.

"Chiffon Butrell? What are you doing here?" Jonelle asked nervously.

"I work here," Chiffon snapped. "Our special today is meat

loaf with a side of—" She stopped short when she saw the message on Jonelle's T-shirt. "What the heck is that supposed to mean?" she said.

Jonelle covered her T-shirt with her hand. "It's just a little joke."

"'I slept with Lonnie Butrell,'" Chiffon said, reading the lettering. "Where in the heck did you get that . . . thing?"

"I had it made at the T-shirt shop in Augusta," Jonelle said as she nibbled on a purple fingernail. "Janie-Lynn Lauren is my all-time favorite movie star; some say we even favor each other. What a coincidence that she and I both slept with *you know who*—"

"Get out of here right now," Chiffon hissed. "Or I'll knock your frizzy-haired self into tomorrow."

Jonelle shot up from the booth and planted her hands on her skinny hips. "Are you threatening me, Chiffon Butrell?"

"You better believe it, you sorry, selfish little—"

"Whoa, Chiffon!" Jewel said, grabbing her arm. "Pull in those horns, girl. What's the problem here?"

Jonelle's face was twisted into a scowl. "Your hired help threatened me with bodily harm."

"Is that true, Chiffon?" a wide-eyed Jewel asked.

"Look at her T-shirt," Chiffon said through gritted teeth.

"What?" Jewel said as her eyes fell on the message emblazoned on Jonelle's flat chest.

"I had no idea she was working here," Jonelle said. "Even if I did, she has no right to come at me like . . ." She fastened her eyes on Chiffon and looked her up and down. "Like a sumo wrestler."

"What's *that* supposed to mean?" Chiffon huffed.

Jonelle clenched her jaw. "I'm saying you're bigger than a moose. No wonder Lonnie always strays. It's not like I'm the only woman in this town who could wear this T-shirt."

Chiffon tried to lunge for Jonelle, but Jewel yanked her back by her apron strings. "That's enough, Chiffon," she said breathlessly.

"Just what kind of crazy establishment are you running here, anyway?" Jonelle said.

"Why don't you just let *me* take your order, Jonelle?" Jewel said, poising a pencil over her order pad.

"Why don't you?" Jonelle said with a flip of her ratty dark hair. "I'll have a Diet Coke, the meat loaf special, a slice of chocolate icebox pie—"

"Sorry, we're out of it," Jewel said neutrally.

"Out of what?" Jonelle asked.

"Everything you ordered."

Jonelle frowned and squinted at the menu. "All right, then, I'll have a Diet Sprite, barbecue chicken, and an apple turnover—"

Jewel shook her head from side to side. "Sorry."

Jonelle tossed the menu on the table and glared up at Jewel. "Just what *do* you have?"

"You're in luck," Jewel said. "Today we're featuring the mystery special. And your server, Chiffon, will personally prepare it for you."

"I'd be delighted," purred Chiffon.

Jonelle's bottom lip twitched. "So that's how it's going to be? Knowing Chiffon, she'll spit in my food." She snatched up her pocketbook. "I'll just take my appetite elsewhere."

As soon as she left, Jewel burst out laughing. "She's one customer I can afford to lose."

Chiffon slumped down in the booth. "You shouldn't have to lose any. I'm sorry, Jewel. I didn't mean to cause a scene. I just saw that T-shirt of hers, and it sent me over the edge."

"It's all right, Chiffon," Jewel said, sliding next to her and squeezing her shoulder. "It was worth it to see the look on her face. She can dish it out, but she sure can't take it."

"I've always had a temper hot as fire," Chiffon said, thinking how simple it was to put Jonelle in her place. How come she couldn't do the same with her mama or Lonnie?

"Why don't you go on home, Chiffon?" Jewel said. "I'll take care of your side work for you. I know you've had a long day."

"Are you sure, Jewel?" Chiffon asked. "I don't want you thinking I don't pull my own weight."

"Go on, now," Jewel said with a wave of her dishcloth.

Chiffon decided to nip by the Winn-Dixie before she picked Gabby up from day care and met the older children's school bus. It was a rare luxury to shop without a buggy spilling over with youngsters. The Winn-Dixie had car-shaped kiddy carts, so there was always the ongoing squabble over who was going to "drive." But the worst part about shopping with her kids was always saying no to all of their requests. Chiffon would like to have said yes now and then, but the family's financial situation left no extra money for the pricey treats that beckoned the kids from the grocer's shelves. Emily, at age eight, was already resigned to the fact that Mommy only bought bags of off-brand cereals like Captain Crisp or Fruity Ohs, instead of the glamorous name-brand varieties dangled under the kids' noses during Saturday-morning cartoons. Dewitt, on the other hand, was still too young to understand why Chiffon purchased the broken cookies on the bargain table instead of Oreos or Keeblers, or why he was never allowed to buy any overpriced drink boxes. Every shopping trip with that child in tow was a trial by tears.

Just once, Chiffon would like to go into the grocery store and toss items into her buggy with abandon, instead of fretting over each purchase, as if she were pricing rubies instead of radishes. Just once she'd like to buy her kids every kind of sugary, teeth-rotting snack they saw on TV.

In the grocery store's parking lot, Chiffon carefully counted out the bills in her wallet, trying to figure how much she could safely spend, deducting the cost of Gabby's day-care bill and Dewitt's sneakers. Her shoulders slumped when she realized how little she'd have left over. Even broken cookies wouldn't make it into her buggy today.

She entered the store and headed toward the produce section. As she checked the price on a bag of Golden Delicious apples, she heard two women whispering near the cantaloupe bin. She tossed a glance in their direction and the whispering ceased.

Chiffon strutted past them with her chin in the air. What did she care what a couple of broken-down biddies thought about her? She did the same when she encountered a clutch of teenage girls in the cosmetics section who went as far as to point and giggle as she passed by.

As she made her way through the store, she deflected every look, murmur, and guffaw, feeling like she had a glass bubble around her. Nothing could touch her; no one could slip past her defenses. She was invincible. She probably would have left the store completely unscathed if she hadn't had to pass through the checkout line. That's when she lost it.

Every magazine cover seemed to feature a photo of Lonnie and Janie-Lynn Lauren together. To see it for herself, to look at all those glossy images of Lonnie lewdly leering at another woman, was more than Chiffon could bear.

Without warning, her wall of protection crumbled and she was stripped clean to the bone. She couldn't stand the scrutiny of the other shoppers for one more second. Shoving her cart to the side, she hightailed it from the store. Tears blinded her as she bolted down the aisle and flung herself toward the exit doors. On her way out, she nearly sideswiped a stock boy holding a mop.

"Watch out," he said. "Somebody spilled some—"

Chiffon's legs gave way, and she skidded several feet before falling in a heap beside a row of gumball machines.

"Wesson oil," he said. "Are you all right, miss? You hit that ground pretty hard."

"I'm fine," Chiffon snapped, struggling to get up. When she tried to put weight on her left leg, she cried out in pain and tumbled to the ground again.

Consciousness is that annoying

time between naps.

Sign outside of a mattress store in Bible Grove

CHAPTER NINE

"You, too, can unearth precious treasures with the MineCo 3000, the most powerful metal detector on the market," blared the TV commercial on Chenille's little ten-inch portable.

Chenille, who'd been lying on her bed in a stupor, propped herself up on her elbows and watched the advertisement with interest. *Metal detecting? Maybe that would be a good way to bring in some extra income.* She could see herself sweeping vacant fields and unearthing misplaced rings or earrings, taking her bounty to pawnshops and bringing home thick rolls of bills. Why, she could have a thriving little business!

"For an investment of only $299.95, you'll soon be finding valuable coins, jewelry, and other riches—"

Chenille aimed the remote at the television. Three hundred dollars was more money than she could safely part with right now. What a shame! Metal detecting seemed like such a restful, solitary type of occupation.

She channel-surfed, looking for *Law and Order*. Ever since she'd been out of work, she'd discovered she could find her favorite show almost any time of the day or night, so she regularly indulged in a near-orgy of episodes. On the rare occasions when she couldn't find the show, her hands trembled and her stomach churned. In a pinch, she'd try to make do with other crime shows such as *CSI* or HBO's *Autopsy series*, but it just wasn't the same.

Chenille wriggled contentedly into her covers when she found an episode of *Law and Order: Criminal Intent* on USA. As an added bonus, it was an episode she'd seen only twice before. She patted the place beside her, expecting to find Walter, but there was only a slight indentation in the bedclothes where his little body had recently lain.

He must have jumped off the bed *again*. There was no denying it: Walter had been distant lately. At first she attributed his standoffishness to his bout with eczema, but even after she applied an itch-soothing topical cream, Walter remained aloof. He no longer followed her from room to room, his stubby legs hurrying to match her long strides. When they relaxed side by side on the bed, he showed her the gray hump of his back instead of his sweet, bewhiskered face. But most disturbing of all, whenever she tried to hug him, he now squirmed to escape her embrace.

Sometimes Chenille swore she saw a look in his eyes that went beyond mere annoyance and bordered on disdain. Was it possible for an animal to lose respect for his owner? Did he somehow sense her decline in status?

He slunk across the carpet with Boo Bear in his mouth, looking so dear, so guileless.

"Walter, darling. Come up here with Mommy," she said, her needy fingers reaching out for his wiry compact form.

He didn't even glance up, but quickened his pace and ducked underneath the bed.

Chenille pounded the pillow beside her. *Snubbed again.* How could he treat her this way when she was so vulnerable? If she'd wanted this kind of behavior in an animal, she could have gotten a cat.

A cry of self-pity welled up in her throat, but she swallowed it back. *Buck up, Chenille.* No wonder Walter didn't want to be near her! She needed to quit languishing in bed and start looking for a job. If only she weren't pinned to the mattress by some kind of invisible force field.

On the day after she'd lost her job, Chenille had gotten up at 5:45 A.M. as usual. She'd consumed her customary breakfast of Grape Nuts with blueberries and a cup of decaf. She'd dressed in her nicest outfit, an ecru suit with lavender piping, accessorized with her pearl-inlaid filigree heart and matching earrings.

Leaving her home at seven o'clock on the dot with the *Bible Grove Courier* and her résumé in hand, she'd driven three miles down the road to the Prospect Employment Agency. There she waited in the parking lot for nearly a half hour, until a mousy woman in a cheap brown suit opened the door for business. Chenille marched inside the agency, a self-assured smile on her face. She addressed the woman behind the desk in a clear, strong voice.

"I read your advertisement in the paper—the one with the 'Jobs Galore' headline—and I drove right over."

The woman frowned. "Can I see that advertisement?"

Chenille surrendered the paper to her. She'd circled the ad several times with a permanent black marker.

The woman, who had a dusting of Danish crumbs on her lip, squinted at the ad.

"This is a typo. It should have read '*job* galore,' because I've got only one listing right now." She peered at Chenille. "You aren't by chance a journeyman welder?"

"No," Chenille said, puzzled. "You have just one job?"

"Yup," she said with a nod.

"As a welder?"

"*Journeyman* welder."

"But the word 'galore' means 'in great numbers' or 'an abundance,'" Chenille said in a puzzled tone. "It can't refer to just one job."

The woman took a noisy slurp of her coffee. "What are you? Some kind of English teacher?"

"Yes, actually, I am. Or rather I *was*."

The woman stared at her. "Wait a minute. You're not that English teacher that everyone in town's talking about, are you?"

Chenille's skin prickled at the collar of her blouse. "I have no idea to whom you are referring."

"The psycho one who tried to cut off some kid's head with a chain saw."

"Good grief! It wasn't a chain saw. It was a plastic machete, and I didn't—"

"It *is* you, isn't it?" The woman went pale. She seized a letter opener on her desk and wielded it at Chenille with a shaking hand. "Look, I don't want any trouble here. If you don't leave peaceably, I'll have to call the police."

. . .

Right after Chenille left Prospect Employment Agency, she took to her bed, where she'd been ever since. Each night before she went to sleep, she promised herself that she would get up early and start making the rounds with her résumé, if not in Bible Grove, then in some of the surrounding cities like Pickens, Easley, or even Greenville.

But every morning, as the streaks of sunlight stippled her bedclothes, an overwhelming feeling of fatigue flattened her to the mattress. Simple tasks like fastening the buttons of her blouse or squeezing toothpaste from the tube seemed to require a superhuman kind of strength that she didn't possess. So she stayed underneath her flannel sheets and down comforter, one arm snaking out beneath the covers to find the remote, and remained there for the entire day, except to attend to Walter's needs or snag a bite to eat from the fridge.

A commercial for a business college interrupted her show. Chenille yawned. How she could be so tired after sleeping twelve hours each night?

"Get on the fast track with your degree in information technology, medical assistance, or accounting," said a fresh-faced woman in a nurse's cap.

What exactly does a medical assistant do? Chenille tried to imagine herself in a spotless white lab coat, working elbow-to-elbow with a wavy-haired, cleft-chinned physician. Their eyes would meet over a test tube and he would say, "Miss Grace, you've no idea how much I admire your dedication to pathology."

She foraged in her nightstand drawer for a pencil to copy down the toll-free number on the screen, but by the time she'd struggled out of the covers, another commercial was on.

"If you, or someone you know, has been injured in an accident, call Schlager and Schlager, attorneys at law."

During the day, there was no shortage of ads for people in debt, out of work, or in need of a quick loan. Chenille was being indoctrinated into a brand-new subculture. At the rate she was declining, who knew when she might need the services of Pawn Auto or No-Questions-Asked Loan Company.

Just as the commercial break ended, the phone rang, startling her. Chenille had no idea who could be on the other line; she received so few calls. The ringing was muffled, as if the phone was wedged under one of the many pillows on her bed. Before she could locate it, the answering machine clicked on and Chenille heard her mother's voice.

"Chenille? Are you there? Your sister has gone and sprained her ankle. Can you imagine? And her with a baby and two other children to care for. I blame that husband of hers. If Lonnie hadn't got mixed up in this latest terrible business, Chiffon wouldn't have been so distracted and slipped on that cooking oil."

Chenille clucked her tongue with disapproval. Lonnie's "terrible business" could have been any number of things. He was one of those foolhardy Southern men who were always finding themselves in hot water.

"Obviously I can't help her take care of those kids, not with my trip to Europe coming up. Thank the Lord you're in the position to lend a hand. It shouldn't be for more than a couple of weeks. Please call me just as soon as you get this message."

Some family trees bear lots
of nuts.

CHAPTER TEN

Last Christmas, Chenille had needed an entire week just to decompress from her annual visit to Cayboo Creek. And that was after seeing her sister and mother for only a weekend. It was hard to imagine spending fourteen days or more in her sister's company.

Still, she knew she had no choice but to help out. Family was family, even if they did make her break out in hives. What kind of person would she be if she didn't help her flesh and blood when they needed her most?

After calling her mother to say she was on her way, she

forced herself to get out of bed and stand under a hot shower. Toweling off, she dressed in red leggings, a plaid jumper, and a matching fringed poncho with pom-poms at the hem. Then she dressed Walter in a Chesterfield topcoat that matched her jumper. She'd half expected him to protest, but he willingly slipped into the garment, as if he sensed the new purposefulness in the air. She then packed her bags, a set for herself and one for Walter, and just before leaving, she left a note for her neighbor, asking her to collect mail and newspapers.

On her way out of town, Chenille filled up her car at the convenience store and purchased a bottle of spring water and a tin of breath mints for the trip. While she waited in line to pay, she glanced at the magazine rack and was astonished to see her brother-in-law on the cover of *People* magazine. So *this* was the terrible business her mother had referred to on the phone! Lonnie was fooling around with the movie star Janie-Lynn Lauren. How awful for Chiffon! She had to be devastated.

After gassing up, Chenille double-checked the straps on Walter's booster seat, set her trip odometer, and sped off to the sounds of Michael Bolton singing "Soul Provider." As she traveled, rain occasionally specked the windshield, and the unvaried landscape of fallow cotton fields and ruddy soil made her sleepy. When she reached the halfway point to Cayboo Creek, she could pick up only country stations riddled with static, so she snapped off the radio and listened to the low thrumming of the motor.

"It'll be nice to be around children again. Don't you think so, Walter? There's a baby in the house now."

Chenille had driven to Cayboo Creek for a day visit when Gabby was first born, but she'd only caught a glimpse of the baby's wrinkled red face through the large window in the hospital nursery. That was back in September. The little girl would be about six months old by now. She wondered if she'd be expected to lend a hand with Gabby, not completely trusting herself with very small children. They tended to be slippery.

Chenille vaguely knew Chiffon's two older children. She'd visited with them on the occasional holiday, and each Christmas she went to the Busy Minds store in the mall and selected age-appropriate, educational toys as gifts for them. Emily seemed quiet enough, studious even. But Dewitt was more rambunctious. Once he'd tried to engage Walter in some rough-and-tumble play, and her dog had signified his outrage by nipping the boy on the ankle.

Chenille stole a look at a panting Walter in the backseat.

"Are you feeling okay, sweetie? Are you overheated? You look so distinguished in your coat."

She rolled down the backseat window an inch or so, hoping to stave off any carsickness. Chenille softly whistled "Me and You and a Dog Named Boo" while she observed a forest of kudzu-shrouded trees. She noticed an abandoned lean-to shack with a homemade billboard advertising boiled peanuts. As she passed a peach grove, she saw the first sign for Cayboo Creek. The closer she got to her hometown, the more unsettled her stomach became. Maybe things would be different this time. Maybe she wouldn't feel so out of place with her mother and sister.

"Ha! And maybe Walter will decide to take up needlepoint," Chenille murmured to herself. She couldn't remember a time in her life when she'd felt even remotely comfortable around her family. As a preteen, she used to fantasize that she was the long-lost daughter of Ethel Kennedy. It made sense to her, as she shared none of the curvy blond prettiness of her mother and sister. Instead, she had boyish limbs and a decided horsiness to her features, much like the Kennedy women. She imagined she'd been accidentally left behind on an outing to Hyannis Port. It was plausible. Ethel had eleven children. Was it such a stretch that one had been overlooked? It would explain why she was inept with a Dial-a-Lash mascara wand and a curling iron and why she didn't look like a hybrid of Elle McPherson and Dolly Parton. How many times had she been out with her sister and mother and heard people remark, "Chenille must look like her father"?

If only her father had been RFK instead of Byron Grace, a window cleaner, who, over thirty years ago, had driven away from his family in a van emblazoned with the slogan YOUR PANE IS OUR PLEASURE.

Eventually Chenille had to let go of the notion that she belonged in Greenwich, Connecticut, instead of Cayboo Creek. She no longer daydreamed about playing touch football within the walls of the Kennedy compound or consulting her aunt Jackie for fashion advice. But if she couldn't be a Kennedy, she had decided she would escape the home where she felt like such an oddity. Except for occasional visits, she'd been able to keep her sister and mother at bay for a little over twenty years. Now she was driving straight back into her family's well-endowed bosoms, where she would remain for fourteen days. She sighed. Her former life in Bible Grove already seemed a million miles away.

*The problem with the gene
pool is there's no lifeguard.*

Sign tacked to a bulletin board in the Senior Center

CHAPTER ELEVEN

Chiffon stared into the burnt mess at the bottom of her Cup O' Noodles. Did Wanda really expect her to eat this?

"Mama?" Chiffon called out softly. When she didn't get an answer, she raised her voice a notch. "Mama? Where are you?"

Wanda, who'd been in the children's room, poked her head into the living room. Wearing a look of pure disgust, she held a diaper at arm's length. "What are you yelling about?"

"I'm not yelling, Mama. I just—" She looked again into her Cup O' Noodles. "Did you put water in this?"

"Water?" Wanda snatched the noodle container from Chiffon's hand. "Oh, for pity's sake. You should have told me it needed water. 'Just heat it up in the microwave,' you said. Your exact words."

"I'm sorry, Mama. You're right. I should have been more clear."

Wanda cocked her head and glared at Chiffon. "Do I hear a tone in your voice, Chiffon Amber? Because I have better things to do than wait hand and foot on you and your litter of children. I haven't sat down one minute since I've gotten here."

"No, Mama. There's no tone, I swear," Chiffon said.

"I certainly hope not," Wanda said, moving brusquely to the kitchen with the diaper in hand. "I'm going to the market now. You're fresh out of milk." The back door banged behind her as she left.

Emily scampered out of her room and plopped down next to Chiffon on the couch. "Mama, does your ankle still bother you?" she asked.

Chiffon stroked the end of her daughter's braid. "Not too much, baby. The doctor gave me some medicine to kill the pain."

"Mama, are baloney sandwiches meant to be crunchy?"

"No, honey. Why? Was the sandwich Grandma made you crunchy?"

Emily nodded. "My stomach hurts." She put her head in Chiffon's lap and Chiffon made little circles on her daughter's tummy with her finger.

Besides being the world's longest-suffering martyr, her mother was also the world's worst cook. Growing up, Chiffon had endured every culinary disaster imaginable, from rubbery eggs to hamburgers as hard and black as charcoal briquettes.

"Some kids at school were talking about Daddy," Emily said in a small voice.

Chiffon stiffened. "What kids? Who was talking?"

Emily lifted her head from Chiffon's lap. "Practically *everybody* in the whole class. They say Daddy was kissing that movie star."

Chiffon gently grasped Emily's slight shoulders. "Don't pay them any mind, you hear? They don't know what they're talking about. It's all a big mistake."

"If it's all a big mistake, why hasn't Daddy come home yet?" She popped her thumb into her mouth, a habit Chiffon thought she'd outgrown.

"He will, Pumpkin. He'll come home and everything will be just like it used to be. I promise—"

A high-pitched scream interrupted her, followed by dogs barking.

"What in the—? Emily, hand me my crutches."

On stiff legs, Chiffon rose from the sofa and awkwardly made her way across the living room to the front door. When she opened it, she saw Chenille standing in the front yard, holding her terrier aloft. Lonnie's two dogs were pawing her and Chenille squawked, "Leave my baby alone!"

"Buddy! Beau! Y'all scat!" Chiffon hollered. The two dogs fled, tails between their legs.

Chenille staggered up the lawn, clutching her dog to her chest. "Do those vicious beasts belong to you?" she gasped.

"Yes," Chiffon said. "But there's no call to get upset. They won't hurt a flea."

"Walter is in shock," Chenille said, in a tizzy. "He needs his Zoloft immediately." She pushed past her sister and situated the dog on the couch while she ransacked a black medical bag. Chiffon followed her inside on her crutches.

"What's Zoloft? If it's kibble, I have a ten-pound sack out back," Chiffon said.

"Walter has an anxiety disorder," Chenille said tartly. "Zoloft is the medication he takes to alleviate his symptoms. Without it, he could have a full-blown panic attack—" She heaved the bag to the ground. "Don't tell me I left it at home!"

Chiffon eyed the small gray dog. His dark eyes gleamed like buttons, and he appeared to be grinning. While Chenille retrieved the pill bottles that had fallen on the carpet, he swiped at his bottom with his quick pink tongue.

"He looks okay to me. Happy, even," Chiffon said.

"Maybe I put the bottle in his suitcase," Chenille said, her voice on the verge of tears. "Keep an eye on him while I run out to the car."

Chiffon sat down beside the dog. "What kind of name is Walter for a dog? No wonder you're so anxious."

"Mommy, that dog is wearing a coat!" Emily said in astonishment. She'd never seen such behavior in a canine. Lonnie's dogs always walked around butt-naked.

"Makes him look kind of silly," Chiffon said, inspecting the garment. It was silk-lined, and the tag said "Made in England." "It sure is a fancy little coat."

"Do you think Aunt Chiffon would let me dress Walter up in some of my baby-doll clothes?" Emily asked hopefully.

"I don't think so. She's awfully particular about her dog," Chiffon said. "Besides, I think Walter is confused enough as it is."

Emily left the room just as Chenille rushed through the door brandishing a bottle as if it were the Olympic torch. "I found the pills. I'd packed them with Walter's toiletries."

She pried open Walter's muzzle and shoved a pill inside. "Swallow for Mama. That's a good boy." Patting his head, she wilted back into the couch cushions. "Emergency averted."

"Yeah," Chiffon said. "How was your trip?"

Chenille straightened her posture and arranged her hands primly in her lap. "It was lovely, actually. When I came up the stretch of Highway 78, just before the turnoff to Cayboo Creek, I saw these huge, majestic birds circling around. Hawks, I should think, or possibly falcons. I wished I'd brought binoculars."

"Buzzards, more likely," Chiffon said. "Don't you remember? We call that stretch of highway Roadkill Ridge. There always seems to be a dead possum or raccoon in the road. Last time I was up there, I saw a belly-up armadillo."

"Oh my. I'd forgotten that nickname," Chenille said. "I'm going to have to get accustomed to being in a quaint country town again."

"Bible Grove is hardly the big city," Chiffon said.

"True, but it's a suburb of Greenville, so it's much more cosmopolitan than Cayboo Creek." Chenille loosened her poncho. "In fact, we got a Starbucks this fall. It's two blocks from where I live."

"Impressive," Chiffon said.

The sisters fell into an uncomfortable silence, both thinking the same thing: If their first interactions were a forecast of the rest of their visit, it was going to be a long two weeks.

Chiffon glanced over at the dog, hoping he'd serve as a topic of conversation. "Can I take Walt's coat?" she asked.

"Oh no, he should wear it. He's sensitive to drafts." Chenille paused. "And he prefers to be called Walter."

"I see," Chiffon said, wondering how Chenille could possibly know how her pet liked to be addressed.

Chenille glanced around the living room. "Did you know this is the first time I've ever been in your house? We've always had our gatherings at Mother's. Where is Mother, by the way?"

"She went to the Quick Curb for some milk. She'll be back in a minute," Chiffon said, jiggling her good foot. Wanda's absence made things even more awkward. The two sisters had rarely spent time alone.

As if on cue, Wanda bustled through the front door carrying a grocery bag. "Chenille! Thank God you're here! I was going stark raving mad." She dumped the bag on the coffee table. "Here's that milk, Chiffon. Chenille, you're looking kind of scrawny. Maybe you can share your diet secrets with Miss Piggy over here." She put her pocketbook on her arm. "Chenille, I'll let you take over. I've got all kinds of packing to catch up on. This accident of Chiffon's has put me way behind. I'll call you before I leave. Good-bye, girls."

Until you walk a mile in

another man's moccasins,

you can't imagine the smell.

Message in a fortune cookie at Dun Woo's House of Noodles

CHAPTER TWELVE

Chenille stood shivering in her bathrobe watching Walter lift his leg to an azalea bush. It was four A.M., and the frozen ground crunched beneath her bedroom slippers.

"Come on, sweetie," Chenille coaxed. "Don't dillydally. Mama's freezing." Walter shot her an indignant look as she tugged on his leash.

Ever since she'd arrived at Chiffon's house, Walter's schedule had gone haywire. Three nights in a row he'd roused her in the middle of the night, demanding to be let out for his morning constitutional. She'd tried reasoning with him, patiently explaining that it was too dark and cold to go outside, but Walter would have none of it. He'd stand over her, his hot breath in her face, until she pulled back the bedcovers on the rollaway bed and placed her feet on the cold floorboards of the living room.

Dragging a reluctant Walter inside, she put on water for her sugar-free hot cocoa. Walter's early-morning forays were the least of her worries. Yesterday she'd attempted to throw a supper together for everyone, but when she opened Chiffon's refrigerator, it was no cooler than a breadbasket. When she suggested calling a repairman, Chiffon acted as if she'd proposed a trip to China.

"How am I going to pay him?" she'd said flippantly. "With my good looks?"

Chenille ran out to the grocery store and purchased three Styrofoam coolers, along with several ice bags to prevent the contents of the refrigerator from spoiling. Then she prepared a hasty supper of pizza topped with sprouts, kale, and zucchini. Surprisingly, the children failed to appreciate her efforts. Dewitt said the sprouts looked like worms, and Emily scarcely ate a bite. Chenille was surprised. She'd assumed all small children liked pizza.

After dinner, she'd talked with her sister and learned that Chiffon was down to her last dime. And since she wouldn't be waiting tables until her ankle healed, it would be a long time before there were any household funds. Chenille promptly went to the phone to discuss Chiffon's situation with Wanda and discovered the line was dead.

"I'm not surprised," Chiffon said. "It looks like Lonnie forgot to pay the bills last month."

Chenille was horrified. How could a man abandon his responsibilities to his family? And how had her sister put up with him for so long? She'd expected Chiffon to share her outrage, but instead of anger, her sister's primary emotion was nostalgia. She sat for hours on the couch, poring over her wedding photo album and listening to weepy country songs.

Chenille insisted on going through Lonnie's desk, hoping to unearth a passbook savings account or other evidence of hidden funds, but all she found were a tangle of fishing lures, back issues of *American Cooner*, and a plaque honoring him as the first-place winner of a dart championship at the Tuff Luck Tavern.

She'd left the desk in frustration and proceeded to paw through Lonnie's dresser drawers. She blushed as she discovered several pairs of novelty briefs printed with suggestive phrases such as "hot stuff," "Energizer bunny," and "oversize load." She also ran across a bottle of blue liquid called Wet Passion Lube. Just as she was about to slam the drawer shut in embarrassment, her hand touched a stack of papers.

Pay dirt! The papers were money orders made out to utility companies and other creditors. When Chenille had shown them to her sister, she smiled vaguely. "I knew he wouldn't leave us high and dry. He just forgot to pay the bills again."

Chenille had spent the next day making rounds to all of her sister's creditors, distributing the money orders. Out of her own pocket, she paid reconnection fees so the satellite dish and phone were turned back on. She also paid to have a repairman from Whirlpool come and fix Chiffon's refrigerator. Once the phone was working, Chenille called her mother and began to describe Chiffon's dire circumstances.

"I know all about it," Wanda said. "But I can't deal with Chiffon right now. I'm leaving on my trip tomorrow. Drive her to Family Services to see if they can help her any."

Chenille knew she couldn't foot Chiffon's expenses indefinitely. She'd accumulated some savings over her teaching career, but she had her own bills to pay, and she wouldn't be able to look for another position until Chiffon's ankle was better.

When she'd brought up the possibility of contacting Family Services, Chiffon was insulted.

"I refuse to go on the dole," Chiffon said, her blue eyes flashing. "There's my pride to consider."

When Chenille had gently mentioned that pride wouldn't put Similac in Gabby's bottle, Chiffon picked up the phone and called the classified department of the *Cayboo Creek Crier*. She placed an ad offering for sale a pool table, guns with rack, a bass boat, two purebred Labrador retrievers, and three all-terrain vehicles.

"Bravo!" Chenille said after her sister got off the phone. "You're selling all of Lonnie's things instead of your own. It's exactly what he deserves."

Chiffon shot her a strange look. "I'm selling his stuff because *I* don't have anything that's worth any money." She'd glanced down at her hand. "Except my wedding rings. But I've always had a sneaking suspicion that the stone's cubic zirconium."

That was yesterday. Chenille tutted to herself as she rinsed out her cocoa cup. Clearly Lonnie was the type of man who blew all his money on himself, leaving his family with thrift-shop clothing and tattered furniture. Thankfully, the ad would come out in the paper today, and maybe Chiffon could raise some cash soon.

Since Walter had awakened her so early, Chenille decided she would use the time to organize her sister's kitchen. When she'd first seen the interior of Chiffon's home, she'd been shocked by the disorder she'd encountered in the grim little rooms. Dust bunnies huddled under the furniture, and piles of dirty clothes towered in the corners. Chenille couldn't take a step without flattening some cheap plastic toy.

Initially she'd raised an eyebrow at Chiffon's utter disregard for housekeeping, but after a day or two of living with her sister, she realized how taxing it was to stay ahead of the children's messes and to keep things tidy in such a cramped space. Still, the rooms didn't have to be nearly as chaotic as they were, and during her stay, Chenille was determined to bring some organization to the household.

She'd been sorting through a jumble of condiments, wondering why on earth Chiffon needed over thirteen bottles of barbecue sauce, when the mistress of the house limped into the kitchen with Gabby clutched to her breast.

"Coffee. Hot. Now," she mumbled.

"It's perking, Chiffon," Chenille said. "Why not have a glass of warm milk while you wait? I've heated some on the stove for the children."

Chiffon gaped at Chenille as if she'd suggested a mug of mud. Then she hobbled into the living room, the tie to her leopard-print robe trailing behind her.

There's nothing wrong with a bit of warm milk. Certainly it had to be healthier than the three cups of coffee loaded with cream and sugar that Chiffon downed every morning. And why did all of her sister's sleeping garments look as if they came directly from a harlot's trunk? Last night when the Weather Channel predicted a frost, Chenille offered to lend Chiffon her nicest full-length flannel nightgown, but she'd snorted at the suggestion.

Chenille appraised a row of salad dressings on the counter, each with an inch of sludge-like liquid in the bottom. She thought about asking Chiffon permission to toss them, but her sister wasn't civil until she'd gotten her caffeine fix and her dose of Katie Couric.

"Executive decision," she whispered to herself as she tossed the bottles into the trash can.

The children were up by this time. They loped to the kitchen table in their pajamas, and Chenille placed a soft-boiled egg and a cup of warm milk at each of their places.

"Where's my Frostees?" Dewitt asked with alarm.

"I thought an egg would be a nice change of pace," Chenille said breezily. "All that refined sugar in the morning isn't good for young tummies."

Dewitt poked at the egg with his fork, releasing the liquid yolk. "It's bleeding! My breakfast is bleeding!" he wailed.

Emily, who was normally a pleasant and accommodating child, took a sip of her milk and immediately made a sour face. "Something's very wrong," she said ominously. "This milk is warm."

"European children always drink warm milk. It's quite healthful," Chenille said.

"I don't want to be 'pean,'" Dewitt whimpered.

Noticing the ruckus, Chiffon clomped over to the table with her crutches. "What are y'all whining about?" She glanced at the children's plates. "Chenille, what is this mess?"

"It's breakfast," Chenille said. "A healthy breakfast without unnecessary additives and fillers."

Chiffon sighed loudly. "Hand me a couple of bowls and the bag of Frootees."

"Do you know what this cereal will do to their blood sugar levels?" Chenille said.

"Give me the flipping Frootees," Chiffon said darkly.

· · ·

Chenille was still stinging from the breakfast debacle long after the children had tramped off to school. When Chiffon asked her to look after Gabby while she went out for an hour or so, she had a hard time keeping the hurt out of her voice.

"Go along," she said with a weak wave of her hand. "Gabby and I will manage."

If Chiffon noticed her distress, she ignored it. She was much too busy shellacking her hair with White Rain.

"I promised Elizabeth and some of the others that I'd come to this meeting," Chiffon said, shielding her eyes from the hair spray. "We're trying to raise funds for the Senior Center."

Chenille's ears perked with interest. She'd never thought of Chiffon as a civic-minded individual.

"I just hope there'll be some decent chow," Chiffon said with a smack of her freshly glossed lips.

"Did you want me to drive you?" Chenille asked.

"Nope. Mavis is picking me up. The meeting's at Elizabeth's

house and the number's by the phone. Wake up Gabby if she's still asleep in an hour from now."

Chiffon, wearing a rabbit coat with several bald spots, looked out the front window. Chenille imagined how much smarter her sister would look if she borrowed her wool navy pea coat, but she knew better than to suggest it.

"Here's Mavis. I'll be back soon," Chiffon said. She slung her pocketbook over her shoulder and treaded out the door in a cloud of imposter Obsession perfume.

Chenille was grateful to have the entire house to herself. It was a relief to enjoy some solitude, plus it gave her the opportunity to indulge in her favorite diversion. She unearthed the TV clicker from the sofa cushions and started searching for *Law and Order* episodes. Ever since she'd arrived at her sister's house, she'd been forced to go cold turkey with her television habits.

Luck was with her. She sighed with pleasure when she found an episode featuring Benjamin Bratt as Detective Rey Curtis. He was so smooth and suave. When he squinted into the camera, Chenille felt the gooseflesh rise on her arms. Just as she'd settled in, the phone rang. Halfheartedly, she rose from the couch, her eyes still on the TV screen.

"Hello," she said distractedly.

"'Morning," a male voice said. "Are you the folks with the bass boat for sale?"

The call turned out to be the first of many. For the rest of the morning, Chenille was forced to field questions regarding the items her sister had up for sale.

"What kind of bilge pump is on the bass boat?" "Do you

know the model year of the ATVs?" "Have the Labradors been dewormed?"

"I'm sorry. I don't know the answer to that question," Chenille kept saying. "I'll have to let my sister call you back."

By noon she'd taken fifteen phone messages and had completely missed her television show. During a lull in the calls, she had time to wake and feed Gabby and to make an avocado salad. After putting Gabby in the playpen, she sat down at the kitchen table and was poised to take a bite of salad when the phone rang again.

"Oh dear," Chenille murmured as she went to answer it.

"Is this Mrs. Butrell?"

"No, she's out. Can I take a message?"

"But there *is* indeed a Mrs. Butrell? Married to Lonnie Butrell?"

"Yes, that's right, and as I said—"

"Who's speaking?"

"This is Mrs. Butrell's sister, Chenille Grace. Listen, I've just sat down for a nibble—"

"Ms. Grace. This is Heidi Conner, a reporter from *People* magazine. I want to make sure I have my facts straight. Lonnie Butrell, Janie-Lynn Lauren's new boyfriend, is he a married man?"

"He most certainly is," Chenille said in a piqued voice. "Not only is he married, he also has three children. One's still in diapers."

"Is that so? Tell me, Ms. Grace, how does Lonnie's wife feel about her husband having a very public affair with Ms. Lauren?"

"She's barely gone out of the house since it happened. Not that she gets around that well since she sprained her ankle."

"Mrs. Butrell has a sprained ankle?" the reporter asked.

"Yes, she was so upset about Lonnie and his dalliance with Janie-Lynn Lauren that she slipped on a puddle of Wesson oil in the grocery store. Now she can't work as a waitress at the Chat 'N' Chew anymore. She's selling Lonnie's things just to pay the bills."

The reporter gasped. "Do you mean to tell me that Mr. Butrell isn't providing for his family?"

"Heavens no! He had his paycheck forwarded to California, and he hasn't sent Chiffon a penny. He's left the whole family to starve."

"That's shocking! Tell me, Ms. Grace, is 'Chenille' spelled like the fabric?"

"Yes." A pause. "Is this going to be in the magazine?"

"Most likely. And 'Chiffon,' is that spelled like the fabric as well?"

"Yes, it is."

"I don't suppose you have a brother named Cashmere?" The woman laughed at her own joke.

"I didn't realize this was going to be printed." It occurred to Chenille that Chiffon might not want her personal business plastered on the pages of a magazine.

"I did say I was with *People*, Ms. Grace."

"I know, but my sister has a lot of pride, and I'm afraid—"

"Ms. Grace, don't you think Mr. Butrell should be held accountable for what he's done?"

"Of course, but I'm just worried—"

What was she worried about? So Chiffon might get a little upset that Chenille talked about her plight with *People* magazine. Chenille was only telling the truth. Lonnie deserved to pay for all the pain he'd caused her sister. Maybe for once in his life he'd feel ashamed of himself.

"You're right, Ms. Conner. Lonnie's made his bed. Now he should lie in it."

*If our food and drink don't
meet your standards, please
lower your standards.*

Sign outside the Chat 'N' Chew

CHAPTER THIRTEEN

Chiffon stared out the window of Mavis's Chevy
Lumina as it glided down Main Street. Jerry, from the Stuff
and Mount Taxidermy Shop, shivered outside his door as he
pulled on a cigarette, the smoke mingling with the condensa-
tion from his breath. A pair of old ladies tottered out of the
Dazzling Do's, clutching each other so they wouldn't slip on
patches of ice. Their hair color was the same steel blue as the
sky above.

It was a few minutes after noon, and street traffic was sparse.
Many of the businesses in Cayboo Creek rolled up the sidewalks during the lunch hour.

"Are you enjoying your sister's visit?" Mavis asked, adjusting the temperature of the car heater.

"She's been a real help," Chiffon said with a tight smile.

"I haven't seen her since she was a senior in high school. Hardly anyone has. Maybe I should throw together a little luncheon in her honor."

"Maybe," Chiffon said, tapping her fingernails against the window.

Truth was, Chenille was stepping on Chiffon's last nerve. Yesterday she'd caught her sister sorting and folding all of Emily's Barbie doll clothes.

"They were cluttering up the Dream House," Chenille had said in explanation.

And the meals she cooked: wheat loaf instead of meat loaf, tofu in place of turkey, and bulgur in lieu of biscuits. Chiffon had to smuggle cookies into her room after meals just to stay satisfied.

And as if being a neat freak and a health nut weren't enough to drive Chiffon crazy, her sister had undertaken a relentless campaign to cheer her. Chenille hummed "Zippity Do Da" as she went about her household chores, and on gray, dark mornings she flung open the curtains and exclaimed, "What a glorious day!" Frequently she left Post-it notes on Chiffon's pillow with hackneyed words of encouragement such as "When life hands you lemons, make lemonade" or "It takes more muscles to frown than to smile."

Chiffon knew her sister meant well, but it was hard to be cooped up all day with a cross between Mr. Clean, Dean Ornish, and Rebecca of Sunnybrook Farm.

Mavis turned off Main Street and headed toward Elizabeth's

house near the creek. As she reached the clapboard bungalow, she parked between Mrs. Tobias's white Cadillac and Attalee's elderly Buick Skylark.

"Looks like everyone's here except Birdie," Mavis said as she opened the car door.

The two of them scaled the stone steps leading up to the bungalow. Camellia bushes bursting with bright pink blossoms stirred in the breeze coming up from the creek. At the sound of their steps on the porch, Elizabeth's dog, Maybelline, pressed her nose up against the window and started barking.

The front door swung open and Timothy clomped down the front steps in work boots and a blue shirt with the words "Bait Box" embroidered on the pocket.

"Hi, Mavis, Chiffon. Everyone is in the nursery admiring the new crib. Go on in."

"Are you going back to work?" Mavis said.

"Elizabeth shooed me off," he said, sweeping a hand through dark curly hair. "I hate to leave her when she's so close to the delivery date. But she's tired of me fussing over her all the time."

"I doubt that," Mavis said with a wink.

Timothy placed a sun-faded cap on his head and yanked it low on his forehead. "If she has even the slightest stitch or twitch, please call me. I don't care if it's a false alarm."

"Will do," Mavis said, ruffling the neck of Maybelline, who'd ventured out to the porch and was sniffing the toe of her tennis shoe.

Timothy ambled to his truck parked in the driveway, whistling Brahms' "Lullaby."

"Timothy treats Elizabeth like a princess," Mavis said. "He'll be a top-notch father."

"Yeah, he's sweet all right," Chiffon said wistfully.

"Oh, sorry. I wasn't comparing—"

Chiffon held up a hand. "Of course you weren't. Come on. Let's take a look at the new crib."

They passed through the airy living room, which had been thoroughly childproofed with window guards, corner bumpers, and outlet covers. As they walked down the hall to the nursery, Elizabeth motioned them inside.

"I'm so glad you're here!" she said, bubbling over with excitement.

The nursery was painted a pale yellow, bordered with a row of baby ducks. Lace curtains, tied back with satin ribbons, hung from the windows, and two oak rocking chairs sat on a rag rug near the crib.

"His-and-hers rocking chairs," Elizabeth said, touching the back of one of the chairs.

Attalee and Mrs. Tobias hovered over a white-spindled crib with a yellow gingham bumper and dust ruffle.

"I'll have to get you more bedding, Elizabeth," Mrs. Tobias said. "This crib doesn't even have a pillow."

"Actually, less bedding is better for babies," Elizabeth said gently. "That's what the doctors say."

"It's a baby wonderland in here," Chiffon said, touching the plush foot of an oversize teddy bear on a shelf.

"Chiffon, you're the expert," Elizabeth said. "Do I have everything I need?"

Chiffon mentally inventoried the baby paraphernalia in the room: bassinet, plastic bath, changing table, Diaper Genie, and baby monitor.

"Where's the swing?" she said after a moment.

"I don't have one," Elizabeth said. "Do I need one?"

"Does a goat need briars?" Chiffon said.

"Nonsense," Mrs. Tobias said. "I raised twin daughters and they didn't have any swings."

"Me either," Attalee said as she tweaked a horn on the Busy Box hanging from the crib. "I reared eight young 'uns and got no help from any contraptions."

"Oh really?" Chiffon said. "And what did you do when your babies cried bloody murder?"

"It was so long ago, it's hard to recall," Mrs. Tobias said, laying an index finger on her cheek. Her eyes suddenly brightened. "I remember. Our driver, Heinz, got out the Packard and took the girls for a ride. Both found the noise of the engine soothing when they were infants. It *had* to be the Packard. For some reason the Olds wouldn't do the trick."

"I gave the little nippers a dose of paregoric in their bottles," Attalee said with a big, toothless grin. "Worked like a charm."

Chiffon crossed her arms over her chest. "Seeing how there isn't a Packard in the driveway, and seeing how paregoric is illegal in every state, Elizabeth might want to give the swing a whirl."

"Paregoric is illegal?" Attalee asked in surprise. "What a load of hokum! Next they'll say you shouldn't take a switch to a young 'un's bottom. Then where will we all be?"

The doorbell chimed and Maybelline yelped.

"That's probably Birdie," Elizabeth said. "Why don't we go into the den and start?"

. . .

As the meeting got under way, Elizabeth served blueberry buckle and coffee while the rest of the women brainstormed on money-making ideas for the Senior Center.

"A bake sale is always profitable," Birdie said from her perch on a wicker love seat. "The citizens of this town have fierce sweet tooths."

"Only thing is, with the holidays over, lots of people are watching their waistlines," Mavis said, patting the soft bulge of her stomach. "I know I am."

"It's too cold for a car wash," Chiffon said. She gazed forlornly at the gray slate of sky visible from the bay window.

"What about a craft fair?" Elizabeth asked. "They always bring out the crowds."

"Isn't there enough macramé in this world already?" Attalee said with a yawn.

"It's just a suggestion, Attalee," Elizabeth said. "But I suppose you have a much better idea."

"You bet your sweet bippy I do," she replied.

"Let's hear it," Mavis said.

Attalee's faded blue eyes danced as she spoke. "I was up all night thinking about it. My idea will make a whole pot of money for the Senior Center, but I'll give you fair warning—" She lowered her voice and grinned. "It ain't for the faint of heart. Elizabeth, you might want to have a bottle of sherry on standby."

"Land sakes alive, Attalee," Birdie said. "Drop the dramatics and tell us your plan."

"On second thought, sherry's too weak," Attalee said. "You got any corn whiskey?"

"Attalee!" Elizabeth said, "Just tell us."

"All right, ladies," Attalee said, her bad eye flickering like a shorted lightbulb. "Hang on to your corsets."

They listened as Attalee explained her plan for saving the struggling Senior Center. Her liver-spotted hands flew around her face in a frenzy as she spoke. The more she said, the more stunned her audience became. Mrs. Tobias clutched at the bit of lace around her throat; Mavis rubbed the newly bleached hair above her upper lip, and Birdie's mouth dropped open so wide a parakeet could have flown inside.

When Attalee finally finished speaking, she was met with stone-cold silence.

"Don't sit there like a bunch of glazed hams," Attalee demanded. "Tell me what you think."

Mavis took a hasty gulp of coffee. "It's outlandish," she said.

A shaken Mrs. Tobias dabbed at her forehead with an embroidered hankie. "It's scandalous."

Elizabeth, who was standing over the group holding a coffeepot, said, "It's, it's, it's . . ."

"What?" Attalee said anxiously. "Put it out there where the goats can get it."

Elizabeth slammed the pot on the table and clamped a hand to her belly. "It's coming! My baby is coming!"

"See what you've gone and done," Birdie hissed. "You've driven the poor girl into labor."

"Get Timothy. Grab my suitcase! Help me out to the car!" wailed Elizabeth.

Mrs. Tobias called Timothy at the Bait Box, and moments later he screeched into the driveway. He sprang out of his truck just as Mavis and Birdie were settling Elizabeth into the front seat of her mommy-mobile, a brand-new Ford Expedition.

"Is she okay? Will we make it on time?" Timothy said.

"Don't get yourself all into a dither," Attalee said, putting a hand on his shoulder. "This is her first young 'un, so she's liable to be in labor for a while. When I had my Posy, I was seized up for more than thirty hours."

"Thirty hours!" Elizabeth said, her eyes darting frantically. "I can't last that long."

Mrs. Tobias squeezed her hand. "It's all right, dear. She's exaggerating. Women always subtract years from their age and add hours to their labor."

Elizabeth moaned and her body bucked with another contraction. "I don't know," she said as Timothy backed out of the driveway. "These contractions are right on top of each other."

As it turned out, Elizabeth's labor didn't last anywhere near thirty hours. In fact, it lasted scarcely thirty minutes. By the time Timothy pulled into the emergency room entrance of University Hospital in Augusta, Elizabeth was close to crowning.

Chiffon, who'd ridden to the hospital with Timothy, Elizabeth, and Mrs. Tobias, couldn't believe it when Elizabeth screamed, "The baby is coming *right now!*"

As soon as Timothy came to a stop, Chiffon leaped out of the car and made tracks on her crutches to the entrance of the emergency room. She grabbed the sleeve of the first white-coated man she saw and said, "My best friend is having a baby in the car. Help her, please."

In moments, a stretcher was dispatched to the parking lot

and a sweat-drenched Elizabeth was gingerly strapped aboard by a doctor and an orderly.

Just as the mommy-to-be and her entourage disappeared into the emergency room entrance, Mavis's car squealed into the parking area.

"Where are they?" Mavis asked, with a slam of her car door. Attalee and Birdie scrambled onto the pavement.

"They just took Elizabeth to delivery," Chiffon rasped. "She's having the baby this very second."

"Out like a ball from a cannon," Attalee said. "Atta girl."

"Let's find out what's going on," Birdie said.

. . .

Five minutes later, Glenda Daisy Hollingsworth came into the world, weighing seven pounds, three ounces, and kicking mad. The baby girl was named after Elizabeth's late grandmother, better known to everyone in Cayboo Creek as Meemaw. A beaming Timothy strutted into the maternity waiting room to deliver the news to the women.

Just as everyone cheered in delight, baby Glenda's other namesake, Daisy Hollingsworth, swept into the room. Timothy had called her on his cell phone.

"Have I gotten here on time? How's Elizabeth?" Daisy said, kissing her son on the cheek and eagerly listening as he announced his daughter's birth.

"I'm thrilled to the core. Imagine. Me as a grandmother," Daisy said. She rushed to hug Mrs. Tobias. "And Mother, you're a great-grandmother. Just think, we now have four generations of our family under this very roof."

Chiffon had only seen Elizabeth's mother-in-law on a couple

of occasions, but she was always awed by her presence. Daisy Hollingsworth lived on a sprawling estate in Augusta and carried herself like royalty. Today she wore a soft blue cashmere dress accessorized with a single strand of pearls. Her hair was up in a simple chignon, emphasizing the slender stem of her neck.

Daisy addressed all of Elizabeth's friends warmly. When asked about her ankle injury, Chiffon felt the urge to curtsy and kiss Daisy's large sapphire ring.

"I need to get back to Elizabeth and my daughter," Timothy said with a face-splitting grin. "I know she'll want to see all of you as soon as she catches her breath."

After Timothy left, the group settled themselves on the vinyl-cushioned chairs in the waiting room. Attalee drummed her fingers on her knee.

"So, now that the dust is settled, what did you think of my idea for saving the Senior Center?" she asked.

"Attalee, this isn't the time or the place," Birdie said with a brittle smile. She adjusted her reading glasses on her nose and picked up a copy of *Modern Maturity* from the stack of magazines on the glass table.

"I think it's the perfect time," Attalee said. "We're just sitting here, twiddling our thumbs. Maybe Mrs. Hollingsworth can toss in her two cents. Don't you got some experience with fundraising, ma'am?"

Daisy Hollingsworth smiled brightly. "Why, yes, I do, and I'd be delighted to hear your—"

"No!" Mavis shouted, startling everyone. "What I mean to say is . . . Attalee's idea is . . . off the beaten track."

"Those are often the best kind," Daisy said.

"So true," Birdie said. "But not only is Attalee's idea bizarre, it's also somewhat . . ." She swallowed hard and blushed. "Indecent."

"Obscene is the word I'd use," Mrs. Tobias said with a sniff.

Daisy arched a perfectly shaped eyebrow. "You've aroused my curiosity. I *have* to hear this idea of yours, Attalee."

Before anyone could stop her, Attalee rattled off her entire plan for the Senior Center. The others listened with white-faced dread. When she finished, Attalee chuckled and said, "Ain't that a doozy?"

Mavis cleared her throat. "Here's the thing about Attalee, she's a little—"

"Senile!" Birdie interjected. "Dotty. Daft."

"Infirm," Chiffon said with a sad nod.

"Brilliant," Daisy said softly. "Absolutely brilliant."

"What did you say, Daisy?" Mrs. Tobias asked.

"Attalee's idea is sheer genius," Daisy said. "You'll make a mint for the Senior Center."

The women looked at one another in disbelief, but no one dared object, not even Mrs. Tobias. After all, Daisy Hollingsworth was the most well-regarded socialite in Augusta. If she thought Attalee's fundraising idea was respectable, who were they to argue? While the women discussed Attalee's plan, Chiffon borrowed Birdie's cell phone to tell her sister she'd be later than expected.

"That's fine. But I should warn you," Chenille said in a strained voice. "There's people hanging around outside."

"Good," Chiffon said. "Tell them I'll be back in about an

hour and a half. If any of them have cash in hand and want to buy now, go ahead and let them. Just don't stand for any dickering. My prices are firm."

"Actually, they aren't here to buy Lonnie's stuff," Chenille said, clearing her throat. "They want something else."

"What do you mean? What people are you talking about?" Chiffon asked.

"ABC, NBC, *People, Hollywood Hijinks, US*, and a bunch of tabloids."

"Who do they want to see?" Chiffon said in bewilderment.

Chenille paused for a moment. "You, Chiffon. They want to see you."

I get enough exercise just

pushing my luck.

Graffiti in the ladies' room at the Tuff Luck Tavern

CHAPTER FOURTEEN

As Mavis turned down Chiffon's street to drop her off, they counted four vans and five cars clustered near the little purple house.

"Mavis. What am I going to do?" Chiffon said. "I don't have anything to say to those people."

Mavis took a moment to assess the situation. "How about if I drop you off at the package shop behind your house?" she said. "Then I'll pull up in the drive to distract them. You can sneak through the back and get into the house through the kitchen door."

"Sounds good. Let's do it," Chiffon said, ducking low in her seat.

Mavis turned the car around and motored along Chickasaw Drive, which ran behind Chiffon's street. Parking in front of the liquor store, Mavis turned off the ignition and looked at Chiffon. "Are you going to be able to manage on those crutches? You'll have to maneuver your way through some brush and bramble."

"I'll be fine." Chiffon opened the passenger door and placed the tips of her crutches on the asphalt. "Here goes nothing!" she said as she hefted her weight out of the car.

"I'll call you later." Mavis blew her a kiss. "Don't forget to give me time to get back to your house."

Chiffon crouched behind a scrub of bushes bordering her lawn until she heard the crunch of Mavis's tires on the gravel driveway out front. Then she sprinted across the backyard on her crutches, maneuvering her way around an abandoned tire, a collection of rusted lawn furniture, and a deflated kiddy pool.

She made it to the back door without being spotted and put her hand on the knob. *Locked!* And she didn't have her keys. She rattled the doorknob. "Chenille!" she said in a low voice. "It's me. Let me in."

The dogs, whose pen was located on the side of the house, started raising a fuss.

"Chenille!" Chiffon said, this time in a louder voice. She rapped her knuckles on the aluminum frame of the door. "Open up."

Chiffon heard a shout coming from the side of the house. "There's someone out back!"

A herd of people carrying cameras and microphones stampeded into the backyard. As soon as they spotted Chiffon, they thronged her like hyenas to a zebra carcass.

"Are you Chiffon Butrell?"

"How do you feel about your husband sleeping with Janie-Lynn Lauren?"

Chiffon backed away from them until she was flattened against the siding of the house. "Chenille! Open up this door!" she yelled.

"I'm from *People* magazine," said a tall woman with a severe haircut. "Is it true that Lonnie has left you and your children penniless?"

A winded man in a rumpled suit shoved in front of her. "I'm from *The Globe*. Have you heard that Janie-Lynn is carrying Lonnie's love child?"

A woman in a pair of stiletto heels tottered to the front of the crowd. "I'm from *Style* magazine," she said, eyeing Chiffon critically. "Are those acid-washed jeans you're wearing? With a fun fur?"

The cameras whirred wildly, and Chiffon felt like a cornered fox. As the reporters and photographers pressed in closer and closer, she was seized with a sense of increasing panic. She banged on the door until her knuckles were raw, but Chenille didn't answer.

Then, out of the corner of her eye, she glimpsed Dewitt's Super Soaker lying on the ground by her feet. He'd played with it on an unseasonably warm day last month, so Chiffon reckoned it might still be filled with water. She reached down to grab it and aimed it at the crowd.

"Come any closer and you'll get it between the eyes," she warned. The gun had weight, so she knew it was loaded.

Murmurs rose from the surrounding crowd. "It's just a child's toy." "What, is she crazy?" "She's bluffing."

Adjusting the nozzle to the highest possible setting, Chiffon put her finger on the trigger. "I'm warning you. This is a Super Soaker Elite 2500. It's a high-powered assault weapon. I want all of you off my property. Now!"

"It's a squirt gun," said a man wearing horn-rimmed glasses. He stepped forward and aimed his camera at her. "Smile pretty!" he said as he snapped a photograph. Chiffon pulled the trigger and gave it to him with both barrels. His glasses flew off his face. For good measure she sprayed the rest of the group.

People screamed and scurried as Chiffon stumbled past them on her crutches. She made her way to the front stoop, snatched the spare key under the mat, and unlocked the door.

"Chenille, darn it! Why didn't you open the back door for me?" Chiffon shouted as she entered the house. Her question was answered with silence. Baffled, she walked down the hallway and peered in each of the bedrooms. The house was too quiet for anyone to be inside. When she entered the kitchen, she saw a note stuck on her refrigerator with a magnet.

Chiffon, there's been a medical emergency. Had to rush to the doctor. Will call soon with news.

Chenille

Chiffon's heart fluttered. *Gabby!* She was probably running a high fever again, or maybe it was something worse. Her daughter could have swallowed a button or fallen from her changing table. Chenille wasn't used to looking after small children and probably didn't know you had to watch them every second.

Chiffon grabbed the telephone book beside the fridge and frantically flipped through the pages looking for the number of the hospital emergency room in Augusta. Maybe Chenille had taken Gabby to her pediatrician, Dr. Peterson. Chiffon had left his number on a pad in the kitchen.

The phone rang and Chiffon snatched the receiver. "Chenille, is that you? What's happened to Gabby?"

The voice on the other end was husky and oddly familiar. "Is this Chiffon? This is Janie-Lynn Lauren."

For a moment, Chiffon was so stunned she couldn't speak. A terrible mixture of anger and sadness roiled inside of her.

"Where's Lonnie?" Chiffon demanded, tears splattering her cheeks. "I need to speak to my husband. Something is terribly wrong with our baby."

"What's wrong with it?"

"The baby's a *she*, not an *it*, and that's none of your business," Chiffon said. "I want you to put Lonnie on the phone now!"

"Lonnie isn't here right now. Besides, he doesn't want to talk to you," Janie-Lynn said evenly. "But I do."

"There are all kinds of people here, and they're camped outside the house. Please let me talk to Lonnie."

"Reporters? I was afraid of that. Have you said anything to them? It's best not to speak with them at all."

"I can't speak to anyone right now, because I need to find out what's wrong with Gabby. You tell Lonnie that if he cares anything about his daughter, he'd better get his butt home right now!" Chiffon slammed down the phone.

It rang again immediately.

"Yes?" Chiffon shouted.

"Chiffon, it's Chenille—"

"Thank God! What's going on? Where are you?"

"There's nothing to be worried about," Chenille said in an unruffled voice. "It was just a minor seizure; there's absolutely no permanent damage."

"A seizure? Oh my Lord! Where are you?"

"At the doctor's. But everything's okay," Chenille said, exhaling with relief. "I did have quite the start, seeing those dear little eyes rolled back and those four legs twitching uncontrollably."

"Four legs?" Chiffon said, dumbfounded. "What are you talking about? *Who* has four legs?"

"Walter, of course. Whose legs did you think I was talking about?"

"Gabby's! Where is Gabby? What have you done with my daughter?" Chiffon screamed.

"Settle down. She's with me, of course. Where else would she be?"

Chiffon took a deep breath. "There is a note on my refrigerator from you saying there'd been a medical emergency. Naturally I assumed something was terribly wrong with Gabby. I had no idea it was just that stupid pooch of yours."

"First of all, Walter isn't stupid," Chenille said with a huff. "Second, I thought I mentioned Walter in the note."

"You did not. Your note says nothing about that mangy mutt." Her voice turned shrill. "Do you have any idea what I've been through today?"

Some days you're the dog;

some days you're the hydrant.

Sign outside of Dr. Dupree's veterinarian office

CHAPTER FIFTEEN

After unsuccessfully trying to calm her distraught sister, Chenille put down the telephone receiver. She smiled at Dr. Dupree, who was stroking Walter behind his ears.

"I want to thank you again, Dr. Dupree, for everything you've done. I'm extremely grateful."

She cast her eyes to the floor when she realized she'd been staring at the veterinarian. But who could blame her? His hair was dark and wavy, and his features looked as if they'd been hand-chiseled by Michelangelo.

"It was my pleasure. Walter's a lucky little dog. And please, call me Drake," he said in tones so sultry and masculine it caused sweat to bead on Chenille's upper lip.

"Drake," Chenille said breathily. It was the name of the hero from her favorite romance novel, *The Rogue and the Rose*.

"I've put some Valium in your bag. You can use it if Walter has an especially severe seizure."

"Administered orally?"

"Rectally," he said smoothly. "If it happens again, just keep calm. Speak gently to him and turn off any loud music."

"I don't care for loud music. I'm an easy-listening fan," Chenille said, forcing back a stray hair that had loosened from her headband.

"Really?" He studied her with intense green eyes. "I don't suppose you're a fan of Kenny G's?"

"I'm mad about him," she gushed. "When he performs his rendition of 'My Heart Will Go On,' I get all teary-eyed. Not, of course, to take anything away from Celine Dion's interpretation," she added quickly.

"There's only one Celine, eh?" Drake said in respectful voice.

"Do I detect a Northern accent?" she asked shyly.

"I'm from Wisconsin. A very cold state. I much prefer the balmy weather of the South."

Gabby interrupted their chat with a loud belch.

"I should go," Chenille said, picking her up from the carrier. "Gabby needs to go home to her mother, and Walter needs his rest."

He touched her on the hand. "This is highly irregular, considering our professional relationship, but—"

"Yes?"

"Would you accompany me to a Kenny G concert? He's coming to Columbia next weekend."

Her cheeks blazed. "Why, Dr. Dupree . . . I mean, Drake, I'd love to go."

. . .

Chenille's heart performed aerial stunts in her chest as she pulled into the driveway of her sister's house. Hugging Gabby to her breast, she waltzed through the media crowd gathered outside.

"No comment," she responded gaily to the questions volleyed her way. She tugged on Walter's leash as he paused to sniff the leg of a reporter from *Inside Edition*.

When she finally entered the house, she found Dewitt and Emily parked in front of the television set, swiftly making their way through a box of Little Debbie Swiss rolls.

"Those snacks are terrible," she said. "Didn't you see the carob cookies I bought for you in the pantry?"

"We thought they were dog treats for Walter," Emily said.

"They sure tasted like dog treats," Dewitt added. "Yuck!"

"Never mind. Where's your mother?" Chenille asked, putting Gabby in her walker.

"In the kitchen," said Emily, methodically licking cream from her fingers. "Aunt Chenille, why are those people outside the house?"

"Don't pay them any mind," Chenille said. "They're shameless opportunists who prey on other people's misery. They'll go away eventually if we just ignore them."

She went into the kitchen and saw Chiffon sitting at the

table with her head in her hands. A pillaged bag of gummy bears lay nearby. Only the green bears had been spared.

"Are you all right?"

Her sister laboriously lifted her head. A decapitated red bear clung to her bottom lip. "One of the reporters said Janie-Lynn was carrying Lonnie's love child," she said in a vacant voice.

"Oh heavens!" Chenille dropped into a chair next to her sister. "You can't believe a word they say. They're just trying to rattle you."

Chiffon shook her head. "My husband has completely abandoned us. I spoke with Janie-Lynn Lauren after I saw your note. I thought Gabby was sick, and I told her that, but I haven't heard a word from him. He doesn't care about us anymore."

"You spoke with Janie-Lynn Lauren?"

Chiffon nodded, telling Chenille the gist of her conversation with the movie star.

"I wonder why she wants to talk with you," Chenille said. "Has she called back?"

"Tons of reporters have called, so I have the machine screening calls, but she hasn't left a message."

Chenille picked up the notepad by the phone. "Here's the numbers of those people who were interested in buying Lonnie's things. We should contact them. You need the money."

Chiffon glumly eyed the long list of names and numbers, saying, "I don't know. The buyers will want to come over here and look at everything. I don't have the energy to go outside and face all of those reporters."

"I'll handle that," Chenille said. "As a matter of fact, I'll even call these people back. You just stand by in case they ask questions I can't answer."

Chenille started returning calls, and several potential buyers made arrangements to come by the house that evening. Then she prepared a supper of tempeh tacos and carrot sticks, but Chiffon, recovering from her gummy gorge, just picked at her food. Chenille coaxed her to finish her taco, but Chiffon folded it up in a napkin.

"I'll eat it later as a snack," she said. Then she went back to her bedroom and closed the door behind her.

Later that evening, Bert from the post office came over and bought the ATVs. While he loaded them onto his truck, Chenille stood in the carport, ignoring the questions fired at her from the media.

Shortly afterward, Garnell Walker dropped in and agreed to buy both of the Labradors. As he went to release the dogs from their pen, the questions from the press came at Chenille so insistently that her patience started to fray.

"Who's that man?" "Are you selling the family pets?" "Do the dogs belong to Lonnie?"

Dewitt came outside just as Garnell was herding the dogs into the backseat of a van.

"Aunt Chenille, where's that man going with Buddy and Beau?"

It hadn't occurred to Chenille that Dewitt might be attached to the animals. She'd never seen him play with them or feed them.

"Honey, why don't you go inside? I'll explain it to you later."

Dewitt stuck out his bottom lip and his hands tightened into small fists. "Those are my daddy's dogs! Where are you taking my daddy's dogs?" he asked Garnell.

Garnell took a step in Chenille's direction. He was older than she, in his early fifties, she guessed.

"I could come back and pick the dogs up at a more convenient time, if you'd like," he said in a low voice.

"That's very nice of you," Chenille said gratefully.

Garnell whistled for the dogs to get out of the car and led them back to the pen. When he got back, he addressed Dewitt. "See, sport, Buddy and Beau are back, safe and sound," he said, squatting down to the child's level.

While Dewitt ran off to pet his dogs, Garnell got up from his haunches and said, "Call me tomorrow and let me know if they're still for sale."

"I apologize for the trouble, Mr. Walker."

"No harm done," he said with a kind smile. His head jerked in the direction of the reporters. "You got quite a commotion going on here."

"I know. It's ridiculous."

"Want me to try to run these folks off for you?" he asked.

Chenille noticed his eyes were the light blue color of his dungarees. "Thanks, but no," she said.

After Garnell drove away, Chenille walked over to Dewitt and squeezed his shoulder. "All right, mister. I want you in your jammies by the time I come in. Aunt Chenille has to take the trash can out to the curb."

The members of the media had been watching this latest drama unfold with great interest. As soon as Dewitt climbed the steps to the house and shut the door behind him, Chenille was bombarded with questions.

"Were you planning to sell that child's dogs under his nose?" "Who was that man?" "What kind of person sells the family dogs?"

Chenille looked at the profusion of microphones and cameras aimed in her direction and lost her composure. She was tired, angry, and fed up.

"If you must know, those two dogs *are* indeed pets. The gentleman buying them will give them a good home. The family is only selling the animals because they desperately need the money. While Lonnie's been off drinking champagne with Janie-Lynn Lauren, his wife struggles to put dinner on the table. He's completely neglected his financial responsibility, and he's left behind three very young children who don't understand why their daddy won't come home."

Her statements, rather than quelling the crowd, only launched a flurry of further questions. Chenille ignored them as she rolled the trash can down the driveway. When she left it behind, a reporter took off the lid and started rifling through it. Chenille shook her head as she watched him toss aside Chef Boyardee cans and orange rinds. Then she shoved her way through the throng of bodies and went back inside the house.

Stop, Drop, and Roll won't
work in Hell.

Sign outside the Rock of Ages Baptist Church

CHAPTER SIXTEEN

"Janie-Lynn Lives in Sin!" "America's Sweetheart Diddling Deadbeat Dad!" "Kiddies Starve While Lonnie Drinks Dom Pérignon!" "Dog-Gone 'Cause Daddy Won't Pay the Bills!"

A few days later, headlines about Janie-Lynn Lauren and Lonnie shouted from every weekly magazine on the rack. Both Chiffon and Chenille had become overnight media sensations. One publication announced: "Move Over, Hilton Sisters! South Carolina Sibs, Chenille and Chiffon, Take Country by Storm."

The film of Chiffon spraying the press corps with a Super Soaker had been played on almost every television station, as had Chenille's angry tirade to the media. Neither of the sisters was very happy with the way they were portrayed by the press.

" 'Schoolmarmish'?" Chenille said as she thumbed through one of the many magazines that were lying by her feet. "That's something of an insult, don't you think?"

"It's better than 'Rambo in a Rabbit Coat,'" Chiffon said from her recliner. "Every time I see that film, I cringe. I look like Sasquatch."

"I thought you looked sweet, in a fierce kind of way."

Chiffon held open a magazine. "Check out this hideous shot of me in *The Globe*. I look like I'm sucking on a lemon."

Chenille was surprised at how much she'd been enjoying the company of her sister the last couple of weeks. Avoiding the press camped outside, the two women rarely left the house except to run out for groceries, diapers, and, of course, magazines. Being in each other's constant proximity had pulled them closer together.

The intense media attention, though annoying, served as a distraction for Chiffon, who no longer spent her days mooning over Lonnie. The family's financial situation had also improved. The sisters had managed to sell all of Lonnie's things, enabling Chiffon to sock away over six thousand dollars. (Garnell did buy Lonnie's dogs, promising Dewitt that he could visit them at any time.) And ever since Chiffon's circumstances had been made public, checks from all over the country had trickled into the household. So far they'd gotten nearly fifteen hundred dollars in the mail.

"Chiffon, do you like my hair up or down?" Chenille said, pulling her locks into a topknot.

"I like it down around your shoulders," Chiffon said, looking up from her magazine. "It's sexier."

Chenille released her hair and eyed herself critically in the mirror above the TV. "I think it needs a bow or a barrette."

"Bows make you look too fussed over. Your hair's much better loose," Chiffon said. "Who are you getting all prettied up for? I heard you talking to Garnell on the phone the other day. Have you taken a shine to him?"

"Heavens, no," Chenille said. "He's a dear man, but not really my type. Walter's veterinarian, on the other hand, is completely gorgeous."

"Rubert Pitt? He weighs over three hundred pounds and is covered with moles."

Chenille shook her head. "I took Walter to a specialist in Augusta. His name is Drake Dupree, and he asked me to a Kenny G concert."

"Can't say much for his taste in music," Chiffon said with a frown.

"I don't know what he sees in me," Chenille said as she continued to gaze into the mirror. "Would you help me with some makeup?" She pinched her cheeks to coax some color into them. "I don't want to look painted, but a touch of cosmetics—"

"We'll have a makeover night!" The magazines slid from Chiffon's lap as she leaped from the chair on her good foot. "We'll give each other pedicures and manicures. I can even put some highlights in your hair."

"Highlights? I don't know—"

"We'll dance to old records. Did you know I still have my hi-fi from high school? I'll pop popcorn and make strawberry daiquiris. We'll even do mud masks on each other."

"Mud masks?" Chenille had a sudden memory of a crew of Chiffon's high school friends, dressed in baby-doll nightgowns and giggling uncontrollably at their blackened faces in the mirror. She'd been holed up in her room trying to study for an AP history exam. "Maybe highlights would look nice," she said, fingering a strand of her hair.

"We'll have a girls' night in. It'll be a hoot. I haven't done anything like that since Lonnie and I . . ." Chiffon trailed off. "It's been too darn long."

The phone rang and the two women waited for the answering machine to click on.

"Hi, Chiffon, it's Mavis. I'm checking to see if you remembered the meeting this noon at the store."

Chiffon scrambled for the handset hanging on the wall. "Hey there, I'm glad you called. It's been so crazy around here that I almost forgot."

Chenille eavesdropped as her sister laughed and gossiped with Mavis in a low voice. Chiffon's friends called every day to check up on her and exchange chitchat. Chenille, who'd always been somewhat of a wallflower, was envious of her sister's easy repartee with her female friends.

"Would you mind watching Gabby again this afternoon?" Chiffon asked after she ended her phone call. "I've got a meeting at the Bottom Dollar Emporium."

"I don't mind at all," Chenille said. She averted her eyes so her sister couldn't read the hurt in them. Despite the recent closeness they'd shared, nothing had *really* changed. She was still the odd woman out.

"Elizabeth is bringing her new baby, so it's a huge deal. There's some bottles prepared in the fridge—" She snapped her fingers. "Hey! Maybe you'd like to come to the meeting. You knew Mavis, Attalee, and Birdie growing up. You probably don't remember much about Elizabeth. She's younger than both of us. But I'm sure you'll like her."

"What about Gabby?" Chenille said, flattered by the invitation.

"We'll just take her with us. She's usually napping around that time, and we'll be back before the other kids get home from school." Chiffon grabbed her sister's hand. "So, what do you say?"

Chenille couldn't remember the last time her sister had included her in anything. She was so touched, she feared she might cry.

"Thank you for asking. I'd love to come with you."

. . .

With scarves wrapped around their heads and big Jackie O–type sunglasses on their noses, the two sisters prepared to sneak out of the house. Chenille cracked open the back door.

"Wait a minute," Chiffon whispered just before they were going to slip out. "We might need some defensive ammunition."

She peered inside the refrigerator and grabbed two aerosol cans of whipped cream and handed one to Chenille. "If they give us any trouble, they'll get a snoutful of Reddi-wip," she said with a wicked snicker.

Chenille examined the can. "I've been meaning to ask you, Chiffon. Why *do* you have so many cans of whipped cream in your refrigerator?"

A sly grin flitted across Chiffon's face. "I'm not so sure you'd want to know."

Chenille blushed. "Are you ready to go?"

"Yes," Chiffon said, sliding a crutch under each arm. "But you carry Gabby, since you can move faster. I'll get the diaper bag."

The two slunk out the back door with their fingers poised on the spray buttons of the whipped cream. They inched along the perimeter of the house and were a short dash away from Chiffon's car when two reporters and a photographer burst out from behind the azalea bushes.

"Have you seen the photos of Janie-Lynn and Lonnie dancing on top of tables at the Garden of Eden nightclub?" "Did you know that Lonnie got a tattoo on his bicep that says 'Janie-Lynn Lauren Forever'?"

"Ready," Chiffon said in a low voice.

"Aim," Chenille answered.

"Fire!" the two sisters shrieked. They sprayed the interlopers full in the face and then sprinted to the car. As soon as they were safely inside, they were both seized by a fit of giggles.

"Next time we'll get seltzer water," Chiffon said as she pulled out of the driveway and down the road.

"Or maybe some Silly String," Chenille said, holding her quivering belly.

"Let's pull over somewhere and calm down for minute." Chiffon parked at the curb and wiped tears from her eyes.

"The look on their faces. Lord, I wish *I'd* been the one with the camera."

Chenille continued chuckling as she opened the door and crawled to secure Gabby in her car seat. "You'd think they'd be prepared for us after the Super Soaker incident," she said, adjusting the straps over the squirming baby. "If they're smart, they'll start wearing raincoats." She emerged from the backseat and opened the passenger door. "That reporter from *US* is cute, in a John Stamos kind of way. Don't you think?

Chiffon stared straight ahead with both of her hands on the steering wheel.

"Chiffon? Are you all right?"

Chiffon slowly swung her head around to look at her sister. Her playful expression had been replaced with a pained look. "Do you think what that reporter said about Lonnie's tattoo is true?" she asked in a little-girl voice.

"Who knows?" Chenille tsked. "But I think tattoos are a tacky way of expressing your feelings for someone."

"I have a tattoo," Chiffon said softly.

"You do? I've never seen it."

"You're not meant to." She paused. "It's in a private place."

"Oh."

"Lonnie's my love bear," she mumbled.

"What?"

"That's what the tattoo says. It's my nickname for him. 'Love Bear.' "

Chenille reached over the console and touched her sister's hand. "I'm sure your tattoo was very tastefully done."

"Lonnie was supposed to get a tattoo that said 'Tweety Bird,' his pet name for me, but the tattoo artist only got to the first 'e' before Lonnie begged him to stop. He never could abide much pain."

"I've heard the procedure is uncomfortable."

Chiffon swiped at her tears with her sleeve. "Don't you see? He endured twenty-one letters for her, but he could only stand three letters for me." Her voice cracked as she slumped over the steering wheel. "He's been with her for just a few days, and he already loves her *eight* more times than he ever loved me!"

"Now, now," Chenille said, resisting the urge to correct her sister's math. "Maybe he just had a stronger anesthetic this time around."

Chiffon lifted her head and stared at her sister with mascara-smeared eyes. "You think I'm an idiot, don't you? Sticking by a man who treats me like a doormat."

"You're not an idiot," Chenille said soothingly.

Fumbling in her jacket pocket, Chiffon extracted a balled-up tissue. "I still love him," she said. "It's not like I can just turn my feelings off with a spigot."

"I've never had a serious love relationship, but I'm very familiar with the feeling of longing," Chenille said, handing her sister a fresh tissue from the travel-size package she always kept in her purse. "But sometimes women put up with shabby behavior from men because they think that's all they deserve."

"He's never treated me well," Chiffon said, banging the dashboard with the palm of her hand. "Not when we were going steady, not when we got married, and especially not after we had kids." She looked helplessly at Chenille, gulping back tears. "I don't deserve anyone better than Lonnie. What do I have to offer? I'm a middle-aged, broken-down waitress living in a rickety purple house. I'm a lousy housekeeper and cook and a so-so mother. The one thing I've relied on all my life was my good looks, but wrinkles and worries are fading those fast."

"You have lots of things going for you!" Chenille insisted. "What about all your friends? You've always managed to attract people to you. And you have a chutzpah that's irresistible. The media noticed it right off."

Chiffon snorted. "Yeah, I have chutzpah to spare when it comes to folks I barely know. But I've never been able to stand up to Lonnie, or Mama, for that matter."

Chenille sighed. "Mama's in a class by herself. I think even George Bush would think twice about tangling with her. Don't allow her to badger you. You're fantastic. I've always wanted to be like you."

Until she'd said it aloud, she hadn't realized how much she truly meant it. In the past, her jealousy of her sister had always overshadowed her admiration.

"That's funny," Chiffon said with a sniff. "I've always thought *you* were the one who had it all together. You had the best grades, you went to college, and you worked at a career instead of just a lousy job. I've always respected you."

"I never knew," Chenille said softly. "Thanks for telling me."

Chiffon smiled at her sister as she put the car into gear. "I guess we should go or we'll be late for the meeting."

For the second time that day, Chenille basked in the new, unfamiliar way of relating to her sister. She and Chenille had more in common than she could possibly imagine. How sad that they hadn't discovered each other sooner.

The higher the hair, the closer to God.

Sign outside Dazzling Do's

CHAPTER SEVENTEEN

Ignoring the sign that said CLOSED FOR LUNCH, Chiffon pushed open the door to the Bottom Dollar Emporium. The two sisters crossed the creaky wooden floor and followed the chorus of "coochie-coochie-coo" that came from the soda fountain area. There they found Mavis, Attalee, Mrs. Tobias, and Birdie clustered around baby Glenda, while a beaming Elizabeth looked on.

"That baby's a dead ringer for my uncle Hoot, jowls and all," Attalee said, chucking the baby's chin.

"Hush, Attalee," Mrs. Tobias said. "Little Glenda is a carbon copy of her beautiful mother. Aren't you, precious?"

Elizabeth noticed the two sisters as they joined the group of admirers circled around Glenda.

"Hi, Chiffon. And you must be Chiffon's sister, Chenille?" Elizabeth extended her hand. "You're a legend in this town. Everyone still talks about how you took first place in the county-wide academic bowl during your senior year in high school."

"I remember," Chenille said. "George Eliot won it for me."

"Who's he?" Attalee asked.

Chenille laughed. "*She* is the author of *Middlemarch*. I was the only one on the panel who knew that."

"I covered that event," Birdie said. "That same year you were named valedictorian of Cayboo Creek High School. You brought a lot of pride to our little community."

"Thank you, Birdie. I remember you. You publish the *Crier*," Chenille said. "And I certainly remember Mavis and Attalee. I used to come in the Bottom Dollar Emporium for after-school sweets." She glanced at Mrs. Tobias. "I'm sorry. You don't look familiar. Have we met?"

"I've forgotten my manners," Elizabeth said. "Gracie Tobias, this is Chenille Grace. Chenille, my grandmother, Gracie Tobias."

"Charmed," Mrs. Tobias said with a friendly nod.

"Your baby is adorable, Elizabeth," Chenille said. "She's sleeping so peacefully."

"Thank you." Elizabeth stifled a yawn and covered her daughter with a receiving blanket. "She *should* be tired. She was awake all night."

Gabby had also fallen asleep, so Chiffon carefully lowered her into her carrier beside Glenda. Gazing at two sleeping children, she said, "Gabby looks like Gulliver next to Glenda. I've forgotten how tiny newborn babies can be."

The women tiptoed away from their sleeping children and took their seats in a circle of chairs that Mavis had set up for their meeting.

"Let's call the meeting to order, shall we?" Birdie said. "Who would like to be responsible for taking the minutes?"

"I will," Mrs. Tobias said, waving a gold-plated fountain pen.

"Excellent," Birdie said. "Now that we've chosen a fundraising project for the Senior Center, I want to emphasize how important it is to keep the specifics of our project discreet. Can everyone in this room keep a secret?"

"I probably shouldn't be here," Chenille said. "I'm an outsider, and maybe you'd rather not—"

"Nonsense," Birdie said. "You're Chenille's sister, so that makes you one of the family. Besides, we could use some objective input."

"I'd love to hear all about it," Chenille said.

"Very well." Birdie's eyes nervously scanned the room. "Who would like to tell Chenille about our little project? Mavis?"

Mavis's face turned crimson. "Me?" She cleared her throat. "All right, then. Um, we've decided— That is, we're going to—"

"Oh, for pity's sake," Attalee said. "It ain't nothing to be ashamed of. We're just putting out a nudie calendar."

"Attalee!" Mrs. Tobias said. She fanned her face with the minutes. "No one will appear *nude* in our calendar. Undressed, perhaps, disrobed, maybe, but nude, never!"

"Let me explain," Elizabeth said. "We've decided to produce and sell a calendar that will feature very tasteful shots of the matriarchs of Cayboo Creek, wearing little more than a smile."

"True Southern exposure," Attalee said slyly.

"Nothing titillating will be on display," Birdie added. "With the strategic placement of flowerpots, hats, and other props, the photographs will actually be quite tame."

Chenille's eyes widened. "All of you are going to take your clothes off for the camera?"

"Just us old gals. In order to be in the calendar, you gotta be over fifty," Attalee said. "The four of us are going to alternate months. For instance, I'm Miss January, May, and October."

"Oh my," Chenille said.

"We were initially stunned when Attalee proposed the idea," Birdie said. "But when we discussed it with Elizabeth's mother-in-law, Daisy Hollingsworth, she thought it was an excellent way to raise money. In fact, she'd heard of another group in England called the Ladies of Rylstone who'd published a similar calendar and raised over half a million dollars for the fight against lymphoma."

"And we all know how *very* proper the English are," Mrs. Tobias said with a wag of her finger.

"Since I have a marketing background, I'll be doing all of the publicity for the calendar," Elizabeth said.

"Chiffon tells us that you used to teach English," Birdie said to Chenille. "Maybe you'd be interested in coming up with some of the captions that will go with the photographs."

"I'd like to," Chenille said, "if I'm still here in Cayboo Creek."

Chiffon sat uneasily in her chair, pushing back her cuticles. No one had thought of a way for her to contribute, but then again, she didn't have any valuable skills.

"First we must come up with a catchy name for the calendar," Birdie said, folding her hands on her lap. "Does anyone have any suggestions?"

"'Birthday Suit Biddies'?" Attalee offered.

"Certainly not," Mrs. Tobias said, flinging her pen down. "Attalee, please do *not* participate in this discussion unless you can exercise decorum."

"There goes 'Lusty, Busty Broads,'" Attalee said with a sad shake of her head.

As the women conversed, Hank Bryson unexpectedly poked his head around the corner. He wore paint-splattered overalls and held a fishing cap in his hand. "Hey there, Bottom Dollar girls. I saw the 'closed' sign, but I was wondering if—"

"Hank!" Mavis screeched. She unconsciously covered her chest with her hands. Mrs. Tobias dropped her notepad.

Hank read the flustered looks of all the women present and backed toward the exit. "I'm sorry. I see that I'm interrupting. I'll just let myself out."

"As I was saying—" Birdie began after Hank left.

"'Bottom Dollar Girls,'" Chenille said, suddenly. "That's what you should call yourselves. And you can have all your photographs taken right here at the Bottom Dollar Emporium. Behind the soda fountain, kneeling over the candy barrels—there's dozens of different possibilities."

Mavis cocked her head in thought. "I love it," she announced after a beat.

"It does have a certain panache," Mrs. Tobias said, toying with the top button of her blouse. "You don't suppose the 'bottom' part is a shade too naughty?"

"Maybe," Birdie said with a smile. "But it fits us to a tee. Congratulations, Chenille, for coming up with not only the name but the theme of our calendar." She glanced at her legal pad. "Finding a suitable photographer is the next item on the agenda."

"We want to look like a pack of glamour-pusses," Attalee said.

"Sepia tones, I think," Mrs. Tobias added. "There should be a lovely, muted feel."

"Lots of airbrushing and retouching." Mavis nodded. "Like they do for the celebrities."

Glenda whimpered in her sleep and Elizabeth rose to check on her. "Birdie, you take great pictures for the *Crier*," she said over her shoulder. "Why don't you be our official photographer?"

"I'd like to, Elizabeth, but my hand isn't as steady as it used to be," Birdie said. "Last week I took a picture of the mayor and sheared off his forehead. Besides, who would take *my* pictures for the calendar?"

"How about Chiffon?" Chenille blurted out. "She's a talented photographer. She even won prizes for it in high school."

"That was a long time ago," Chiffon said quickly. "I haven't looked through a viewfinder in ages."

Elizabeth jiggled Glenda against her chest. "You'd be perfect, Chiffon. The women would feel comfortable around you, and we wouldn't have to bring in a stranger."

"I don't even have a camera anymore," Chiffon said.

"You can use mine," Birdie said.

"Chiffon can also do everyone's makeup and hair before the shooting," Chenille added. "She was on the pageant circuit for years, so she knows lots of beauty secrets."

"It's settled," Birdie said. "Make a note in the minutes that Chiffon Butrell is the official photographer and stylist for the Bottom Dollar Girl Calendar Project."

Mrs. Tobias completed the minutes with a flourish. "We're certainly lucky to have two such talented sisters in our midst," she said. Everyone echoed her sentiments.

Chiffon couldn't believe it. A couple of minutes ago she'd felt as useless as a pothole, and now she was practically running the whole show. She glanced at her sister, who tossed her an exaggerated wink. *What a character she is!*

Marriage is a three-ring

circus: engagement ring,

wedding ring and suffering.

Sign outside a divorce lawyer's office

CHAPTER EIGHTEEN

After the meeting, Elizabeth invited the two sisters out to the Chat 'N' Chew for lunch, but Chenille declined.

"You go ahead, Chiffon," Chenille said with a wave of her hand. "I'll drive your car home."

"You sure?" Chiffon said. "The Chat 'N' Chew ain't all grease and grits, you know. Mort tosses together a decent chef salad."

Chenille shook her head. "Walter's been alone all morning, and he's due for a walk. You two go out and have some fun."

So Chiffon and Elizabeth loaded up their babies in Elizabeth's car, and they pulled into the Chat 'N' Chew parking lot just after the noon rush. Chiffon was grateful that the diner wasn't too crowded, because as soon as they slid into a booth, everyone abandoned their braised beef tip specials and descended upon her.

"Can I get your autograph on the back of this menu?" Alice Faye Pruitt said, thrusting a pen under Chiffon's nose.

"What do you want my autograph for, Alice?" Chiffon asked. "You've known me since I was in kindergarten."

"You're famous," she said. "I saw you on the cover of a magazine."

When Chiffon reluctantly scribbled her signature next to the $3.99 egg-and-sausage platter, Alice said, "Do you think you could get me Mel Gibson's autograph, too?"

"Mel Gibson? I don't know him from a hole in the ground. How would I get his autograph?" Chiffon said.

"Really?" Alice said, a mystified look crossing her weathered face. "I just assumed all you celebrities knew one another."

"I'm not a—"

"Smile pretty, Chiffon," Buck Dillard said, snapping her photo with an Instamatic. "Wait until my kin in Sylvania get a load of this."

Thus it went, for nearly half an hour. The same folks she'd waited on at the Wagon Wheel, or had chatted with on Main Street, suddenly saw her as some kind of pop icon.

"Looky here, y'all," Elizabeth finally said. "Chiffon can barely eat her shaved ham sandwich. Why don't you give her some peace?"

After the crowd reluctantly scattered, Jewel sauntered over and said, "I need to get me a engraved brass plaque for this booth that says, 'Chiffon Butrell sat here.'"

"Oh, don't you start, too," Chiffon said, tossing a dill chip at her former boss.

Jewel's thick red hair was piled up on top of her head, and she wore a form-fitting forest-green uniform that matched her eyes. She leaned down to address Glenda, who dozed in her carrier.

"Everyone was so distracted by Chiffon that they missed the real celebrity dining in our midst," Jewel said. "She's just adorable, Elizabeth."

"Thank you," Elizabeth said. "Now, if she'd only learn to sleep at night, we'd be doing fine."

"You need to get a baby of your own, Jewel," Chiffon said, groping in her purse for Gabby's pacifier.

"They're both cute as bugs' ears," Jewel said. "But I'd have to find me a man first, and as I told you, I'm not in the market just now."

From the kitchen, Mort dinged a bell.

"Order up. I better hustle," Jewel said. "Remember, Chiffon, as soon as that ankle mends, you'll have a place here."

Chiffon smiled, but her expression lacked sincerity. She didn't look forward to going back to the Chat 'N' Chew or to any waitress job. She was tired of being a soup jockey.

"She's so pretty and friendly," Elizabeth said, her fingers laced around a coffee cup. "I've always liked Jewel."

"I know. I've offered to set her up with some fellows, but she won't have any of it. Says she's content to be alone." Chiffon rolled her eyes at the idea.

"Is that such a terrible thing? Maybe she got burned in the past, and she's relieved to be on her own. Sometimes no man in your life is better than the wrong man."

A stray curl worked its way into Chiffon's mouth. "What are you trying to say?"

Elizabeth pushed a noodle around her plate with her fork. "Nothing." Dabbing at her lips with a napkin, she regarded Chiffon. "It's just that I've seen a real difference in you today. For the first time since I can remember, everything hasn't been all about Lonnie—what he's thinking, what he's doing, where he's gotten off to. Have you even given him a second thought since we've been together today?"

"No," Chiffon said quietly. "I really haven't."

"It shows," Elizabeth said.

"But I still love him," Chiffon insisted. "I'd be miserable without him."

"Any more miserable than you are when you're with him?" Elizabeth asked.

Chiffon took a sip of her sweet tea. She wondered if her friend might have a point.

. . .

"Is that a stretch limousine in your driveway?" Elizabeth asked as she turned onto Chiffon's block.

"Lord only knows what's going on," Chiffon said, staring at the gleaming black vehicle. "Looks like there's twice as many reporters around. Tell you what. Drop me off at the liquor store on Chickasaw Drive. I'm going to try the sneak approach through the back."

"Are you sure?" Elizabeth's face clouded with concern. "Mavis said you tried that last week and they descended like ants on a sticky bun. Plus, you have Gabby and your crutches to deal with."

"The dogs gave me away last time, but they're not around

back anymore. Besides, I've gotten so used to these crutches, I can do some serious trucking with them. I'll just carry Gabby in her Snugli."

Chiffon checked her purse to make sure she had the key to the back door. "This will be a cinch."

"If you say so," Elizabeth said. She turned the car around and drove to the liquor store.

When they stopped, Chiffon eased Gabby into the front carrier and positioned her crutches under her arms. She waved good-bye to Elizabeth and swiftly crossed the backyard, alert for any reporters, but saw no one. As her heart hammered in her temples, she reached the back door, stuck the key in the lock, and darted inside.

Sagging against the kitchen counter to catch her breath, she saw a huge black man barreling toward her at the speed of a tornado. He raised a boxing-glove-sized fist.

"No sudden moves," he ordered.

"Oh my God, please don't hurt me or my baby! You can have anything you want." She heaved her pocketbook at him. "There's seventeen dollars in there and a half-off coupon for a large two-topping pizza at Domino's."

The man ignored the pocketbook and scowled at her. "Who are you?"

"I'm Chiffon Butrell. I live here."

"Come with me." He jerked his thumb in the direction of the living room.

Before they could move, Chenille came scurrying into the kitchen. "Tork, what's going on?" She spotted Chiffon cowering near the back door. "Chiffon, you're back. And I see you've met Tork."

She opened a kitchen drawer and took out a pot holder. "I certainly hope my brownies aren't burning. I'd hate to serve guests burnt goodies. Now, Chiffon, these are guiltless brownies, so you can have as many as you want. They're made from silken tofu and wheat pastry."

"Chenille, who is this . . . *person*?" Chiffon demanded. "He scared me to pieces."

"He hasn't told you?" Chenille said. She plunged a toothpick into the batch of brownies she'd just removed from the oven. "Chiffon, do you know anyplace in town that carries Evian water?"

"What is going on here?" Chiffon asked.

Tork extended his hand. "I'm sorry if I frightened you, ma'am. I'm just trying to protect my client. Lots of crazies in this world. Those brownies smell mighty good, Ms. Grace."

"Call me Chenille," she said, twirling a strand of hair around her finger as she smiled at the huge man. "And wait until you taste one. Chiffon, Tork is Jay-Li's bodyguard. Can you believe it? Jay-Li is right here in this very house!"

"Jay-Li? Who is Jay-Li?" Chiffon asked in exasperation. "And why can't I get a straight answer from you?"

"Excuse me, ladies," Tork said. "I need to make sure the front door is still secure." He slunk out of the room like a big, sleek panther.

Chenille's eyes fastened on his broad, muscular backside. "There's just something about a brawny man," she said with a sigh.

"Chenille!" Chiffon said.

"I'm sorry," Chenille said, cutting the brownies into squares. "I'm just flustered from all the excitement. Jay-Li is Janie-

Lynn Lauren. She's here! Sitting in Lonnie's La-Z-Boy." She lowered her voice. "I put down a clean afghan first. That chair's seen better days."

"*What?*" Chiffon sputtered. "That hussy is here in my house? And you're serving her brownies?"

"Actually, the brownies are for Tork. Jay-Li won't touch any food that contains flour," Chenille said. She grabbed her sister's wrist. "Chiffon, Jay-Li is so beautiful and nice. She's like a goddess walking the earth."

Chiffon jerked away. "She's a husband-stealer!"

"She's a very *sweet* husband-stealer."

"Here. Take Gabby," Chiffon said, handing her sister the baby. "I'm fixing to open a can of whoop-butt on that sweet husband-stealer."

"No, Chiffon. Don't!" Chenille said, but Chiffon had already stomped into the living room. Chenille plunked Gabby in her walker and hurried after her.

There on the recliner was five feet, five inches of the most pampered and primped specimen of female that Chiffon had ever seen. The dazzling creature had one dainty foot extended as a small Asian woman hovered over the appendage with a pumice stone. Toffee-colored eyes alighted on Chiffon as she stood in the doorway to the living room. An ever-so-familiar husky voice addressed the Asian woman. "Thank you, Sake. That'll do."

Enveloped in an exquisite-smelling cloud of sandalwood and jasmine, the woman rose from the chair and extended a hand. Her impeccably manicured nails were pale pink, like the interior of a seashell. "You must be Charmin. Like the toilet tissue."

"Chiffon," Chiffon said slowly.

Dozens of big-screen images reeled through Chiffon's mind. She'd seen all of Janie-Lynn Lauren's movies. The big box office pictures like *Foxy Girl, Stand by Your Rock Star,* and *Meter Maid in Milwaukee* she'd seen more than once. But she'd also seen her duds, such as *The Autobiography of Madame Curie* (when Janie-Lynn Lauren wanted to be regarded as a serious dramatic actress) and *Rollerblade Renegades* (which she starred in because she was having an affair with the leading man, Matt Maverick).

"Oh my Lord," Chiffon said as she melted into the chair across from the movie star. "It really is you. You're Janie-Lynn Lauren."

"You can call me Jay-Li. All of my friends do."

"As do some of your enemies," said a woman who was stabbing at a Palm Pilot with long red fingernails.

"That's my personal assistant, Ariel," Jay-Li said. "Sake is my manicurist, and you've met Tork, my bodyguard."

As Chiffon sat in stunned silence, Chenille merrily chatted with Jay-Li. "I'll never forget that scene in *Foxy Girl* when you took a champagne bath with Brad Pitt. Is he really as good-looking in person as he is on the screen?"

"Girlfriend, he's even better-looking." Jay-Li showed teeth that glowed bright white, as if under a black light.

Chenille clapped her hand to her chest. "'Girlfriend'?" She turned to her sister in a tizzy. "Jay-Li called me 'girlfriend.'"

Chiffon nodded dumbly, still too shocked to speak.

Just then Ariel, who was sitting by the fireplace, dropped her Palm Pilot with a noisy clatter. Chiffon glanced up toward the mantel and caught a glimpse of the family photograph they'd posed for at Olan Mills only two months ago. Lonnie was in the center of the picture, holding Gabby on his lap. Chiffon and the two older children framed him. In an instant, the celebrity spell that Jay-Li had cast was broken.

"You've stolen my husband," Chiffon said in a threatening voice.

"Steady, girl," Tork said as he took a step in her direction.

"Chiffon!" Chenille said. "We were just getting along so nicely. Why doesn't everyone have a brownie?"

"It's okay, Tork," Jay-Li said. She was wearing a curve-hugging salmon-pink jumpsuit with the word "Juicy" stamped on her bottom. "She has a right to be upset. That's why I'm here. To take some of the sting away. Ariel?"

The woman, thin as a knife's blade in a black tailored dress, jumped to attention.

"In exchange for the pain and suffering of losing your husband, we are prepared to compensate you with this"— Ariel stuck a calculator in Chiffon's face—"generous monetary gift."

Chenille peeked over Chiffon's shoulder at the glowing numbers. "Am I counting right? Do I see six zeros?"

"That's correct," Ariel said, snapping the calculator shut. "We'll have a cashier's check prepared with that amount."

"Please promise me you'll buy those sweet doggies back for your son," Jay-Li said as she toyed with a gold necklace thick as a rope shank. "*That* was a public relations nightmare. Also, could you give me your recipe for corn pones? Lonnie has a 'hankering' for them, and my cordon-bleu chef doesn't have a clue."

"What am I supposed to do in exchange for this money?" Chiffon asked.

"Divorce him," Jay-Li said, yawning prettily.

"So *you* can have him?"

"That's the idea," Jay-Li said. "We're planning a wedding, but keep that under your hat. My publicist claims we're just good friends."

Chiffon shook her head in disbelief. "I have three children with him. We've been married for ten years, and you expect me to pass him off to you like he's some kind of baton in a relay race?"

"Charmin," Jay-Li said in a syrupy tone. "Let me explain. I love him; he loves me. He spray-painted my name on an over-pass in Hollywood. Now, if that isn't devotion—"

"The name's Chiffon!" Chiffon snapped. "And you have some questions to answer. Did Lonnie get a tattoo with your name? Are you carrying his love child?"

"Yes, Lonnie commemorated our love with a tattoo. And no, I'm not carrying his love child." Jay-Li sensuously ran a hand over her concave belly. "But not for a lack of trying."

"You wench!" Chiffon lunged toward Jay-Li, but Chenille yanked her back.

"Calm down!" Chenille said to her sister, who struggled to be released from her grip. "Attacking Jay-Li serves no purpose."

"Did you hear what she said?" Chiffon said.

Tork stepped between Chiffon and Jay-Li. "Miss, I'm going to have to ask you to stay at least three feet from Ms. Lauren," he said.

"She'll be fine," Chenille said, leading her enraged sister to an armchair. "Just sit here for a minute and regain your composure. I'll talk to Jay-Li."

Tork loomed over Chiffon like a tank, so she had no choice but to remained seated.

"Jay-Li," Chenille began. "I know that some people consider Lonnie to be something of a looker—"

"He's stunning," Jay-Li purred.

"But you have your pick of gorgeous men. Why would you want Chiffon's husband? You can't possibly have much in common." She lowered her voice to a whisper, so Chiffon couldn't hear. "After all, you can dress Lonnie up in the finest cashmere and leather, but underneath it all, his neck will always be red."

"That's precisely why I find him sexy," Jay-Li said. "He's a real man, not some sort of plastic Hollywood substitute. I'm tired of vegan men who have weekly facials at Elizabeth Arden. I want a man who likes his steak rare and bloody; who has strong, callused hands; who—"

"Always leaves the toilet seat up," Chiffon said with a smirk.

"Who makes me feel like a woman," Jay-Li said with a sultry pout. "Lonnie taps into my wild feminine side like no other man before him. He's my soul mate."

"But he's also Chiffon's husband," Chenille pointed out. "It's wrong to be a home-wrecker."

"The marriage was broken long before I entered the picture," Jay-Li said dismissively. "Lonnie tells me that he hasn't made love to Charmin since the conception of his youngest child."

"That's a lie!" Chiffon sprang up from her chair, and Tork

glared at her until she sat back down. "We made love three times the night before he left for California," she whimpered.

"You poor, deluded soul," Jay-Li said with a flick of her silky auburn hair. "Lonnie hasn't been attracted to you in a very long time. If he's made love to you in the last year, it was only out of a sense of duty."

"I won't listen to this," Chiffon said. She screwed her eyes shut, willing herself not to cry.

"What about his children?" Chenille said. "Lonnie still has a responsibility to them."

"That's one of the reasons you're getting such a large check," Ariel said, looking up from her Palm Pilot. "Child support is included in the amount."

"There's more to being a father than money," Chenille said.

"On occasion, we'll fly the children out to L.A. in my private jet," Jay-Li said, rising from her chair. "I'll rent Disneyland for the day."

"You stay away from my children," Chiffon growled.

"I've no interest in your brood," Jay-Li said coolly. "Lonnie and I plan on adopting our own Asian baby soon after we marry."

"A Chinese baby?" Chenille asked.

"That's last season's nationality," Jay-Li said. "We'll be adopting a Cambodian child."

"I'm disappointed in you, Jay-Li," Chenille said sadly. "Where is that heroic woman who single-handedly saved an entire town from mercury poisoning in *The Winsome Whistle-Blower*?"

"That was the movies," Jay-Li said, picking up her fringed bag. "This is real life. And in real life, whatever Jay-Li wants—"

"Jay-Li gets," said Tork, Sake, and Ariel in unison.

"Exactly," Jay-Li said. She flashed her big-screen smile. "I'll be sending over divorce papers via messenger. Sign them, and you'll get the check." Her smile turned hard. "Don't sign them, and I just might have to get nasty."

Are you following Jesus this closely?

Bumper sticker on Reverend Hozey's Chevy Lumina

CHAPTER NINETEEN

"I want go to Garnell's house and see Buddy and Beau today," Dewitt said, tugging on his aunt's hand. *"Peeeze."*

"I don't know." Chenille glanced uneasily at her sister, who was camped out on the couch in a nest of balled-up Kleenexes and junk-food containers. "I'm a little concerned about your mother."

"You promised," Dewitt pleaded.

"I'm perfectly fine," Chiffon said, waving her sister off. She'd just polished off the last Great Berry Reef Pop-Tart and kicked the empty box to the floor.

"Did you know Pop-Tarts are loaded with trans-fatty acids?" Chenille asked.

"And your point is?" Chiffon said. She flicked crumbs off her chin onto her bathrobe.

"I'm worried about you. You haven't moved from that spot for two days."

"I'm fine," Chiffon said, and turned her attention back to a rerun of *Green Acres*.

Chenille glanced out the window. "It's awfully bright outside. Dewitt, go get Walter's leash and his Doggles. They're both on a stool by the back door."

"Doggles?" Chiffon looked up from the TV screen.

"Doggles are goggles for dogs. Walter is sensitive to UV rays."

"Ha!" Chiffon guffawed. "You're putting sunglasses on a dog and you're worried about *me*?"

Chenille ignored her sister and scooped up the car keys from the coffee table. Dewitt returned with a bespectacled Walter trotting behind him.

"This is the episode where Oliver uses Lisa's hotcake batter to make a head gasket," Chiffon said with a snicker. She propped her bare feet on the armrest.

"Can I get you anything while I'm out?" Chenille asked.

"How about a jumbo package of fried cherry pies?"

"Chiffon," Chenille began. Before she could continue, the phone rang.

The voice coming over the answering machine was Drake's. "Hello, Chenille, this is your veterinarian. I was calling to check on Walter."

"Not *him* again," Chiffon remarked.

Chenille pounced on the phone. "Hello, Drake," she trilled.

"There you are. I wanted to make sure our patient was still in good stead."

She looked down at Walter, who was batting at his Doggles with his paws. "Walter's in excellent health, Doctor. How nice of you to inquire. Are you so attentive to all of your patients?"

"Only when their owners are as captivating as you are."

"Oh, Drake. You're embarrassing me."

Chiffon pantomimed sticking a finger down her throat. Chenille turned her back on her.

"I can't wait until our rendezvous this Saturday night," Drake said.

"Nor can I," Chenille said, sighing.

"Until this weekend, my lovely one."

Chenille gently replaced the receiver and pressed the palm of her hand to her chest. "I just might faint."

"Would you cut the corn? I'm trying to eat here," Chiffon said as she grazed on a fistful of Scooby-Doo cereal.

"Mommy, that's *my* cereal," Dewitt said with a pout. "You're eating everything in the house."

"Not everything." Chiffon pursued a marshmallow that had fallen between the cushions. "I haven't touched a single celery stick."

"Dewitt, why don't you get Walter strapped in his booster seat?" Chenille said. "I'll be there in a minute."

After Dewitt left, Chenille stood in front of her sister. "Look at you. Your hair's a fright, your skin's broken out from all that junk food, and you haven't taken a shower for two days. What's happening to you?"

"Janie-Lynn Lauren happened to me," Chiffon said through a mouthful of cereal.

Chenille knelt beside the couch. "I suppose you think you're entitled to stew in your own juices, but it's just hard for me to reconcile *this* Chiffon with the one I used to know."

Chiffon scratched her stomach beneath her nightgown. "Which Chiffon was that?"

"The one who used to have the world by a string. The one who carried herself like a beauty queen."

"Anyone with a pretty face can collect tiaras and scepters."

"Not so," Chenille said. "You had more than just beauty. You possessed a charisma that made you stand out from every other girl. It was true star quality."

"Me? With star quality?" She fingered a strand of her lank locks. "That'll be the day."

"Yes, *you.* And if you had it once, you still have it. Maybe it just got buried underneath the weight of marriage and children. But you can retrieve it."

A car horn bleated from outside the door. "Your son's summoning me," Chenille said. "I'd better go." She kissed her sister on the cheek. "Love you," she said.

Chiffon turned toward her sister with a stunned look on her face. "Love you, too."

. . .

With a deft turn of a spatula, Garnell flipped the hash-brown concoction sizzling in the skillet. Walter lay by his feet, watching with worshipful eyes.

"I don't know why these things are called creek banks," Garnell said, adjusting the height of the flame on the gas stove. "But that's what my daddy called them, and that's what his daddy called them."

He winked at Dewitt, who was seated at a battered oak table in the kitchen, chugging a glass of chocolate milk. "All I know is they'll put hair on your chest."

"I want lots of hair! Like Wolverine," Dewitt said as he swiped at his milk mustache with his sleeve.

"Can Walter have a smidgen of ham?" Garnell asked.

Chenille shook her head. "Walter is a vegetarian, but thank you. It was gracious of you to have invited us to dinner, Mr. Walker. I hope we haven't taken advantage of your hospitality."

"Shoot, I love me a little supper company," he said over his shoulder. "You two are doing me a favor. And please, call me Garnell."

Garnell had refused to take no for an answer when he'd asked them to stay for dinner. Dewitt had played for over an hour with the Labs in the front yard while Chenille and Garnell watched from two Adirondack chairs on his wraparound porch. The man clearly loved animals. In addition to the dogs, he had two cats, a potbellied pig, three ferrets, and a skunk.

"Don't worry about PU," he said when the skunk ventured on the porch to use the litter box. "He's been descented."

Their chat had been pleasant enough. Garnell mainly talked about his woodworking hobby. He'd made the chairs on the porch, as well as most of the furniture in his house. As they conversed, he'd whittled a whistle for Dewitt out of a sapling. Then, as soon as Chenille made a motion to leave, he launched his fervent campaign to get them to stay for dinner. Her protests were useless, particularly after he mentioned there'd be black-bottom pie for dessert and Dewitt crawled up her legs pleading, "*Peeeze*, Auntie Chenille, *peeeze.*"

So there she was, listening to Johnny Cash sing "Ring of Fire" on a transistor radio and waiting to eat greasy bachelor fare. On the bright side, Dewitt was having a grand time. She supposed it was healthy for him to be exposed to a positive male role model like Garnell.

While Garnell cooked, Chenille drifted around the den situated just off the kitchen. She spied a bookshelf against the wall, expecting to find a set of Foxfire books or a collection of woodworking volumes. She withdrew the nearest book on the shelf and examined it.

"Balzac?" she said with a start. As she flipped through the pages, she saw the book was in the original French. She continued to scan the spines: Euripides, Aristotle, Virgil, Voltaire, and Descartes.

"Mr. Walker—I mean, Garnell. Whose books are these on the shelves?" Chenille asked.

"They're mine," Garnell said, transferring the steaming creek banks to a serving platter.

"But why do *you* have them?"

"To read, naturally. What else are books good for?" he said with a grin. "Well, on second thought, I did once use the Aristophanes to put under the leg of a wobbly table, but other than that—"

"But some of these books aren't even translated."

"I know. I dabble some in foreign languages. 'Course, don't ask me to *parlez français*. These country-boy lips don't wrap around French syllables too good. I'm much better at reading it."

"I never would have guessed."

"I don't suppose I come across as a scholar. Probably 'cause I'm self-taught. Never did go to college, even though Miss Beezle at the high school kept after me about it."

"Miss Beezle?" Chenille said in surprise. "She was *my* teacher! You must have been in the accelerated program at Cayboo Creek High School."

"I don't know what they called it back then, but, yeah, I took all my main subjects from Miss Beezle until eleventh grade, when I quit. My daddy got sick, and I had to get a job."

"Miss Beezle was my mentor. I have such an admiration for her! She must be in her eighties by now. I wonder what's happened to her?"

"She's still at the high school, teaching the smart kids. Matter of fact, she comes to visit me now and again. She's making noises about retiring. I could invite the two of you over for a visit sometime."

"I'd love to see her."

"Then it's a date," Garnell said. He plunked three mismatched plates down on the table. "Time to eat. Y'all come and get it."

Chenille opened her mouth to say that a visit with Miss Beezle at his house really didn't qualify as a date, but she thought better of it. There was no sense in hurting his feelings. She'd just have to make certain he didn't get the wrong idea about her. Although he was a decent and obviously bright fellow, he wasn't the man for her. Only Drake could make her heart do somersaults.

. . .

When Dewitt and Chenille returned home from Garnell's house, Emily was sitting on the La-Z-Boy in the living room, watching Nick at Nite. Chiffon had finally vacated her spot on the couch.

"Where's your mother?" Chenille asked.

"In the bedroom," Emily said, hopping up from the couch. "Mama, Chenille is back!"

Chenille started toward the bedroom, but Emily blocked her path. "Don't go in there. She wants to make an entrance."

Emily made a megaphone with her hands and shouted, "Are you ready, Mama?"

"I'm ready, baby!" came Chiffon's answer from the back of the house.

"Ladies and gentlemen," Emily announced. "May I please present a woman with star quality, charisma, and a queenly bearing. The *one*, the *only*, Chiffon Amber Butrell!"

Chiffon strode regally down the threadbare hall carpet. Her blond ringlets were piled high up on her head, and winking atop her hairdo was a rhinestone tiara. She wore a long black velvet skirt and a rose blouse that complemented her creamy complexion.

"Good evening," Chiffon said, flashing a toothy smile. "I was born under the sign of Scorpio. My favorite color is mauve, I'm an animal lover, and every day I pray for world peace."

"Yay!" Emily cheered. Dewitt let loose a wolf whistle (learned at the knee of his daddy, no doubt) and Chenille started clapping.

"You're beautiful," Chenille gushed. "How elegant you look."

"Thank you. Although I do feel kind of funny." She showed Chenille a shiny red bra strap. "See, it's still just me underneath."

"I'm speechless," Chenille said.

Chiffon caught her sister's hand and sat beside her. "I want you to know I really appreciate all the nice things you said to me. Made me remember a time in my life when I was confident. I could walk the runway of any pageant and know I'd be taking home that crown. When I put this old tiara on my head, that cock-of-the-walk feeling came rushing back to me. I can do it, Chenille. I'll get through this thing with Janie-Lynn without falling apart."

"Of course you will," Chenille said.

Chiffon kissed Dewitt and Emily on the top of their heads. "Y'all two need to get into your jams," she said. "Go on, scoot."

After the children left, Chiffon picked up a manila envelope from the top of the television and tossed it to her sister. "This came by overnight mail."

Chenille peeked inside. "Divorce papers?"

"That's right," Chiffon said with a nod.

"What are you going to do?"

"Send them right back where they came from." She took the envelope and fastened it. "Movie star or no movie star, queens don't hand their man over to another woman without a fight."

"Are you sure he's worth the trouble?"

Chiffon shrugged. "Maybe not. But Janie-Lynn Lauren isn't getting the better of me."

When Everything's Going Your Way, You're in the Wrong Lane.

Message in a fortune cookie at Dun Woo's House of Noodles

CHAPTER TWENTY

"Stop," Drake said as Chenille climbed the steps leading to Chiffon's house.

She paused on the landing underneath the yellow bug light. "What's wrong?"

"Be still for just a moment, please." Drake arranged his hands into a viewfinder and gazed at her. "I wish you could see yourself right now. Standing there, bathed in moonlight, you look like a statue carved from alabaster."

Chenille's cheeks grew hot. "Drake. The things you say!"

He seized her hand and covered her knuckles with butterfly kisses. "All of them are true." He was so close to her now, she could smell the citrus of his cologne and feel the heat of his breath on her cheeks. Under dark, lush eyelashes, his eyes searched her face.

"Tonight my life has begun anew." His lips lightly brushed hers in one brief, electric moment. After the kiss, he stepped back and regarded her with a penetrating gaze. "Good evening, my sweet."

After he left, Chenille stood on the step, watching the red trail of his departing taillights. Enveloped in a haze of euphoria, she groped for the doorknob and floated inside the house. Chiffon was sitting on the sofa in her bathrobe with Walter by her side.

"Did the two of you wait up for me?" Chenille asked as she shut the door behind her.

" 'Course we did. How was Kenny G?" Chiffon asked.

"Fine. I think."

"What do you mean *you think*?" Chiffon yawned. "Was it any good or wasn't it?"

Chenille hugged herself. "Who cares about saxophone music when a handsome man like Drake whispers wonderful things in your ear during the entire concert?" She slid into a chair beside her sister.

"What sort of things?"

"Beautiful, poetic things. He said my hands looked like little white doves."

Chiffon laughed. "Don't you think that's a mite over the top?"

"No, I don't," Chenille said defensively. She held her hands out to inspect them. "My hands *are* nice, and I'm flattered he noticed."

"I don't know," Chiffon said, shaking her head. "Something about him seems kind of hinky."

Chenille had been extremely nervous about introducing Drake to Chiffon. In the past, whenever the two sisters were together, men would practically trample over Chenille to gain her sister's attention. So, earlier this evening, when Chiffon answered the door wearing a very snug sweater, Chenille had braced herself for Drake's appreciative glances and flirtatious banter. To her relief, Drake didn't drool, grovel, or preen when he met Chiffon. Perhaps her sister wasn't used to being ignored. Was it possible she was just jealous?

"I've always dreamed of going out with a physician," Chenille said.

"He's a vet," Chiffon said in a snide voice.

Ah, so she is jealous!

"You know, I could always ask Drake if he has a nice friend or colleague. Maybe we could double-date."

"Chenille, I'm married!"

"I know that. I just thought—" Chenille plucked a bit of lint off her skirt. "Never mind."

Chiffon fluffed a sofa pillow and wedged it underneath her head. "Call it intuition, but I don't think Drake's the guy for you. Plus, I've asked around and nobody knows a thing about him."

"He lives in Augusta. He probably travels in much more sophisticated circles than Creek people."

Chiffon sprang up from the cushions. "Chenille Chastity Grace, I can't believe you said that."

"I'm just stating the truth. Creek folk and city people don't mix much."

"You're hardly citified yourself, hailing from Bible Grove."

"A suburb of Greenville," Chenille reminded her.

"Big whoop. Greenville ain't exactly Gotham," Chiffon grumbled. "Speaking of Bible Grove, did you know I have an appointment with the doctor day after tomorrow? My ankle feels a lot stronger. I'll probably be able to turn in my crutches."

"Which means you won't need *me* anymore," Chenille said softly. "Which means it's time to go back home to Bible Grove."

"You don't have to, you know," Chiffon said.

"Drake asked me out for another date next weekend."

"There's also the Bottom Dollar Girl calendar. We're counting on your input."

Chenille toyed with the beads of her necklace. "Would I be putting you out if I stayed here for a little bit longer?"

"You're welcome here for as long as you like," Chiffon said as she got up from the couch and slid her feet into a pair of terry-cloth mules. "Although I'm sure you're tired of sleeping on a rollaway bed in the living room."

"It's not so bad. But I'll have to go home soon. I've got to find a job."

"Me, too. I dread going back to waiting tables. Good night, Chenille," she said. Chiffon started shuffling off to her bedroom, but then paused to glance back at her sister. "I almost forgot, Garnell called. He wants you to give him a ring in the morning. Something about getting together with Miss Beezle." She waggled her eyebrows. "You've certainly been the belle of the ball lately."

"We're just friends," Chenille said brusquely.

"Too bad. I think Garnell is precious."

"He's nice, but I've wished for a man like Drake all my life."

"Well, you know what Granny Eugenie used to say. Be careful what you wish for, because one day—"

"It might just kick you in the fanny," Chenille interrupted. "Granny certainly had her own way of saying things. But believe me, Drake is the exception."

. . .

The next Monday, Chiffon was able to walk without her crutches for the first time in days. Although she was grateful to regain her mobility, she didn't want Chenille to go back to Bible Grove just as the two of them were getting along so well. Both sisters were subdued when they left the doctor's office.

"What's going on at the Bottom Dollar Emporium?" Chenille asked as they traveled down Main Street on their way home. Chiffon glanced out the window to see Mello Vickery, Prudee Phipps, and several other women from the Baptist Ladies' League picketing outside. She slowed the car and read the signs aloud. "'Bottom Dollar Girls, Keep Your Drawers On.' 'How Dare You Bare?' 'Just Say No to Carnal Calendar.'"

"Oh my goodness! How'd they find out about the calendar?" Chenille said.

Chiffon jerked her gearshift into park. "I don't know, but let's go in and see."

She hoisted Gabby from her car seat, grabbed the carrier, and strode to the store entrance with Chenille following behind her. Mello stepped in front of Chiffon before she could open the door.

"If you cross this threshold, you're entering a pagan's den," Mello said, flinging her fox fur over her shoulder.

Chiffon brushed past her. "I've always been partial to a little sinning."

Prudee pressed a button into Chenille's hand that said HAR-LOTS REPENT. "Wear it with pride, sister," said Prudee.

Chenille followed Chiffon into the store. Birdie, Mrs. Tobias, and Mavis were chatting in a tight knot near the cash registers, and Attalee was stationed behind the soda fountain.

"How did they find out?" Chiffon asked. Three heads swiveled in Attalee's direction.

"I only mentioned it to my roommate," Attalee said peevishly.

"Myrtle, aka Mouth of the South," said Birdie with a smirk. "Telling Myrtle is like hiring a skywriter to fly over Cayboo Creek."

"I told her about the calendar because I thought she might want to be one of the models," Attalee said. "Don't know why I even bothered to ask her. She has a face like a bulldog chewing on a wasp."

"It's all right, Attalee," Mavis said. "You meant well."

"Are those ladies outside driving away business?" Chiffon asked.

"Some," Mavis said. "I've seen a few Rock of Ages congregation members turn around in the parking lot when they spotted the picketers."

"Perhaps this calendar isn't such a good idea after all," Mrs. Tobias said. "It's much too racy."

"And this community is so conservative," Birdie added. "Maybe no one would even buy it."

Chiffon poured herself a cup of coffee and leaned against a

wooden barrel filled with sour chews. "Well, we can't have Mavis losing business over this."

Just then the front door swung open and Reverend Hozey from the Rock of Ages Baptist Church stormed in wearing a charcoal suit and a stormy expression.

"This is a house of heathens," he rumbled, his face the color of stewed tomatoes. Tugging on his graying sideburns, he scanned the room with the cold, narrow eyes of a copperhead. When he spotted a pale-faced Mavis by a display of oil lamps, he thundered, "Mavis Loomis, do you consider yourself a sister in Jesus Christ?"

"Yes, yes, I do," Mavis said.

"Then why have you invited Satan into our midst?"

Attalee sidled over to the reverend, holding a drink in her hand. "Why don't you simmer down with a nice, frosty glass of root beer?" she said. "No sense in rattling the windows when no one's going to pass around the plate."

"There are no cold drinks in hell, Attalee Gaines," he said, ignoring the draught she'd offered.

"For goodness' sake," Chiffon began. "I don't know what you've heard, but this calendar is perfectly respectable."

"Who are you?" he asked, regarding Chiffon. "I've never seen you in the Lord's house."

"I go to the Methodist church," Chiffon said. Although her last visit had been Easter Sunday two years ago.

"That godless place with a woman at its helm?" he said. "What do you know of goodness?"

Mavis meekly stepped forward. "Reverend Hozey, the girls and I, we were just discussing—"

"I've heard you call yourselves the Bottomless Girls," he said. "How could you befoul our fair community in such a wanton manner?"

Chiffon planted her hands on her hips. "It's called the Bottom Dollar Girls, and—"

"Silence, strumpet!" he roared.

"Now, wait a darn minute—" Chiffon said.

"*You* wait," he continued. "Mavis, if this project continues, you'll be banned from the church nursery. Likewise for Birdie and her piano playing. If this calendar is published, your services as a musician will no longer be welcome at Wednesday-night suppers. Am I understood?"

"Yes, Reverend," Mavis said in a small voice.

"That's very good to hear, sister. I knew you were an instrument of the Lord." His bellowing voice softened into benevolence. "May y'all have a blessed day," he said, lifting his hand to his forehead.

"There's nothing dirty about the human body," Chenille interjected, surprising herself by speaking out. "Besides, the calendar was going to be very tasteful."

Reverend Hozey fixed his dark eyes on her. "The only person who would find something tasteful about old, flabby bodies is the devil himself." He turned on his heel and slammed the door behind him.

"Who you calling old?" Attalee hollered after him. "Bet you don't look so hot in your skivvies, either!"

Mrs. Tobias smoothed her skirt over her knees. "I take exception to his comment about flabby old bodies. I still fit into the same Chanel suits I wore as a young bride. And lately I've embarked on an exercise regimen with Campbell's soup cans which has yielded pleasant results."

Birdie patted her middle. "I cut out my morning doughnut run, and I think I may have lost a pound or two. It's a shame we'll have to think of some other way to raise money for the Senior Center."

"Why *should* we come up with something else?" Mavis said, a resolute look in her eyes.

"You know how stubborn Reverend Hozey is," Birdie said, tugging on the ribbon of her hat. "Plus, I think we were all beginning to agree that maybe this idea wasn't right for us."

"I was having my doubts, too," Mavis said. "But then Reverend Hozey called me 'an instrument of the Lord.' If I was truly the Lord's instrument, I wouldn't worry about what Reverend Hozey and his flock thinks; I'd focus on what project would best serve the Senior Center. And I truly believe this calendar will make us the most money."

"How will we deal with Reverend Hozey?" Birdie said. "He'll have our heads for lying to him."

"I didn't lie to him," Mavis said. "I just said I understood him. That's not the same thing at all."

Chiffon linked her arm with Mavis's. "But what about the nursery? I know you love looking after those babies."

"Sometimes you have to make sacrifices," she said. "Being an instrument of the Lord isn't always pleasant."

Mavis glanced at Attalee. "Don't breathe a word of this to anyone. What Reverend Hozey doesn't know won't kill him. He'll find out when the calendar comes out, and I'll deal with his wrath then."

"My lips are sealed," Attalee said, zipping her fingers over her mouth.

"They'd better be," Birdie said. She studied the faces of the women around her. "It looks like operation Bottom Dollar Girls is full steam ahead. Is everyone in?"

Mrs. Tobias nodded. Chiffon and Chenille smiled, and Attalee danced a jig around the room.

"We're going to be calendar girls!" she shouted.

God wants spiritual fruits,

not religious nuts.

Message in a Methodist church bulletin

CHAPTER TWENTY-ONE

When Janie-Lynn Lauren had said things were going to get nasty if Chiffon didn't sign the divorce papers, she wasn't just whistling "Dixie." After Chiffon and Chenille left the Bottom Dollar Emporium, they drove home to find the yard crawling with news trucks and reporters.

"What now?" Chiffon said, parking behind an NBC van.

"I thought they were finally going to let us alone," Chenille remarked.

As the sisters warily emerged from the car, the reporters and photographers closed in on them, like bullworm moths on a corn ear.

"Chiffon, how do you respond to Lonnie's allegations that he didn't father any of your children?"

"Is it true that you seduced other men while your husband was at work?"

Gabby started whimpering and clutched frantically at her mother's T-shirt. Chiffon stood motionless in the swirl of questions, eyes glazed with shock.

Chenille tugged at her sleeve. "Chiffon, are you okay?"

Chiffon ducked her head down, saying, "I don't know anything about this."

"Have we struck a nerve, Chiffon?" asked a male reporter with spiked blond hair and a sharp nose. "I don't see you breaking out the squirt guns or the whipped cream."

Chiffon's chin trembled, and she looked helplessly at the mob bustling around her. "I want to go inside. I feel sick."

"It's a simple question, Chiffon," the same reporter continued. "Did you get some nookie underneath Lonnie's nose?"

She didn't answer but instead stood motionless, blinking back tears.

"Of course she didn't," Chenille said, putting a protective arm around her sister. "Chiffon is loyal as the day is long. This isn't Hollywood; it's Cayboo Creek, South Carolina, and we have morals around here."

She took Gabby from Chiffon's arms and nudged her sister gently toward the house.

"Chiffon, people claim you're the town tramp," said a male reporter from *The Star*. "Care to comment?"

"That's enough!" Chenille said, pushing past him. "Scat, you vulture! Why don't you get a job with a decent magazine, like *Family Circle* or *Guideposts*?"

When they finally squeezed their way through the jam of journalists and into the house, Chenille sat her sister down on the couch and made a cup of hot tea.

"Those people don't have a smidgen of decency," Chenille said, covering her sister's shoulder with a frayed afghan. "And I will not buy a ticket to see a Janie-Lynn Lauren movie ever again."

Chiffon held the cup of tea to her lips with shaking hands. "I don't know what I would have done without you. I froze out there."

"You were in shock, and who could blame you? After listening to such vile lies. To suggest that your darling babies were conceived with strange men. I've never heard such a—"

"Chenille," Chiffon interrupted. "I'm suddenly feeling exhausted. I think I want to crawl into bed."

"You do that. This terrible situation is wearing you down. I'll look after Gabby and see that the kids do their homework when they get off the bus. Then I'll prepare all of us a healthy supper."

While Chiffon slept, Chenille kept busy screening phone calls. Attalee checked in saying she'd seen reporters hanging around Main Street, grilling folks about Chiffon. Chenille told her about the rumors surrounding her sister.

"Those scandal sheets cut no squares with me," Attalee said. "Our Chiffon would never cheat on Lonnie. She's a regular Tammy Wynette."

A break in calls during the afternoon allowed Chenille to help Emily find a shoe box for a social studies diorama and to play a game of Chutes and Ladders with Dewitt. Later, as she prepared supper, the phone rang and Garnell's voice drawled over the answering machine.

"Hello, Garnell," Chenille said, picking up the receiver. "I know I was supposed to call you today, but everything's gone haywire around here."

She told him about the reporters camped outside the house and what they'd been saying about Chiffon. "Poor thing," Chenille clucked. "The fight's gone right out of her."

"Is there anything I can do?" Garnell asked.

"Nothing." She parted the curtains to look out into the yard. A reporter, chewing on a slice of cheese pizza, spotted her and waved. "I need to walk Walter, but I don't want to face all those people. We're practically prisoners in our own home."

"That's a crying shame. Those folks should have better manners," Garnell said. "Tell you what, why don't you let me come over there? I'll chase off those nosy reporters."

"I don't want to put you to any trouble," Chenille said. On the surface, Garnell seemed a gentle sort, but she was familiar with the behavior of riled Southern men. Buckshot and battle cries of "yee-haw" were the usual modus operandi.

"No trouble at all. Just let old Garnell take care of this for you."

Minutes later, Garnell rumbled up the drive in a red twin-cab pickup truck the width and girth of a steamroller. The grille gleamed with what looked like sharp silver teeth, and Garnell revved his engine, spewing a blue-gray cloud of exhaust. Any minute, Chenille expected to see the barrel of a shotgun poke out the driver's-side window.

Instead, Garnell cut the engine and hopped out. He wore blue jeans and a tight T-shirt that emphasized long, ropy arm muscles. Nodding curtly at the reporters, he swaggered to the side of the vehicle to open the door of the back cab.

Here it comes. Chenille squeezed her eyes shut, imagining anything from a battalion of pit bulls to a cache of firearms. Peeking out from the narrowed slits of her eyelids, she saw Garnell tugging on the leash of a small animal. It was PU.

It took a moment for the little skunk to make his impact, but as soon as his tail twitched, the effect was immediate. Pizza slices and notebooks were tossed aside as their owners scattered like seeds in a windstorm.

Garnell grinned as he watched the vans and cars spit gravel, trying to depart. Once the area was cleared of vehicles, he and PU ambled up the drive. Chenille met him at the door.

"That was clever," Chenille said. "It's no wonder you were in Miss Beezle's honors class."

"All in a day's work. Good thing those city people didn't know PU is descented," he said. In the last lingering light of day, his eyes looked bottle-fly blue.

"I'm grateful, and I know Chiffon will be, too."

Garnell sniffed the air. "Is that pork I smell?" Pork came out as "poke."

"Heavens, no. Pork's much too fatty. I'm making lentil cutlets. I have an extra cutlet if—"

"Don't mind if I do." He slipped his cap off his head and entered the house.

She settled him in the living room with a magazine so she could finish dinner. Not a minute later, he peered over her shoulder as she put a head of broccoli on to boil.

"That would be even tastier if you added chicken bouillon to the water," he remarked.

"I try to limit my consumption of animal products," Chenille said quickly. He made her nervous, standing so close to her. "Aren't you comfortable in the other room?"

"I didn't want you to get lonesome in here." He slapped a rolled-up copy of *TV Guide* on the speckled counter. "This was on the coffee table. Maybe we have something else in common besides Miss Beezle."

"Like what?" Chenille asked.

"Every episode of *Law and Order* is highlighted. Who's the fan? You or Chiffon?"

"Me," she said casually. "I watch it now and then."

He hooted. "You're lying, girl. Nobody watches it *now and then*. Admit it. You're a full-blown addict. You haven't missed a listing in this guide."

She turned to face him, her spatula playfully aloft.

"You're awfully pretty in this light," he said softly.

Embarrassed, she whirled back to attend the cutlets sizzling in the skillet. He wasn't nearly as poetic as Drake, but his compliment had caused an odd flowering feeling in her chest.

At dinner, Garnell told a string of knock-knock jokes that had Emily and Dewitt in stitches. Chenille found herself smiling at a couple as well. Just as the children got up from the table to play in their rooms, Chiffon slogged into the kitchen, a waffle-like imprint on her cheek from her blanket. When she saw Garnell at the table, she straightened her shoulders and her face lit up like a Wurlitzer.

"Garnell Walker! What are you doing here? Come here and hug my neck."

Chiffon was happiest whenever there was a trace of testosterone in the room. Seeing her sister glow in Garnell's presence gave Chenille an idea.

"We should go out some evening," she said. "To a nightclub. Why not that place on Mule Pen Road? What's it called?"

"The Tuff Luck Tavern?" Garnell said.

"Yes. That would be fun," Chenille said.

Chiffon rattled the ice in her tea glass. "The old Tuff Luck. I haven't been inside that dive in a coon's age." She sighed. "I've gotten too old and creaky for clubbing."

"Nonsense," Chenille insisted. "I've heard they have a dance floor. We could drink Jell-O shots, dance the boot-scooting boogie, and have a jolly time."

Garnell squinted at her. "You do Jell-O shots?"

"No," Chenille said. "But I could give it a go."

Chiffon snickered. "Somehow I don't think you'd much like the Tuff Luck."

Before Chenille could protest, the phone rang, and Chiffon picked up when she heard Mavis's voice.

"You're kidding?" she said after listening for a moment. "I guess I should watch, but I need moral support. Why don't you and Attalee come over?"

She hung up the phone. "Mavis said Janie-Lynn Lauren is a guest on *Hollywood Hijinks* tonight. It's on in twenty minutes."

"Do you really think you're up to it?" Chenille asked.

"Yeah." She nodded. "I want to know what's going on."

Garnell slung an arm over Chiffon's shoulder. "I caught wind of some gossip at the barber's today, and it all sounds like a load of hoo-ha. Don't know how they can make up them kind of stories."

A strand of hair had made its way into Chiffon's mouth, and she was gnawing away at it. "Me, either," she said.

Beauty is in the eye of the beer holder.

Sign outside of the Tuff Luck Tavern

CHAPTER TWENTY-TWO

Attalee rattled a box of Junior Mints in front of Mavis's nose. "Want some?"

Mavis shook her head and adjusted the sofa cushion behind her neck.

"How about some Wonka Runts or Hot Tamales? Anyone?" Attalee asked, looking around Chiffon's living room for any takers.

"It's no wonder you don't have any teeth," Mavis said.

The women were assembled on the dilapidated couch, and Garnell had commandeered the La-Z-Boy. The only light in the room was the blue flicker of a TV commercial peddling tampons.

"Pearl girl, she's a pearl girl," Attalee warbled along with the jingle.

"Are those Tamales regular or extra hot?" Garnell asked.

"Shhh!" Mavis said. "The show's coming on."

The theme music for *Hollywood Hijinks* swelled from the television, and the kittenish visage of Godiva Jones, the host, filled the screen.

"Good evening," said Godiva, wearing a sequined red evening gown with a plunging neckline. "Tonight we take you far from the glamorous and moneyed hills of Hollywood to what could literally be called Hillbilly Country."

Banjos twanged in the background, and a wide shot of Cayboo Creek appeared on the screen.

"Cayboo Creek, South Carolina, is a sleepy backwater town with no particular distinction, until today," Godiva continued.

"Who they calling backwater?" Attalee said. Her dentures whistled as she bit into a Milk Dud.

"Cayboo Creek is the home of Chiffon Butrell, the wronged yet madcap wife of Lonnie Butrell, Janie-Lynn Lauren's latest squeeze."

The screen showed taped footage of Chiffon spraying reporters with the Super Soaker; it switched to a shot of Janie-Lynn and Lonnie frolicking on a private beach in Malibu.

"But maybe it's Lonnie Butrell who's been the wronged one all along. According to Janie-Lynn Lauren, Chiffon Butrell won't earn any Girl Scout badges for loyalty."

The camera zoomed in on Janie-Lynn, dressed in a long

ivory dress, looking like a vestal virgin. She sat on the edge of a white leather sofa, her legs crossed primly at the ankles.

"Lonnie told me he can't be sure he's the father of any of Chiffon's children," said Janie-Lynn, her fawnlike brown eyes taking on a serious cast. "He's supported them out of the goodness of his heart. I'm trying to help him recover his pride."

"Why doesn't Lonnie speak for himself?" an unseen reporter asked gently.

"Because he's liver-lillied!" Attalee heckled.

"Hush," warned Mavis.

Janie-Lynn bit her lip in a dramatic gesture. "He finds it too painful. It's hard for a man as sensitive and strong as Lonnie to have the whole world know his wife is a cheat."

The camera showed footage of reporters firing questions at a zombie-like Chiffon with Chenille by her side.

"Chiffon Butrell was unusually subdued when confronted with questions about her supposed infidelities," said Donovan Tate, *Hollywood Hijinks*'s on-location reporter, as he stood on the edge of Chiffon's lawn. "She refused to confirm or deny the allegations. But her sister, Chenille Grace, vehemently defended Chiffon against the rumors."

"Thank you, Donovan," Godiva said. "Let's go to Darcy Day, who interviewed some citizens of Chiffon's hometown."

"I'm at a restaurant called the Wagon Wheel in Cayboo Creek, talking with a former employer of Chiffon's, a Mr. Wilbur Peet," said Darcy, a bouncy-looking blonde in a short pink skirt. She thrust the microphone in Wilbur's face. "What can you tell us about Chiffon?"

"She was an inferior employee," said Wilbur, his skinny face screwed up with self-importance. "She wouldn't suggestive-sell our Flowering Onion, which, by the way, is made from farm-fresh Vidalia onions, lightly breaded and fried to a golden—"

"Was she overly friendly with her male customers?" Darcy interrupted.

"Yes, ma'am," Wilbur said. "She called them sugar pie, honey lips, and other inappropriate names. She flirted constantly."

"We talked to another resident of Cayboo Creek, who asked not to be identified," Darcy continued. "Her face and voice have been digitally altered."

There was a shot of a blurred face, belonging to a woman in a navel-skimming sweater and skintight blue jeans. "Chiffon Butrell is the biggest tramp this town has ever seen," said the woman.

"Jonelle!" shouted everyone on the couch.

"I'd recognize those snug blue jeans from twenty paces," Chiffon said bitterly.

"She thinks she's so hot, just because she won a beauty pageant or two," continued the blurry-faced Jonelle. "But does anyone really care who won Miss Catfish Stomp fifteen years ago?"

"*She* does!" Chiffon said, pointing at the TV. "Jonelle competed with me in that pageant and didn't even place. Someone needs to tell her that playing the kazoo isn't a talent."

The camera panned back to a pensive-looking Godiva. "This just in," she said. "Apparently a group of reporters gathered outside the Butrell residence were scared away by a man with a skunk on a leash. Were you on the scene for that incident, Donovan?"

Donovan was framed in a small box on the right-hand side of the screen. He guffawed, showing rows of capped teeth. "No, Godiva, I missed it. But I heard it caused quite a stink."

Godiva smiled. "Well, Donovan, I guess you're not in Kansas anymore. Next up on *Hollywood Hijinks:* Who is that new lady on George Clooney's arm?"

Chenille clicked off the television. "Enough of that bunk."

Mavis scowled. "How can a TV show get away with such outrageous lies? Chiffon, you probably have a case against these people. I know a crackerjack lawyer in Augusta. Want me to call him for you?"

"No," Chiffon said abruptly. "I want to put all of this behind me."

"Mavis is right, Chiffon," Garnell insisted. "You shouldn't let them get away with those lies."

Chiffon snapped her fingers. "You know what? I've changed my mind."

"You want to sue?" Mavis said.

"No, but I *do* want to go out drinking and dancing, just like you suggested, Chenille. I could use a night out."

"Tonight?" Chenille asked. "Where would we get a sitter at this hour?"

"If it's a sitter you need, I'd be glad to oblige," Mavis said. "A night out will do you good."

. . .

Forty-five minutes later, Chenille crawled out of the backseat of her sister's Firebird and tentatively put the toe of her borrowed cowboy boot on the pavement.

"I don't know about this. I look . . . strange," she said.

Chiffon yanked the rearview mirror toward her face and dabbed at her eye shadow. "You look fine," she said.

"Fine and dandy," Garnell said, taking her by the elbow and helping her out of the car.

As she stood, Chenille tried to pull down the short flared skirt that Chiffon had loaned her. "I was more comfortable in the clothes I was wearing."

Attalee wriggled out from the front seat in a pair of electric-blue Lycra pants. "You can't wear Hush Puppies and a cardigan sweater to a place called the Tuff Luck Tavern," she said.

Attalee twirled in front of them. Her pants sagged noticeably in the rear. "How do I look?" she asked.

Like a refugee from an '80s roller-boogie film, Chenille thought, suppressing a giggle. Then, fearing her unkind thought registered on her face, she said, "Those are darling trousers."

"You look mighty sharp, Ms. Gaines," Garnell added.

Chiffon stood by the door of her car and eyed Attalee. "Those pants bring back so many memories. My girlfriends and I drove into Augusta every Saturday night to a disco called Studio Five. I must have danced to a hundred ABBA songs in those pants. 'Course now I'd bust the zipper just trying to squeeze into them."

She pointed at the lemon-sherbet moon, wedged between two branches of a crepe myrtle. "It's our night to howl. Yee-haw!" Chiffon emoted, in homage to the full moon.

"Whooop! Whoooop!" Attalee chimed.

"Meow!" Chenille said, trying to get in the spirit of things.

"Darn it, if you aren't the cutest thing," Garnell whispered in her ear.

"Will they have a mechanical bull?" Chenille asked, bashfully pulling away from him.

"They got rid of that years ago," Garnell said. "It was an insurance worry."

"That's too bad," Chenille said, hoping for an ersatz *Urban Cowboy* experience.

The Tuff Luck Tavern, a low-slung cinder-block structure, looked seedier close up than from the street. The entrance was lit up with a Pabst Blue Ribbon sign, and DIE DAWGS was spray-painted on the side of the building. Chenille's nose wrinkled at the smell of sour beer in the parking lot. As they reached the entrance, Chiffon flung open the door, and the air buzzed with the song "Whose Bed Have Your Boots Been Under?"

"Y'all step right up," she said, ushering them in. She wore a black-and-white-spotted cowboy hat atop her froth of honey-blond hair and a skintight pair of Wranglers that—thanks to a heavy-duty girdle—didn't betray her taste for sweets.

An awning of cigarette smoke hung in the entrance, and as Chenille stepped inside the hazy gloom, a dart whistled past her ear.

"Dang, Harlan, you've got the worst aim I've ever seen," Garnell said, retrieving the dart and handing it to a grizzled man in overalls.

Their group walked through the gloom and took seats at an empty table. Above hung a framed picture of a revolver with the slogan IN DIXIE WE DON'T CALL 911.

Garnell pulled out a padded wooden chair for Chenille. Just as she was about to sit, someone screamed, "Stop!" A middle-aged woman wearing a leather miniskirt stumbled toward them.

Chenille glanced back at the seat, looking for gum or something else equally unsavory. "What's wrong?"

"That's Earl Widener's memorial chair. Can't you read?" she slurred. She pointed a long press-on nail at the plaque affixed to the back of the chair.

"Memorial chair?" Chenille said.

"He choked on a maraschino cherry right here," the woman said, patting the cushion. Her eyes glowed red underneath the light of a neon Gamecock sign. "He was trying to tie the stem into a knot with his tongue." Suddenly she flung her narrow frame upon the back of the chair. "God, I miss him!"

Garnell gently helped her up. "Come on, Claire. It's all right. She didn't mean to sit in Earl's chair. It's usually by the video poker machine."

"I thought he could use a change of scenery," Claire said through sooty black tears.

Garnell guided the weeping woman back to her bar stool. He whispered something to the bartender and then returned to Chenille's side. He snatched a chair from another table and gestured for her to sit.

"You know a lot of people here," Chenille said, squinting at the row of patrons who were bellied up to the bar.

"I come here now and again. Mostly for the darts and sometimes for the company."

And for the whiskey. Chenille knew how much small-town Southern men loved their sauce.

A red-haired waitress, wearing a pair of overtaxed Daisy Dukes and a T-shirt with a rebel flag, plodded to their table. "What'll it be?" she said, flipping open her order pad.

"A wine white spritzer, easy on the wine," said Chenille.

"A shot of tequila," Chiffon said.

"A cosmopolitan," Attalee said with a toss of her long gray ringlets.

"The usual," Garnell said. "An O'Doul's in a frosty mug."

"Party pooper," Attalee said.

Garnell shrugged. "What can I say? I've never been much of a drinking man."

Chenille glanced at Garnell, who was bouncing his knee to the beat of the music. The man was constantly surprising her.

After the waitress delivered their drinks, Chiffon got up from her chair and surveyed the action. "I think I'll put a couple of quarters in the jukebox," she said, licking her lips. As she shimmied across the room, several heads at the bar swiveled in her direction.

"I don't think she'll be buying any of her own drinks tonight," Chenille mused.

The strains of "Honk if You Honky Tonk" blasted from the jukebox. Attalee snapped her fingers and hungrily scanned the barroom. "I feel like shaking a leg."

"I'll take you for a spin," Garnell said, extending his hand to her.

"Hold on a minute," Attalee said. "I think I may have snagged me a bull."

Chenille followed Attalee's gaze to a man who was propped up on the corner of the bar, sucking on a longneck. He was dressed mostly in black, from his spurred boots to his felt cowboy hat. The fluorescent light behind the rows of mini-bottles lining the bar bounced off his silver Smith & Wesson belt buckle. He ambled toward their table, a chain from his wallet slapping against his relaxed-fit Levi's. His shirt was unbuttoned to his breastbone, showing off a pelt of wiry white hairs.

"Hot damn!" Attalee whispered as he made his slow approach to the table.

The neon picked up the glint of his trifocals as he stood in front of them. He smiled, revealing a set of teeth so white and uniform they had to be mail-order dentures. Then he extended a gnarled hand across the table to Chenille and said, "Care to cut a rug?"

"Me?" Chenille said, nearly toppling her spritzer with her elbow. Attalee shot her a poisonous look. "I can't," Chenille said, scooting her chair closer to Garnell. "My boyfriend wouldn't approve."

Garnell draped his arm around her. "That's right, Dooley. I'm kind of the possessive type."

Dooley's glance lighted on Attalee. "How about you, miss?"

Attalee popped up like bread from a toaster. "Don't mind if I do."

As the pair strolled to the small sawdust-covered dance floor, Garnell whispered in Chenille's ear, "So I'm your boyfriend now, am I?"

Chenille shivered at the feel of his warm breath on her neck. He hadn't moved his arm, and the well-muscled heaviness of it across her back gave her a pleasant and unfamiliar sense of security.

"I'm sorry," she said shyly. "I'm not used to fending off the advances of men, and I panicked."

He looked down at her with his crinkly blue eyes. "Pretty thing like you? I bet you have to fight them off with a two-by-four."

"Not really. This is the first time I've ever been in a night-club."

"Mmmm, mmmm," he said. "They just don't make girls like you anymore."

A slow song came on the jukebox, Willie Nelson crooning "Always on My Mind," and couples bobbed like buoys on the dimly lit dance floor.

"That's my favorite song," Garnell said. "May I have this dance?"

Chenille started to decline, but instead nodded and ascended from her chair. Garnell grinned and slid her fingers through his belt loop to lead her through the crush of bar patrons.

Once on the dance floor, he put a firm hand on the small of her back as they swayed to the rhythm of the music. He wasn't the most graceful of dancers. Several times he stepped on her toes, but Chenille felt so light-footed she barely noticed.

Woozy from the wine and the sleepy pace of the song, she longed to rest her head on his shoulder. Just as she was about to surrender, Garnell started singing to the music in a raspy off-key voice. Jolted out of her soporific state, an image of Drake's classic features flashed in her mind. Her dream mate. The man she'd been waiting for all her life.

She scrutinized Garnell through heavy eyelids. He was congenial, fun, and smart, but all of those qualities couldn't save him from being as ordinary as a vanilla bean.

"Chenille," he said in a drowsy voice. "You are some kind of woman."

Even his compliments were mundane. He was burlap to Drake's batiste, rhinestone to his rubies, Fritos to his frittata.

"I'm sorry," Chenille said without thinking. "I don't think it can work between us."

Hurt stole over his face like a shadow. With downcast eyes, he opened his mouth to speak, but was interrupted by a high-pitched scream behind them.

A burly man lumbered out from behind the bar and pulled the plug on the jukebox. The crowd pushed toward the noise, and Chenille was caught up in its current.

When the throng reached the source of the disturbance, Chenille stood on tiptoe and peeked over the broad shoulder of one of the onlookers. Through the blue fog of smoke, two women rolled on the floor, locked in a bizarre embrace.

"Catfight!" shouted a bandied-legged cowboy standing next to her. It was difficult to discern much from the writhing tangle of legs and arms, but as she blinked in the faint light, Chenille spotted a mass of blond curls and the toe of an alligator boot.

"Chiffon!" she cried out. "That's my sister!"

A bushy-haired woman straddled Chiffon's chest, getting the better of her. The woman shook her so hard that Chiffon's head lolled from side to side.

"Stop it!" Chenille shrieked. "You're hurting her!"

No sooner had she shouted than an electric streak of blue burst from the crowd, squealing like a banshee.

It was Attalee in her Lycra pants. She pounced on the back of the woman with all her force, but was instantly flung off like a pile of rags. The bushy-haired woman, her bony denim-covered bottom twitching in the air, renewed her assault on Chiffon with a vicious vigor.

The surrounding mob clapped and shouted, "Fight! Fight!"

Chenille looked behind her and spotted Garnell trying to jostle his way through the crowd. He seemed so far away.

She frantically rifled through her purse, searching for some kind of weapon, but found only Walter's rubber bone. She snatched it up, shouldered through the crowd, and started hitting the bushy-haired woman on the butt with the bone.

"Get off of Chiffon, now!" she demanded. The girl whipped around and tried to rake her face with a set of long blue fingernails. Now that she was close enough to smell the bourbon on her breath, Chenille recognized the wild-eyed creature: It was Jonelle Jasper.

"Easy, Jonelle, easy," Chenille said, ducking before Jonelle could shred her cheeks with her talons. Jonelle hissed like a cat and lunged for Chenille at the waist. Chenille's knees buckled underneath her, and just as she was about to hit the floor, she felt someone grab her underneath her arms. She spun around to see Garnell holding her up.

Meantime, both Attalee and Chiffon had recovered, and they were yanking a screaming Jonelle around the floor by her long dark hair. A bouncer bullied his way through the crowd and shooed the pair away from Jonelle. Adding to the confusion was the insistent pop of flashbulbs and the whirr of cameras.

Chenille staggered toward Chiffon, looking like a wrung-out rag doll. "Come on! Let's get out of here," she said.

Attalee was behind her, and the three stumbled to the exit. Garnell followed on their heels as they pushed open the door and fled into the cold night air.

"We gotta get to the car," Chiffon said, swiping at a smear of blood on her lip. "I saw them, they were—"

Before she could finish her sentence, two photographers burst out of the exit door holding their cameras.

"Aren't you a picture, Chiffon?" one hollered out. "Is that a collagen injection, or did someone use your lip as a punching bag?"

"Make a run for it," Garnell said. "I'll distract these boys."

Chiffon and Attalee had already sprinted toward the parking lot, but Chenille lingered.

"How will you get home?" she asked Garnell.

"I'll catch a ride. Go," he urged. He turned his back and walked away, and Chenille felt an unexpected feeling of loss. Had she made a big mistake?

If God wanted me to touch my toes, he would have put them on my knees.

Bumper sticker on Attalee Gaines's Buick Skylark

CHAPTER TWENTY-THREE

"How bad is it?" Chiffon asked her sister. It had been several days since the scuffle at the Tuff Luck Tavern, and her bottom lip was still inflated like a toy raft. There was also a quarter-sized bald patch on her scalp where Jonelle had yanked out her hair.

Chenille had just returned from the grocery store with a stack of tabloids under her arm. "Well, it's—" She winced and deposited the magazines on her sister's lap. "It's pretty awful."

Chiffon sifted through the papers, reading the headlines aloud: "'Redneck Mama Rocks Roadhouse.' 'Drunk and Disgraced: Mom Involved in Melee.' 'Chiffon Butrell, Brawling Broad.'"

She shoved them aside. "Are they all like this?"

"Sort of," Chenille said. "I put the nicest ones on top."

"Dang," Chiffon said. She glanced at her watch. "It's time for *Hollywood Hijinks*. They're supposed to be airing another story about me."

"Do you really think you should watch it?" Chenille said, settling beside her sister on the couch.

"I can't help myself," Chiffon said as she aimed the remote at the TV.

Godiva Jones appeared on the screen wearing a gold lamé evening gown as tight as a scuba suit. "Tonight's top story involves tequila, a tavern, and one heck of a tussle," she said with a toss of her lacquered brunette mane. "Let's travel to boondock country in Cayboo Creek, South Carolina, and find out what's up with Chiffon Butrell."

The camera zoomed in on the outside of the Tuff Luck Tavern as "Dueling Banjos" played in the background.

"Enough with the banjos already," Chiffon said as the cameras closed in on a shot of a grinning Donovan Tate interviewing the waitress from the Tuff Luck Tavern.

"Chiffon Butrell was here drinking tequila," the waitress said, using the tip of her pencil to scratch her thigh. "Straight shots. I lost track of how many she ordered."

Chiffon sprang up from the couch. "What's to keep track of? I had *one* shot the entire night."

"She was flirting with all kinds of men," the waitress continued in her heavy Southern drawl. "And strutting her stuff in some mighty tight britches."

The camera panned to Jonelle Jasper, wearing large hoop earrings and jawing on a wad of bubble gum. "I was minding my own business when Chiffon Butrell came at me like a linebacker," she said in a blubbery voice. "I was scared silly because she's the size of a battleship. Then she sicced her friend and sister on me, and I saw my life passing in front of my eyes."

There was footage of Chiffon and Attalee dragging Jonelle by the hair, followed by a shot of Chenille beating Jonelle's butt with a dog bone.

"That's such a lie!" Chiffon shouted at the television. "She was taunting me, calling me a tramp. I turned around to confront her, and she shoved me first. I notice they don't have any pictures of Jonelle banging my head on the ground."

"Thanks, Donovan," Godiva said, shaking her head in dismay. "Such chilling images. Now we have a surprise for our viewers tonight. Earlier this afternoon, Janie-Lynn Lauren granted *Hollywood Hijinks* an exclusive interview. Let's take a look at that tape now."

The camera showed Janie-Lynn curled up in a wingback chair, wearing a tight, cropped T-shirt that said, BE GONE, CHIFFON.

"First off, Janie-Lynn," Godiva said, leaning toward the actress in a chummy manner, "what statement are you trying to make with that T-shirt?"

"I think it's obvious," Janie-Lynn Lauren said, folding her shapely arms over her chest. "Both Lonnie and I are fed up with Chiffon. She refuses to sign the divorce papers and let Lonnie go. It's time for her to 'be gone' from our lives."

Godiva nodded sympathetically. "What do you think about her latest antics at the Tuff Luck Tavern?"

"Completely in character, according to Lonnie," Janie-Lynn said, her eyes flashing with righteousness. "She's a hard-drinking, unfit mother, always on the prowl for a man and a good time."

"What a shame for those three children of hers!" Godiva said.

"Yes. Lonnie and I have talked at length about those dear little tots. Even though he seriously doubts he fathered them, he still loves those children and wants to make certain they're well cared for." She looked straight into the camera. "Chiffon, if you're listening, please get the help you need, for the sake of your children; otherwise, we'll be forced to fight you for custody."

"*What?*" Chiffon said, with bulging eyes.

"Does this mean that you and Lonnie are together for the long haul?" Godiva asked.

"Yes," Janie-Lynn Lauren said with a coy smile. She extended a hand to Godiva, and the camera panned in on a walnut-sized diamond engagement ring. "We're planning a wedding as soon as Lonnie's divorce is final."

Godiva squealed and drew Janie-Lynn into a hug. "You heard it here first on *Hollywood Hijinks*," she said as she signed off.

"That conniving, lying little—" The ringing of the phone interrupted Chiffon's tirade. "Take it off the hook. Everyone in town will be calling."

The answering machine picked up. "Chiffon, this is Janie-Lynn Lauren. If you're there, pick up the phone."

"You listen in on the other extension," Chiffon hissed to Chenille. Chenille darted to the bedroom phone, and Chiffon picked up the cordless phone on the coffee table.

"You have a lot of nerve calling here after that interview on TV. There's no way you're getting custody of my children," Chiffon said.

"Don't start with me," Janie-Lynn said haughtily. "You should have learned by now that I'm the one calling the shots."

"Why are you doing this to me? What did I ever do to you?" Chiffon demanded.

"I warned you that if you didn't sign the divorce papers, things would get ugly." She laughed. "Of course, even *I* couldn't have engineered your little barroom brawl. Luckily I hired a detective and a pair of photographers to tail you constantly, just in case you did something stupid. And you didn't disappoint."

"Why did you tell Godiva you'd try to get custody of my kids?"

"Because you won't sign the divorce papers," Janie-Lynn said with an impatient sigh.

Chiffon paused for a moment. "You're bluffing. Why would you want to be saddled with three kids?"

"Don't test me, Chiffon. I'm a multimillionaire. It's not like *I'll* be wiping their noses. When they're not with a nanny, they'll be in boarding school. I'll never even know they're around." She lowered her voice. "Besides, lately Lonnie has been a little overly sentimental about your tykes, especially the little boy, Dennis."

"Dewitt!" Chiffon said.

"Whatever. He might start pushing the custody issue, but I can dissuade him. He does whatever I say. But you have to sign those papers."

"Of course Lonnie's sentimental," Chiffon retorted. "They're his kids. I don't know why you keep suggesting they aren't. There *are* paternity tests that could make you look like a liar."

Janie-Lynn Lauren yawned. "You're trying my patience, Chiffon. You don't think I'd go on national television and make up lies that could get me in trouble, do you? You and I both know there's some truth in what I said."

Chiffon's heart hitched. "What do you mean?"

"Skeet Watson," Janie-Lynn said, with bravado in her voice. "The traveling satellite dish salesman from Tick Bite, North Carolina? Sound familiar?"

Chiffon gasped. "Lonnie told you about Skeet?"

"He tells me everything."

The line went dead silent. Chenille was afraid Chiffon might have fainted. She was about to run into the living room to check on her sister when Chiffon took a big gulp of air and spoke in a rush of words.

"I only slept with Skeet because I wanted to repay Lonnie for all the hurt his cheating caused me over the years. Skeet was a good listener, he was kind, and it just . . . happened. I had terrible regrets, and I confessed to Lonnie as soon as he got home that evening."

"Yes, you did," Janie-Lynn said. "And nine months later you had your third child. Unfortunately, you couldn't be sure who the baby's father was."

"No, we couldn't," Chiffon said, struggling to talk through her tears. "But we both made a pact that we'd never talk about it again. It was just that one time with Skeet versus dozens of times with Lonnie, so we figured Lonnie *had* to be Gabby's father. Neither of us had the desire to prove anything different."

"Now you can prove it," Janie-Lynn said brightly. "We'll order a paternity test for your dear little daughter. Are you a gambler, Chiffon?"

There was no response.

"Well?" Janie-Lynn prodded.

"No," Chiffon said in a whisper, knowing she'd been licked. "I'm not a gambler. I'll send those divorce papers back to you today. Obviously, my marriage is over."

"Good girl!" Janie-Lynn Lauren said. "I'll be sending you a check for child support, but expect some deductions due to your bothersome delays. Bye-bye."

Chenille hung up the phone and rushed to the living room. Her sister clung to the counter for support.

"What an awful woman she turned out to be!" Chenille said.

"I'm the awful one," Chiffon said, bent over as if she'd been punched in the stomach. "I cheated on my husband, and I'm not even sure who Gabby's father is." She refused to meet her sister's gaze. "I can't imagine what you must think about me."

Chenille picked up her sister's chin and looked her square in the eyes. "I think you've been through the wringer and you've handled yourself with a lot of courage and style."

"Oh, Chenille," Chiffon said, burying her face in her sister's chest as she wept. "I can't believe this has happened!"

Chenille held her sister close as she heaved out her sobs. Once her cries had diminished into a few stalled sniffles, Chiffon weakly lifted her head and mouthed, "Thank you."

"Anytime," Chenille said with a smile. "Is there anything I can do for you? Do you want some sort of treat to eat?"

Roughly wiping away the streaks of tears on her face with her fists, Chiffon regarded Chenille with swollen eyes. "Nothing personal, but I think we have different ideas about treats. Carob cookies just ain't going to cut it for me today."

Chenille handed her sister a fresh tissue from the box on the coffee table. "I was thinking more of a DQ run."

"Dairy Queen?" Chiffon said, cocking her head. "What did you have in mind?"

"I've seen their advertisements for a dessert called the Triple Chocolate Utopia. It sounded so decadent it made me think of you." Chenille picked up her car keys and jingled them in her hand. "Interested?"

Chiffon blew her nose. Gorging on massive amounts of chocolate with her sister wouldn't resurrect the ruins of her life with Lonnie, but it could make her predicament slightly easier to bear.

"I'll get my shoes."

Madness takes its toll. Please have exact change.

Sign in the break room at the Bottom Dollar Emporium

CHAPTER TWENTY-FOUR

Chenille sat across from Miss Beezle at the Wagon Wheel, marveling at how unchanged her old high school teacher looked after twenty years. Same carefully coiffed corona of white hair. Same smear of hot-pink lipstick. Same harlequin eyeglass frames.

"Chenille, do stop slouching so."

Same crabby demeanor. With a round little face and blue eyes, Miss Beezle resembled Mrs. Claus, but there was nothing merry or motherly about her.

Chenille threw back her shoulders and sat up straight. "Miss Beezle, I'm delighted you asked me out for lunch. It's such a treat to see you after all these years, and I've thought of you so often. I'll never forget how you used to wear that scorpion pendant on test days. Do you still do that?"

"Of course. Why would I change?" Miss Beezle said, cutting her fried catfish into precise, uniform pieces.

"No reason, I suppose," Chenille said.

Miss Beezle looked up from her plate and fixed her cool gaze on Chenille. "This isn't a social visit. I'm not in the habit of having reunion lunches with former students, no matter how bright they were. And you were certainly one of my most gifted pupils."

"Thank you, Miss Beezle," Chenille gushed. "What a lovely thing to say!"

Miss Beezle set down her knife. "I'm not flattering you. I'm merely stating a fact. There's nothing extraordinary about genius. It's just a trick of genetics, like a crooked eyetooth or the ability to wiggle your ears. It's what you *do* with your gift that matters, and from what I've heard, you haven't done diddly."

Chenille pushed a pinto bean across her plate. "It's true, I haven't exactly set the world on fire—"

"You haven't even struck the first match," Miss Beezle said, pointing a fork at her. "But I'm going to give you the opportunity to change all that. It's time for me to retire from my teaching position, and the high school needs a replacement. I thought you'd fit the bill."

"*Me?* You think *I* should take your place at Cayboo Creek High School?"

"Are you hard of hearing? That's exactly what I said."

"But, uh . . ." Chenille blinked in confusion. "I didn't even think you liked me."

"Whether I like you or not has nothing to do with the equation. I know that you have the required intelligence for the job, and you come highly recommended by Garnell Walker. That's good enough for me."

"Garnell recommended me?"

She gave Chenille a withering look. "Do you have trouble understanding the King's English? Yes, he recommended you. Highly. According to him, you're the best thing to come to Cayboo Creek since they installed a traffic light on Chickasaw Drive. And I value Garnell's opinion."

Chenille fidgeted in her chair. "At my other school . . ." She paused and cast her eyes to her lap. "There was an *incident*."

"With a machete?" Miss Beezle said matter-of-factly.

"Not *my* machete, and it was made of plastic, but yes."

Miss Beezle dabbed at her lips with a napkin. "Doesn't concern me. If I were forced to teach a horde of lazy underachievers, a plastic machete would have been the least of their worries. In my classroom, students are there to perform, period, or I boot them out. As the only gifted program in the area, we draw students from far-flung parts of the county, and there's always a waiting list. The students understand that if they give me any lip, it's back to learning watered-down mush with the masses."

"I'd love to teach gifted children," Chenille said. "And it would be wonderful to stay here in Cayboo Creek with my family."

Miss Beezle flung down her red-and-white-checked napkin. "Good. I've already discussed it with my principal, and he's expecting you to drop by on Monday morning. Your interview with him will just be a formality, as he trusts me to pick my successor. We'll be starting a new grading period in the spring. Are you prepared to begin teaching then?"

"Yes, I am," Chenille said, thrilled to the core. "Thank you so much."

Miss Beezle rose from the booth, wearing a familiar-looking dark paisley dress with a lace collar. "You can thank Garnell. Now that we've conducted our business, I'll be on my way." She paused for a moment, clutching her patent leather bag. "Incidentally, I don't know the nature of your relationship with Garnell, nor do I care to. But I will say this: If you're not making a mad play for that man, I promise you some other woman will. He is one of the finest individuals I've ever had the privilege to know. Good day, Miss Grace."

Chenille was left speechless . . . and with the lunch check. As she searched through her wallet for a credit card, her thoughts turned to Garnell. Ever since the night of the big fight at the Tuff Luck Tavern, he'd been on her mind. At odd times of the day, she'd hear the distinctive twang of his voice in her ear or imagine his friendly face lit up with a good-natured grin. He'd even started haunting her in her sleep, riding into her dreams, not on a big white stallion but on the back of a mule. Surprisingly, thoughts of Garnell had replaced her fantasies about Drake, and although she had a date with the veterinarian this evening, she wasn't looking forward to his company as much as she had in the past.

After her lunch with Miss Beezle, Chenille called Chiffon from the pay phone outside the restaurant to share the good news about her teaching position. Her sister was so excited she whooped over the phone line, causing Chenille's eardrum to throb.

"I'm stopping by Garnell's on the way home. I want to tell him the news, since he was the one who put in a good word for me with Miss Beezle," she said to Chiffon just before she hung up the phone.

Not wanting to appear at Garnell's door empty-handed, Chenille stopped at the grocery store and purchased a potted African violet plant. Not many men appreciated flowers and plants as gifts, but she knew Garnell would.

She parked in his drive and walked along the cobblestone path leading up to his wooden A-frame house. She knew he was home because both his truck and van were parked under the shade of a large magnolia tree. Just as she ascended the steps leading to the porch, one of Garnell's cats, a gray tabby with eerie-looking blue eyes, wound through her legs.

The faint sound of music came from inside the house. Chenille paused to discern the melody and was surprised to hear one of her all-time favorite songs, "Mandy," by Barry Manilow. Why was a happy-go-lucky fellow like Garnell listening to such melancholy music? Was it possible that he was holed up in his house, listening to sad songs and pining away for her?

"I'm here, darling," she wanted to call out, but instead knocked on the door, waited a minute or so, and knocked again. Hearing no answer, she felt a pang of concern.

She turned the knob, discovered it wasn't locked, and tentatively pushed it open. Silently she padded down his hallway, following the sound of the music to the den. There she spotted Garnell, but he wasn't alone.

His left arm was curled around a woman's tiny waist, and the other grasped her small white hand. Garnell whispered something in her ear, and the woman flung back her long auburn hair, letting out a musical laugh. Chenille recognized Jewel Turner from the Chat 'N' Chew.

She stood in the doorway to the den, unnoticed, African violet still in hand, as the two remained locked in their embrace. Chenille soundlessly backed out of the room and dashed out of the house to her car. Fastening the seat belt over her chest, she gazed miserably out her windshield, remembering Miss Beezle's warning: "If you're not making a mad play for that man, I promise you some other woman will."

Jewel hadn't wasted a second moving in on Garnell, and Chenille understood his attraction to her. She was pretty, sharp, and sweet as sugarcane.

He's not shedding any tears over me, Chenille mused as she pulled out of the drive. Her good cheer had been replaced with an emptiness as pervasive as the hole in a doughnut.

"Guess My Eyes Were Bigger Than My Heart"

Selection B-9 on the Chat 'N' Chew jukebox

CHAPTER TWENTY-FIVE

"What's wrong with you? You're a million miles away," Drake said to Chenille as he grasped her hand over the white linen tablecloth. "Maybe you're gathering lavender in Provence or schussing down the Alps." He brushed his lips over her knuckles. "But you're not here, drinking champagne with me."

"I'm sorry, Drake," Chenille said, withdrawing her hand and balling it into a fist. A single candle flickered in a glass globe on their table in an Augusta restaurant called Bistro 99. Drake's face was shrouded in shadows as he studied her from across the table. "I'm just a little tired." She stared down at her mostly untouched lamb stew.

"I'll summon the waiter," he said, holding up a finger. Then he trailed his thumb along the inside of her wrist. "You look lit from within tonight. Like a golden goddess."

Chenille fought to keep a yawn in her chest. Normally Drake's compliments made her as giddy as a teenager, but tonight his smooth talk failed to move her. He might as well have been reciting his grocery list.

The waiter brought the check, and Drake discreetly slid his platinum credit card into the leather holder.

"Before we leave, there's a little something I wanted to give you." He fumbled in the pocket of his jacket and withdrew a small black velvet box that he placed in front of her. "Open it," he said in a low voice.

"Drake?" She looked up at him with a question in her eyes.

"Go on."

She pried opened the box and gasped at the contents. Nestled inside was a platinum ring with a pear-shaped diamond.

"I don't understand."

"I'll make it clear to you then." He dropped to one knee beside her feet, covered his hand with hers, and said, "Will you marry me?"

"What?" she asked, studying his face in the flickering candlelight. "Goodness gracious! You're serious."

"Serious?" He chuckled as he rose from the floor. "Of course I'm serious. Ever since I set eyes on you, my heart's been your prisoner."

"But Drake, we hardly know each other. We've only been out on a few dates."

"What does time matter?" he said with a wave of his hand. "The French have an expression, *vivre l'instant*, which means 'live for the moment.' At this moment I want to marry you."

"My grandma Eugenie used to say, 'Marry in haste; repent at leisure.'"

"How puritanical," he said, a frown marring his impeccable features. "That's not the Chenille I know. You led me to believe you had a taste for romance."

"I do, but—" She lightly touched the diamond as if it might burn her. "This is so sudden."

"Let me put it on your finger." He removed the ring from its box and slid it over her knuckle before she could protest. "Look at the way the facets pick up the candlelight. It's on fire."

"It *is* beautiful," Chenille said. She waved her hand in front of her face, mesmerized by the glowing gem on her finger.

Drake pushed a fine strand of hair behind her ear. "Let's drive away together tonight," he whispered. "There's a place in the Smoky Mountains called the Forever Wedding Chapel, where we can pledge our love."

"Tonight?" She dropped her hand into her lap. "I can't get married tonight. I'd have to tell my sister. I wouldn't dream of getting married without letting her know."

"We'll pick her up on the way. She can be our witness."

"Chiffon can't just take off for the mountains. She has three children," Chenille said, struggling to remove the ring, which was stuck fast on her finger.

"You see," he said with a silky laugh. "It belongs to you."

Beware of the high cost of
low living.

Sign outside the Rock of Ages Baptist Church

CHAPTER TWENTY-SIX

The check from Janie-Lynn Lauren arrived, and it was for a piddling amount, much less than the figure she'd promised before. The memo on the check said, "One year's child support, paid in full." After speaking with a lawyer, Chiffon discovered that Janie-Lynn had paid the exact amount of money required by the state based on Lonnie's salary at NutraSweet last year. Not a penny more.

Now that her ankle was healed, Chiffon knew she had to earn some money. She'd accepted an offer of five hundred dollars from *The Globe* to tell her side of the story, on the condition that they didn't ask any questions regarding the paternity of her children. (The published story, entitled "I'm Not a Redneck," portrayed her as a hick straight out of Dogpatch.)

She'd turned down an offer to appear on a reality show called *Fame Factor* because she would have been forced to eat mealworms as a stunt. She decided she wasn't eating worms for a million dollars, much less a measly three thousand.

Meanwhile, her story had been usurped almost immediately by the latest news out of Hollywood involving Wessica. "Wessica" was the media's shorthand for the romance between movie star Wes Livingstone and supermodel/pop star Jessica Day. Recently Jess and Wes had had a public argument in the New York hot spot Bungalow 8 over a lesbian affair Jess supposedly had with her stylist. The media couldn't seem to get enough of the couple, and Chiffon and the Tuff Luck Tavern plummeted from the radar screen.

Janie-Lynn and Lonnie didn't completely disappear from the celebrity tabloids, though. A short article in *People* claimed that were keeping a low profile at her spread in Montana until their top-secret wedding date.

"Insiders predict that the wedding will coincide with the June release of Janie-Lynn Lauren's first action flick, called *Kill Another Day*," the article read.

Chiffon finally accepted that her marriage was deader than a dodo bird. That evening, after the kids had gone to bed and Chenille had stepped out with Drake, Chiffon paged through her scrapbook a final time before she stored it in the attic. Ticket stubs for drag races, tractor pulls, and monster truck rallies were pasted throughout the book. If she had a nickel for every time she'd sat on a rickety stand next to Lonnie, a cup of warm draft beer between her legs, she'd be a rich woman.

As she glanced through the book, she recalled some of the more unpleasant aspects of her marriage, such as Lonnie's obsession with fishing and hunting. How often had she been eyeball to eyeball with a bass or a crappie, standing over the cold, clammy creature with her filet knife? And how many weekends had she spent cooped up with the kids while Lonnie lumbered through the woods trying to fell some cute woodland creature with a load of buckshot?

She also wouldn't miss the endless nights, tossing and turning on the waves of their waterbed, knowing her husband was out with another woman. She wouldn't miss the scent of an unfamiliar perfume on his T-shirts, or answering the phone and hearing dead silence on the other end. Most of all, she wouldn't miss the way his cheating made her feel, as if her insides had been stirred with a fireplace poker.

Chenille's key turned in the front-door lock just as Chiffon shut the scrapbook and shoved it under the sofa.

"You're still up?" Chenille said, startled to see her sister wide awake on the sofa. "I'm completely exhausted. I'll take Walter out and then wash up in the bathroom. Is he sleeping in the children's room?"

"I took Walter out an hour ago, so he's fine. How about slowing down for a minute?" Chiffon patted the place beside her. "Tell me about your date."

"It was fine. I'm just pooped," she said with an exaggerated yawn. She covered her mouth with her hand, and then, as if she was hiding something, plunged it back into the pocket of her skirt.

"What was that?"

"What?" Chenille said, oozing innocence.

"You know *what*." Chiffon stood in front of her sister. "Something caught the light. Let me see your hand."

Chenille demurred for a moment and then flopped her hand out of her pocket. "Drake proposed to me tonight. He wants me to elope with him."

"Yow!" Chiffon said, eyeing the ring on her sister's finger. "You didn't say yes, did you?"

"No, of course not." She bit her bottom lip. "But I didn't say no, either."

"When does he want to get married?"

Chenille blushed. "Tonight, actually. Of course, I turned him down."

"I knew it," Chiffon said, jabbing a finger in the air. "There's something hinky about that guy."

"What do you mean?" Chenille asked, shirking away from her sister.

"He must *want* something from you. Maybe he thinks there's a secret fortune in our family."

Chenille twisted her engagement ring. "Why do you think he wants something from me? Isn't it possible he wants to marry me because he loves me?"

"Loves you?" Chiffon said in an incredulous voice. "He doesn't even know you! Besides, the two of you are horribly mismatched."

"I suppose you think I'm too plain for him," Chenille said hotly.

"Of course not. You're just too *innocent* for him. It's like a hammerhead shark dating My Little Pony."

Chenille squared her shoulders. "Drake says I'm refreshing."

"Or naive. Which works to his advantage."

"I'm too exhausted to discuss this," she huffed. "And I'm also insulted that you assume Drake has a sinister motive for marrying me. Maybe he just loves me. Is that so far-fetched? That your spinster sister could find a husband?"

"Chenille—"

"Maybe you're just jealous because he shows absolutely no interest in you."

Chiffon's face fell. "You can't believe that. I'm just trying to look after you. You're not wise to the wiles of men."

"And you are?"

Chiffon flinched.

"I'm sorry." Chenille sighed. "I shouldn't have said that. I'm overly tired and"— she glanced down at her engagement ring— "confused. I'm going to get ready for bed," she said, heading toward the bathroom.

"Chenille, I just want you to be happy," Chiffon said, trailing after her sister. "That's my only motive. You do believe that, don't you?"

Chenille didn't turn around to answer.

. . .

On Monday morning Chenille left for the high school to meet with the principal. She claimed she was no longer mad at her sister, but judging by her wounded expression and stiff posture at breakfast, Chiffon believed otherwise. She feared her negative comments about Drake might shove Chenille right into his arms.

I wonder what his game is, Chiffon thought as she stacked the dishes from breakfast in the sink. No matter what Chenille said about him, Chiffon suspected Drake was slicker than a greased eel. As she wiped down the kitchen counter, the phone rang, and Garnell was on the other end.

"Hey you," Chiffon said cheerfully. "Haven't heard your voice in a spell. What's hanging?"

"Laying low," Garnell said. "I've been picking up some over-time at the kaolin plant. Is Chenille around this morning?"

"She's at the high school today."

"High school? What's going on?"

Chiffon tucked the phone under her chin. "You haven't heard? Chenille's going to take Miss Beezle's place over in the gifted program. I thought she stopped by your house to thank you." Chiffon had hoped her sister would develop an interest in Garnell, seeing how he was such a fine man and obviously fond of her.

"I probably missed her, I've been so busy," Garnell said. "That's the best news I've heard all day. So she'll be staying in Cayboo Creek?"

"Looks like it."

"Great," he said, genuinely pleased. "I'm sorry I missed her, 'cause I've got a little surprise for her."

Chiffon exhaled heavily. "She's got her own surprise, and frankly I'm worried sick about it."

"What's that?"

"Saturday night she accepted an engagement ring from a man she barely knows."

"Say again?" Garnell croaked.

"She's crazy as a boxful of crickets. She's only been out with this Drake character a few times. And I don't trust him as far as I could throw him."

"Who is Drake?" Garnell said sadly. "I didn't even know she was seeing anyone."

"Some fancy pet doctor in Augusta. She met him when Walter was having one of his seizures. He's a sneaky-looking fellow and a Yankee to boot. Hails from Wisconsin." Chiffon spat out the state's name as if it were equivalent to San Quentin.

Garnell cleared his throat. "I know some folks in Augusta. I could ask around. What's this fellow's last name?"

"Dupree. If she marries him, she'll be Chenille Dupree. Sounds like a stripper's name."

"Have they set a date?"

"No, but he's in an awful rush. Wanted to waltz her down the aisle the other night. Thank God she turned him down. She hasn't accepted his proposal yet, but she's thinking about it."

"I'll see what I can find out about him. Don't bother to tell her I called. The surprise I had for her . . ." He trailed off. "It don't matter so much now."

Chenille hung up the phone feeling sorry for Garnell. He had sounded stricken by the news of Chenille's proposal. Was it possible he was sweeter on her sister than she'd realized?

*If we aren't supposed to eat
animals, why are they made
out of meat?*

Sign outside Boomer's Butcher Shop

CHAPTER TWENTY-SEVEN

Dewitt went outside to play ball in the front yard
and nearly tripped over an arrangement of eighteen sweetheart roses on the stoop.

"There's more flowers out here!" he hollered to Chenille,
who was seated on the sofa grooming Walter.

"Just bring them in and I'll put them on the mantel with the
others," she said.

She glanced up at the fireplace, which was beginning to look
like a miniature Garden of Eden, courtesy of Drake Dupree.
Tulips, red as rubies, burst lushly from a clear glass vase. Ger-

ber daisies, in Easter-egg colors, popped their heads out from a white wicker basket. A single orchid, slender and pale pink, curled from a terra-cotta pot.

Dewitt teetered in, looking like a floral bouquet with legs.

"Goodness gracious, that's enormous!" Chenille said, rushing to relieve the child of his burden. "It's too big to fit on the mantel." She moved aside a checkerboard and placed the bouquet on a beveled-glass coffee table supported by a couple of elk horns. "There. That's lovely," she said. She didn't bother to read the card attached to the flowers because they all said the same thing: "I can't wait a minute longer. All my love, Drake."

As she returned to the couch and resumed grooming Walter, Chiffon wandered into the living room, fresh from the shower.

"I forgot to tell you," she said, face flushed and hair wrapped up in a bath towel. "Some lady called while you were gone yesterday, and she said the pet deposit on the apartment you looked at was five hundred dollars."

"Ridiculous!" Chenille said, running a brush through Walter's wiry fur. "Walter is an exemplary tenant. He's clean, polite, and scarcely sheds."

"I didn't know you were looking for an apartment," Chiffon said softly. Things were still tense between the sisters, even though Chiffon hadn't said anything further about her sister's engagement to Drake.

"I need to know what's available in Cayboo Creek. I can't sleep in your living room forever," Chenille said. "Although, if I marry Drake, I won't need to find somewhere to live. I'll just move into his place in Augusta."

"I see he's upping the ante," Chiffon said, noticing the flowers on the coffee table. "Roses. Pretty darn impressive."

Could I have been wrong about Drake? Chiffon was beginning to doubt herself. Last night Drake had stayed for supper and he'd been a perfect gentleman, bringing the kids an assortment of dime-store trinkets and raving over her venison stew. Afterward, they'd all sat down to watch *Chicken Run* on the Family Channel, and Drake pretended to enjoy it—at least halfway through—until he fell asleep. He woke with a start, shouting the name "Veronique!" When questioned, he claimed Veronique was the name of his poodle who'd died of distemper when he was a child.

"Veronique is the reason I went into the veterinary sciences," he said solemnly as they all nodded in sympathy.

Still, she couldn't help but think there was something off about the guy, especially the way he was trying to drag Chenille down the aisle so quickly. But she'd kept her mouth shut, since her sister had made it clear she didn't welcome her opinion.

"What's this?" Chenille said with alarm as she ran her fingers through Walter's fur. "Oh no! It can't be. Walter has a parasite!"

"A parasite?" Chiffon said, leaning over for a closer look. "What kind? Not worms, I hope."

"He has a tick!" Chenille said, hiccupping. "I can't believe it. I never should have brought Walter out here to the backwoods where he'd be exposed to so many predators. Bring me the phone. I need to . . . *hic* . . . call Drake immediately."

Chiffon was surprised at her sister's overreaction. She'd become a lot more relaxed about Walter in the past weeks. Yesterday she'd even let Emily dress him in a Strawberry Shortcake outfit.

"It's just a little tick," Chiffon said in a soothing voice as she gently took Walter from her sister and examined his coat.

"Just a little tick, she says. I suppose . . . *hic* . . . Rocky Mountain spotted fever and Lyme are just *little* diseases."

Chiffon rooted through Walter's coat and extended her palm to her sister. "Is this your tick? Looks like a burr to me."

Chenille squinted at the small brown object in Chiffon's hand. "Oh. I guess I didn't . . . Are you sure? I could have sworn it was a tick."

"I'm sure."

Chenille threw up her hands. "I don't know what's wrong with me lately. I'm so emotional, so raw. I can't concentrate."

"You're going through a lot of changes in your life."

"Yes, I am. And Drake has been just wonderful. He's the most romantic man on the planet, just like one of those dreamy guys in the Mystery Date game we played as kids. It's just happening so fast and . . ."

"Yes?"

Chenille drew up her knees to her chin, like a little girl. "I'm not sure I love him. I might just love the *idea* of him. He's so suave, handsome, and successful. But our relationship feels like a movie set. It looks realistic from a distance, but when you get close, you see it's all fake."

Chiffon nodded. "So don't rush into anything. Give it time."

"That's what I *want* to do, but Drake is so impatient. I'm afraid he'll give up on me and then . . ." She hiccupped. "I'll lose my last chance."

"Your last chance for what?"

"Everything!" she said with a sniff. "White wedding gown, honeymoon, babies, a Cuisinart."

"This isn't your last chance. You've still got time. Nowadays women have babies well into their forties."

Chenille shook her head vehemently. "I'm forty years old, and Drake's the first man who's ever shown serious interest in me. Before he came along, I never got beyond the third date or the first kiss."

"You mean you're a—"

"Yes." She let out a delicate cough. "I am."

"Oh."

"It's freakish, I know," she said in low voice.

"It is not freakish," Chiffon said, squeezing her hand. "And you'll have plenty more opportunities to meet the right fellow. Before, you were closed up like a clam. Now that you've returned to Cayboo Creek, you've blossomed. Other men besides Drake will take notice."

"I don't know about that," Chenille said, remembering how quickly Garnell had forgotten about her.

"I'm not going to tell you what to do," Chiffon said. "But please, remember one thing. If it's true love, it will keep."

Chenille took a tissue out of her pocket and blew her nose. "I'm seeing him tonight. We'll see what happens."

· · ·

By the time Drake was due to pick her up, Chenille had shredded two pairs of pantyhose with her fingernails and poked herself in the eye with a mascara wand. Everything she'd tried on looked about as flattering as a feed sack. Most of her clothes were in a heap in a corner of Chiffon's room. When the doorbell rang, she rubbed her face raw with a washcloth, slipped into an old baggy pair of slacks and a blouse with a button missing, and trudged into the living room.

Drake stood in the hallway, having been admitted inside by Emily. He was patting Walter on the head as Chenille walked into the room.

He wore an exquisitely tailored camelhair coat, with a green silk scarf around his neck. His abundant dark hair, slightly damp from the drizzle outside, curled up around his ears. Chenille stood at the threshold of the living room, drinking him in.

So gorgeous, and so wrong for me.

Chiffon was right; they *were* a mismatched pair. Drake was a Ferrari, with quick acceleration and glamorous sleek lines. But Chenille didn't want or need such a fancy model of a man. Tonight she had to break it off. It wasn't fair to keep leading him all around Robin Hood's barn. She had to tell him she wasn't ready to get married, even if it meant losing the only male attention she'd ever attracted.

"Hello there, lovely one," he said, glancing up at her. "Are you ready for our adventure tonight?"

"Just let me get my coat," she said.

Drake was taking her to a hilltop in Augusta where all the city lights could be viewed. On the drive over, he animatedly chatted to her about his day (a ferret had bitten him on his index finger; he had been forced to put down a cat with feline leukemia). He didn't seem to notice or care that she was slumped against the passenger window, her cheek squashed by the cool glass.

They drove to an area called the Hill, and Drake parked the car on an incline. As Chenille peered out the window, she had to admit that the view was spectacular. The downtown area, with its dark alleys and aging buildings, glowed in the gloom like a lit-up birthday cake. It was hard to imagine anything sad or disturbing occurring among the friendly mosaic of multi-colored lights. Chenille heard a pop and realized Drake had just opened a bottle of champagne.

He poured a glass and handed it to her. She shook her head. "I'm not very thirsty."

He continued to push the drink on her. "Thirst has nothing to do with it. Champagne quenches the soul."

She reluctantly took the glass and ventured a small sip. The bubbles made her tongue itch.

"And now for a small token of my love," Drake said, placing a wrapped box in her hand.

"Oh, how nice," Chiffon said. Her voice held the false enthusiasm of a child who unwraps a package of underwear at Christmas.

"In some ways it's the most special gift of all," he added.

Chenille couldn't imagine how he could top himself. Already, he'd wooed her with Lindt chocolate truffles, a pair of pearl earrings, a fourteen-carat-gold bracelet, a boxed collection of Kenny G CDs, a rhinestone-studded collar for Walter, and a pashmina shawl.

It was all too phony to her. Garnell holding her close as he stepped all over her feet was the genuine article. Drake's brand of courtship, on the other hand, was as real as gold glitter that came in a jar.

She weighed the gift in her hand. It was extremely light. A box of handkerchiefs was her guess. Or maybe another bracelet. She opened the package and tore away the tissue paper to reveal a winged heart made from red construction paper and lace doilies.

"What's this?" She lifted the heart up to see if something was underneath it, but the box was empty.

Drake looked at her shyly. "I cut out that heart when I was in the fourth grade. I promised myself that when I grew up, I'd give it to my wife."

"Oh," said Chenille.

"I always imagined what my future wife would look like. Sometimes she was brunette, sometimes blond. My mother told me, 'Drake, it doesn't matter what she looks like, it's how she makes you feel here,'" he said, jabbing his chest with his thumb. "Before I came over this evening, I added the lace wings," he continued softly. "Because this is how my heart feels when I'm around you."

"Oh, Drake!"

He gently opened her hand, pressed the heart into her palm, and closed her fingers around it. "Please treat it with care."

Chenille felt lightheaded, as if she were swinging at the very top of a Ferris wheel. Had she dismissed Drake too quickly? Here he was, giving her what she'd been looking for all along: some sign of his vulnerability and humanness. With this one small gesture, she felt herself softening like margarine on a baked potato. His eyes seemed to plead for her approval. What had she been thinking? Why was she shoving this wonderful man away?

"I've made up my mind, Drake," she heard herself saying, almost as if in a dream. "I will marry you. And I promise I'll treat your heart as if it were my very own."

Sex after eighty is like trying

to shoot pool with a rope.

Attalee Gaines's favorite one-liner

CHAPTER TWENTY-EIGHT

The morning of the calendar shoot had arrived, and all of the participants, except Elizabeth, were assembled in the break area of the Bottom Dollar Emporium. Elizabeth was at home nursing a croupy baby.

Chiffon tinkered with the settings of Birdie's camera, while Chenille, who was helping Chiffon with the women's makeup, sorted through her sister's kit, trying to find the right lipstick shade for Attalee.

"Ahh, Wicked Red Cherry," Chenille said, unscrewing the top to examine the color. "This ought to do the trick."

"Cherry sounds good," Attalee said. "I'm starving."

"No nibbling on the lipstick," Chenille warned. "It's for beauty, not nourishment."

"I hope you have a whole case of that lipstick," said Birdie, a puckish glint in her eye. "It'll take that much to beautify her."

"You ain't exactly Pamela Anderson yourself," Attalee shot back.

"Purse your lips for me, will you?" Chenille asked Attalee.

She obeyed, and as Chenille applied the lipstick, Attalee squealed. "What's that on your finger? It's scratching up my face." She grasped Chenille's hand. "Well, I'll be a bug-eyed baboon. This girl's got herself an engagement ring."

Chenille smiled. She'd been waiting for someone to notice the ring, being too shy to make the announcement herself, and Chiffon didn't seem inclined to tell anyone. Mavis, wearing a headful of pink sponge rollers, rushed over to examine her ring.

"Why, that sly fox. I just saw Garnell yesterday, and he didn't breathe a word," she said.

"Oh, it's not Garnell," Chenille said quickly.

"Not Garnell?" Mavis frowned. "I was under the impression—"

"My fiancé's name is Drake Dupree. He's a veterinarian in Augusta," Chenille said.

"Dupree?" Attalee said. "Do you reckon he's any relation to the Vidalia Duprees? My third cousin married an Arnold Dupree, although I think they pronounced it 'Dupray.' I've told you about him, Mavis. He's the one who was in that terrible accident at the chicken-plucking plant."

"That's highly unlikely," Mrs. Tobias said, patting her neck down with moisturizer. "Since your fiancé is a professional man, he's certainly related to the Augusta Duprees. A very distinguished family, indeed. Made their fortune from bricks."

"It could be either, I suppose," Chenille said. "Truthfully, I don't know where his people are from."

"What?" everyone said in unison, except for Chiffon, who was curling Birdie's eyelashes.

"Chenille, dear," Mrs. Tobias said. "You can't be serious."

"She hasn't known Drake for very long, so she hasn't met 'his people,'" Chiffon said, searching through her makeup bag for an eyeliner. "She'll get to know them soon enough. They're getting married in a week."

"A *week*?" squawked Attalee. "Where's the fire?" Mavis gave her a sharp look, and Attalee's eyes brightened with understanding. "Oh, I see. You ate supper before saying grace. When's the little bundle due?"

"There's no bundle. I'm not expecting a baby," Chenille said, shaking her head fervently. "Drake and I haven't even—" She swallowed the rest of her sentence.

"I'd advise you to make sure the sap rises in that tree before you set down any roots," Attalee said with a wink.

"That's enough smut," Mrs. Tobias said to Attalee. She rose and looped her arm through Chenille's. "A bride doesn't have to know her groom in the biblical sense before the wedding, but she simply *must* know who's nesting in his family tree."

"Are we all invited to the wedding?" Attalee asked.

"I'd love for you to come," Chenille said. "But Drake and I are getting married in Rome."

"I got me a niece named Delia who lives in Rome," Attalee

said. "She's a waitress at the Feed Mill over there. If you sit in her section and mention my name, she'll slip you extra corn-bread with dinner."

"Actually, we're getting married in Rome, Italy, not Rome, Georgia," Chenille said.

"Rome?" Mavis said, unspooling her hair from the rollers. "How romantic! This Drake must be something else."

"He is," Chenille said. "I told him I wanted to put off the wedding until my mother got home from her European tour, but he was too impatient. So he insisted we meet her in Rome. We'll have a civil ceremony there. Drake's arranging every-thing."

"What about Chiffon?" Mavis asked. "She isn't going to be at your wedding?"

Chenille cast an anxious glance at her sister. "I wanted her to come, of course. Drake even said he'd pay for her ticket, but—"

"How am I going to traipse off to Rome when I have three kids to look after, one still on the bottle?" Chiffon said curtly. "Now, I don't mean to rush you, but we only have two hours before Mavis is open for business. We should get started."

The older women exchanged glances. They would have liked to ask more questions, but from Chiffon's tone it was obvious that she considered the topic of Chenille's marriage closed.

"So who wants to go first?" Chiffon said, loading the camera with film. She glanced around the room. You could have heard a bug sneeze, it was so quiet in the store.

"Come on," Chiffon coaxed. "It's natural to feel nervous." She set a bottle of wine and some cups on the soda fountain.

"That's why there's a little libation, in case anyone wants a taste of courage. Daisy Hollingsworth sent it over."

"I ain't chicken," Attalee said, slowly getting up to her feet. "I'm proud of the body my maker gave me." She picked up the bottle of wine and tried to open it. "This durn thing won't twist off."

Chiffon took the bottle from her and popped it open with a corkscrew. "I put everyone's robes in the storeroom. Just slip into yours and come on out. I'll set up the shot."

"Good luck, Attalee," Mavis said in a faint voice.

Chiffon positioned the camera on a tripod. The first shot called for Attalee to lean over from behind the soda fountain wearing her soda jerk hat, bowtie, and nothing else. A large banana split would hide her "assets."

Chiffon stretched a diffusion filter over the lens that she'd fashioned out of a silk stocking. She was ready to go, but Attalee was taking her sweet time coming out of the storage room.

"Attalee, shake a leg," Chiffon called out. "We're ready to go."

"I'm coming!" she said, stumbling out of the storage room wearing a full-length terry-cloth robe. "It takes a while to chugalug a bottle of wine."

"You drank the whole thing?" Chiffon said.

"I was thirsty," she said with a belch.

"Never mind. Just come behind the soda fountain. Chenille, she's got a merlot mustache. Could you wash it off and reapply her lipstick?"

Chenille readied Attalee while Chiffon peered through the viewfinder. "The lighting is perfect," Chiffon said. "Attalee, you just lean into the banana split and put your hands on each side of the dish as if you were serving it to a customer. I'm ready whenever you are."

"She's all set to go," Chenille said, stepping out from behind the soda fountain.

"All right, Attalee, just drop your robe whenever you feel comfortable," Chiffon said. "I'll take a few shots, and then you can put your robe back on while I set up for the next one."

"Would y'all quit staring at me?" Attalee said. "This ain't no peep show."

"Why doesn't everyone close their eyes so Attalee will feel more comfortable?" Chiffon said. The women dutifully covered their eyes with their hands while Chiffon made one final adjustment to her camera. "There now, Attalee, it's just you and me."

"That's more like it," Attalee said. "I don't need the whole world ogling my goodies." She licked her lips nervously and glanced around the room. "Here goes nothing," she said, but her fingers continued to clasp her robe together. "Sorry," she said with a shake of her head. "Can't do it. It's too airish in here. I'll catch my death."

Chiffon glanced at the thermostat on the wall. "It's eighty degrees in here. But if you're really cold I'll plug in a space heater."

Attalee stared down at her feet. "Last night I took a good long look at myself, and it wasn't a pretty sight." She kicked at the ground with her slipper. "Guess I ain't nearly as brave as I thought."

"Thank the Lord," Birdie said, rising from her chair, her hands clasped together in jubilation. "I've been sitting here thinking there's not enough spirits in this county to make me squeeze out of my support girdle and pose nude for the camera."

"I concur," Mrs. Tobias said with a resigned sigh. "And I thought that I was the only one who wanted to back out."

"I didn't sleep a wink last night, I was so edgy," Mavis said. She gazed glumly at the group. "I guess this means we'll be forced to have a bake sale after all."

Everyone sat in sullen silence. Chiffon reluctantly lifted the camera from the tripod. First Chenille was getting married in Rome, and now the calendar project was falling apart. She'd so looked forward to taking photos again. The opportunity had just slipped through her fingers. Disheartened, she stared listlessly down the store aisles, until a display caught her eye.

"Wait a minute," Chiffon said with a slow grin. "I just had once heck of a thought. What if we still did the calendar, just a little differently than we planned? No one will have to remove a stitch of clothing."

"What do you have in mind?" Birdie asked.

The group of women gathered around Chiffon as she eagerly explained her plan.

"I think it's a novel notion," Mrs. Tobias said after Chiffon finished speaking. "Campy as well as clever."

"And we won't have Reverend Hozey and the hard-shelled Baptists breathing down our necks," Birdie said with a nod of her head.

"Are we all in agreement, then?" Chiffon said, smiling broadly. Everyone murmured words of accordance. "Good. Attalee, let's finish your shoot. The rest of you calendar girls, start getting ready. This is going to be a hoot."

A balanced diet is a cookie in each hand.

Magnet on Chiffon Butrell's refrigerator

CHAPTER TWENTY-NINE

The proofs came back for the Bottom Dollar Girl calendar and they looked scrumptious. Attalee, in particular, was tickled pink at how stunning she appeared in the photographs.

"If you close one eye and squint a little, I'm the spitting image of Ann-Margret," she kept repeating to everyone. Birdie was most impressed by the quality of the photographs. She asked Chiffon if she'd consider working for the *Crier* as a photographer.

"I just don't have the eye anymore," Birdie said. "The pay

wouldn't be much, and you might have to sell an ad or two on the side, but it'd be a start. Plus, if you wanted to do any moonlighting photography work, I'd give you free ads."

Chiffon didn't think twice before she snapped up the opportunity. Anything was better than being a waitress, and she loved taking photos. Never again would she have to come home from work smelling like fried onion rings or with feet so tired she had to soak them in bucket of warm water and Epsom salts. She'd be as happy as a dog with three tails if she weren't worried sick about Chenille.

"What about your passport?" Chiffon asked, a few hours later, as she watched her sister packing for Rome. "Did you pack it?"

"I've got it in a special zippered compartment of my purse," Chenille said, folding a pair of socks and placing them in her suitcase.

Of course she packed her passport. Chiffon was just making idle conversation. Her sister was more prepared than any Boy Scout ever dreamed of being. Among the items she'd packed were two kinds of electrical converters, Euros in several different denominations, a full-color map of Rome, an Italian phrase book, a raincoat that folded up to the size of a postage stamp, a sewing kit, and two extra rolls of Angel Soft toilet tissue. (Chenille had heard that Italian toilet tissue was scratchy as sandpaper.)

Chenille shook out a long white nightgown.

"I've never seen that before," Chiffon said. "Is it new?"

"I bought it to wear on my wedding night," Chenille said with a blush.

The gown looked about as sexy as a nun's habit. Then again,

Chiffon couldn't picture her sister in a feather-trimmed black negligée with peekaboo cutouts.

"Is there anything you'd like to know? I'm not exactly Dr. Ruth, but—"

Chenille took a book from her suitcase and shyly presented it to her sister.

"*Sex for Dummies*?" Chiffon said, reading the title.

"I read it cover to cover. It had many helpful diagrams," Chenille said.

"I guess you're all set."

"And you've got my list of instructions concerning Walter?" Chenille asked.

List? It's more like an owner's manual. But Chiffon didn't care; she'd grown close to the dog, regarding him as her furry little nephew.

"I'll take really good care of him," Chiffon said, meaning every word.

Chenille zipped up her suitcase and looked at her sister. "I know you think I'm making a big mistake, but I promise everything will be fine. The other night I realized Drake *is* the man for me." She smiled dreamily. "Beneath that suave exterior, he's really just a big pile of mush. I'm so lucky."

"I guess I'm like Mavis. I kind of always pictured you with Garnell," Chiffon said.

"Garnell's a lovely man, but it just didn't work out between us. Besides," she said regretfully, "he's already paired off with someone else."

"Garnell? That can't be right. It's you he's taken a shine to."

"Really?" Chenille slung her pocketbook over her shoulder. "He was getting awfully cozy with your friend Jewel. I went by his house to thank him for his influence with Miss Beezle, and he was holding her in his arms."

"There must be some kind of misunderstanding," Chiffon said with a frown. "Jewel isn't interested in dating. She told me herself. Is that why you got serious with Drake all of a sudden? Because I'd wager one phone call could clear this up."

"It doesn't matter anymore. I'm in love with Drake and I'm marrying him." A car door slammed outside. "That's Drake. Don't worry about me so much, Chiffon. I'm beginning a wonderful chapter in my life with the man of my dreams."

Chiffon hugged her sister. "I hope so," she said, kissing her on the cheek. "Send me a postcard of the Eiffel Tower?"

Chenille laughed. "That's in Paris. How about the Sistine Chapel?"

"I never was too good at geography," Chiffon said ruefully. "And Chenille?"

"Yes?"

"Tell Drake he'd best treat you right or he'll have to deal with me. Tell him I'm a sharpshooter when it comes to Super Soakers."

Chenille pulled away from her sister's arms. "Drake loves me. I know he won't hurt me." She wheeled her luggage to the front door. "*Ciao*, Chiffon. I'll see you in a week."

. . .

After her sister left, Chiffon couldn't relax. She organized Dewitt's LEGO collection, straightened Emily's closet, and fluffed the pillows on Walter's dog bed. She sadly gazed at a photograph Birdie had taken of the two sisters at the Bottom Dollar Emporium. "Silly girl," she said to herself, placing the frame facedown on her dresser. "She's going to Rome, not Pluto."

She went into the kitchen looking for something to eat. Peeking into the pantry, she saw that it was impeccably organized, compliments of Chenille. All of the items were in alphabetical order: applesauce, bran cereal, carob cookies. Seeing the box of carob cookies made her instantly sentimental for her sister. With tear-filled eyes, she opened the package and popped one into her mouth. *Yuck!* She immediately spit it out. Dewitt was right. They did taste like dog biscuits.

Chiffon moved on to the "O" section of the pantry and grabbed a box of Double Stuf Oreos. After consuming three in rapid succession, she felt a little better.

She glanced at the copy of Chenille's itinerary, which was stuck under a refrigerator magnet. Right now she was on her way to New York on a direct flight from Augusta. From there she would pick up her connection to Rome.

Walter barked as someone pounded at the front door. Chiffon wiped cookie crumbs from her mouth and dashed to the living room. She squinted out the peephole and saw Garnell, nervously shifting from one foot to another, like he was having trouble holding his water.

Chiffon opened the door. "What's wrong, Garnell?"

"Has Chenille left yet?"

"A couple of hours ago. Why?"

"Darn it!" Garnell said, pounding his fist into his hat. "I was afraid of that. I finally got the goods on that Drake character."

"Oh my gosh," Chiffon said, ushering him in. "What's his story? Ex-felon, con artist, litterbug?"

"He's Canadian," Garnell said grimly.

"Canadian?" Chiffon raised an eyebrow. "Well, that's hardly a crime. Some very decent people are Canadians." She ticked off on her fingers. "Michael J. Fox is Canadian; Jim Carrey; Keanu Reeves—"

"This Canadian's temporary visa has run out, and he didn't win the green card lottery this year," Garnell interrupted. "He'll be forced to return to Quebec in a few weeks. That is, unless he gets married."

She gasped. "So that's why he was in such an all-fired hurry to get hitched. How did you find this out?"

"I poked around a little. One of the assistants in his office, Glory, reads tarot cards for the niece of Elva Mims, who is the housekeeper for my barber's accountant, Norm Hobbs, who sits three stools away from me at the Chat 'N' Chew and told me all about it."

"Lord, sounds like you poked around a lot!"

"Six degrees of Garnell," he said matter-of-factly. "Glory jabbers like a magpie, and her favorite topic is her boss. Turns out Drake Dupree came from Canada with a lady friend. She got her green card, but he didn't. Her name is Veronique."

Chiffon stamped her foot. "He said Veronique was the name of his dead poodle!"

"She's no poodle," Garnell said gravely. "He keeps a separate apartment, but he pretty much lives with her."

"My poor sister is on her way to Rome to marry someone who doesn't love her, and only wants her for her U.S. citizenship." She pointed a finger at his chest. "And it's all your fault!"

Garnell blinked in confusion. "What in tarnation did *I* have to do with it?"

"She went over to your house to thank you for putting a good word in with Miss Beezle and she saw *you* hugging up on Jewel Turner."

"Hold up a minute," he said, scratching the stubble on his chin. "Jewel and I weren't hugging, we were dancing. The night we all went to the Tuff Luck Tavern, everything was jim-dandy until Chenille and I started dancing and I stomped over her feet like a big, dumb dairy cow. I was telling Jewel about it over at the Chat 'N' Chew, and she offered to give me a few lessons." He demonstrated a stiff cha-cha-cha on the braid rug. "See? I was going to surprise Chenille and take her out dancing in Augusta."

Chiffon grinned. "You really do have a soft spot for Chenille, don't you?"

"Oh, Chiffon," he said with a moony glaze to his eyes. "I turn into a heap of goo when I see her."

"Good! Mention that when you call her in New York to tell her about Drake."

"You want me to call her about Drake? You're her sister. Shouldn't you?"

Chiffon shook her head. "She gets real prickly with me when it comes to Drake. You're the one who found the dirt on him. It should come from you."

Garnell set his lips into a stern line. "She's gotta be told before she marries that bum. A fellow like him deserves a good horse-whupping. Lucky for him, I ain't a violent man."

"She arrives in New York at two P.M.," Chiffon said, grabbing a copy of Chenille's itinerary and shaking it in his face. "You'll page her at the airport. We have to catch her before she gets to Rome, because Drake's arranged for them to drop their luggage at the hotel and go directly to the clerk's office to be married. We can't miss her."

"I Would Kiss You Through the Screen Door, but It'd Strain Our Love"

Selection G-5 on the Tuff Luck Tavern jukebox

CHAPTER THIRTY

"When the moon hits your eye like a big-a pizza pie, that's *amore*," Dean Martin crooned on Drake's CD player. Drake told Chenille that he'd selected the music to get her in the mood for Rome. She turned down the volume a notch and leaned back against the leather seat of his Mercedes.

"I can't believe it. We're starting our lives together," Chenille said, reaching over the console to touch Drake's shoulder.

"Not while I'm driving, dear," Drake said smoothly. "Your touch is much too thrilling, and I fear I'd run off the road."

Chenille examined her freckled hand with new respect.

To think she possessed the power to bring excitement to her husband-to-be with a mere brush of her fingertips! She swiveled her wrist so her engagement ring would cast prisms from the sunlight streaming in through the windshield.

"Oh, Drake! I want to know everything about you. What you were like as a little boy. What your dreams were; what your hopes were—"

"Darn it!" Drake said, in a sharp voice that startled Chenille. "I forgot the airplane tickets. They're on the mantel at home." He glanced at his watch. "We have plenty of time. I'll swing by on the way to the airport."

"What a treat! I'll finally get to see your apartment." She sighed happily. "I mean *our* apartment."

"There's nothing much to it," Drake said. "Three stifling little rooms. We'll look for something else after we marry."

"But until then, it will be our love nest." She blushed at the word "love." "I can't wait!" she crooned.

Drake turned up the volume of the stereo system, almost as if he was trying to drown out Chenille's chatter. But she chided herself for thinking he'd behave so boorishly. He loved her, after all. He'd certainly said so enough times. The poor dear was just distressed about leaving the tickets behind.

Within minutes, Drake pulled into an apartment complex called Glen on the Green. It was one of those boxy places for singles with a kidney-shaped pool and a community weight room. A banner stretched across two poles read, IF YOU LIVED HERE, YOU'D BE HOME BY NOW. Chenille had never quite understood what was meant by that phrase, but now it applied to her and Drake.

"Let me go in first," Drake said as he climbed the wooden

stairs to the apartment. "I want to make sure that I haven't left any horrible messes."

Chenille smiled as Drake let himself into the apartment. He didn't have to worry about keeping his living quarters tidy anymore. As soon as they got back home, she'd have his apartment in apple-pie order. As she waited for him, she glanced at her surroundings. *Our banister,* she thought, running her hand along it. *Our mail slot,* she mused, examining the blunt opening in the door. She sniffed a sweetish smell in the air. *Our dry rot.*

After a moment, Drake poked his head outside and said, "You can come in now. But only for a minute. We need to be on our way to the airport."

Chenille stepped inside and was immediately dismayed by the impersonal appearance of the apartment. There were no books, photos, or bric-a-brac in sight. The living room was as clean and sleek as one of those model apartments leasing agents maintain for potential renters. She'd no idea why Drake had fretted about a potential mess. His quarters were immaculate.

"I need to use the facilities," Drake said. "Wander around if you like."

As he disappeared into the bathroom, Chenille glanced into the galley kitchen. *Neat as a pin.* The appliances gleamed as if they'd never been used, and there wasn't so much as a fork in the sink. She peered into the refrigerator. A single bottle of seltzer water. How desperately he needed her! As soon as they got home from Rome, she'd stock it with sprouts, veggies, and other goodies.

Leaving the kitchen, she spotted a closed door down the hall. *The bedroom.* That's where he probably hid all of his bachelor clutter. Chenille excitedly skipped down the hall, expecting to see hillocks of socks or a flurry of old newspapers behind the closed door. Instead she opened it to reveal a room so nondescript, it could have been in the Ramada Inn. Drake's bedroom contained only a bed, an armchair, and a dresser. Chenille examined the double bed, covered with a drum-tight blue blanket. *Hospital corners.* She might have guessed.

She peeked under the bed looking for secrets but found nothing, not even a stray piece of dust. Then, as she lifted her head, she spotted a flash of color: A book was shoved between the mattress and the box spring. She glanced back guiltily, looking for Drake. He was still indisposed, so she decided to grab it. After all, she and Drake would soon be married. It wasn't healthy for a man to keep things from his wife, and the book appeared to be the only personal item in the apartment.

The book was a paperback romance novel called *Wicked Heart.* Chenille glanced at the spine. It was from the Aphrodisiac line, an imprint much too racy for her tastes. She couldn't fathom why Drake was reading it. She'd imagined him as an Ian Fleming fan.

Furtively, she tucked the book into her bag and scurried from the bedroom. She waited in the living room until Drake emerged from the bathroom.

Later, as they drove to the airport in silence, Chenille reflected on the sterile appearance of Drake's apartment and found herself becoming increasingly upset. Twice she remarked to him, "It almost looks as if you don't live there."

But either Drake didn't hear her over the music or was deliberately ignoring her, because he made no comment. She was also disturbed that she'd seen nothing in the rooms to indicate he was readying his apartment for her. There'd been just one pillow on his bed, and if there were any welcoming touches at all, she'd missed them.

"Drake, what's the pet policy at your apartment building?" she said abruptly.

He shrugged. "I don't know. I work so much I haven't had time to care for an animal."

"But what about Walter?" she asked in a panicky tone. "Surely you knew he'd be living with us. Didn't you even think to call or inquire if pets are allowed?"

She felt a hiccup rising up from her diaphragm. "Maybe this wedding is . . . *hic* . . . a big mistake," she said over the sultry strains of Dean Martin.

Drake immediately jerked the wheel and pulled over to the side of the highway. "What an oaf I've been!" he said, massaging his temples. "What with planning this trip, arranging for our wedding, and clearing out my apartment from top to bottom, I completely forgot about your precious pet." He reached over and stroked her shoulder. "Please forgive me. If they have a policy against dogs, we'll just move elsewhere immediately."

A feeling of shame washed over Chenille. He'd been so busy making all of their arrangements, it was only natural that he'd overlooked a detail or two. How selfishly she'd behaved!

"You cleared out your apartment for me?"

"Of course, darling. That way you can decorate it to your own taste. You should have seen the place before the Salvation Army came and carted my junk away. I had all sorts of tacky items, dating back to my college days. A beanbag chair, inflatable beer bottles, bookshelves made from plastic crates. It was revolting."

It was hard to imagine Drake possessing those things; he was such a stylish man. But she was immensely flattered that he'd made room for her in his home. Now she saw his sparsely decorated apartment in a completely different light.

"I'm sorry, Drake. I don't know what came over me. Just pre-wedding jitters, I guess."

"Are you okay now?" he asked, concern in his eyes.

"I'm fine," she said softly.

They arrived at the airport, checked their luggage, and passed easily through security. But as they prepared to board the plane, they discovered they weren't seated together. Drake made a big stink about it at the gate. "This is my honeymoon," he said, sweeping his hand through his dark hair in agitation. "I can't be in 15F while my fiancée is in 4C."

The airplane was filled to capacity, so nothing could be done about their separate seating arrangements. Chenille assured an overwrought Drake that she'd be fine sitting without him on the short flight to Newark. They had seats together from Newark to Rome, and that was what mattered most.

After Drake had made certain she was settled in her seat (he fluffed her dinky pillow, adjusted her overhead air temperature, and tore open the plastic earphone package), he reluctantly left when the captain put on the no-smoking sign. Chenille frowned when she saw that the in-flight magazine was missing from the flap in front of her. She was left with nothing to amuse her but safety instructions. Then she remembered the romance novel she'd taken from Drake's apartment. Slipping the book out of her purse, she started reading.

From page one, she knew she wasn't going to like the story. The protagonist's name was Vixen Fox, a massage therapist whose first client, Devlin Shaft, was looking for more than a rubdown. *What a pity that so many romance novels have turned raunchy!* Chenille longed for the days when phrases like "punishing kiss" or "heaving bosom" were as steamy as it got.

But there was nothing else for her to read, and Devlin seemed like an engaging hero. Having been shot down by Vixen at the beginning of the book, he'd opted for a more subtle and endearing approach. Chenille came to a portion in the book that had been highlighted with a yellow pen.

"Standing there, bathed in moonlight, you look like a statue carved from alabaster," Devlin said with a twinkle in his eye.

Chenille gasped.

The elderly woman sitting in the next seat eyed her with apprehension. "Are you all right, dear?"

"Fine," Chenille said hastily. "Something in this book startled me."

The woman glanced at the tomato-red cover of *Wild Heart*. There was a picture of a man and woman, dressed in wisps of fabric, groping each other in an orange-yellow haze.

"Oh my!" the woman said, disapproval registering in the tight set of her mouth. "I have a copy of the first book in the 'Left Behind' series. Maybe you should be reading that instead."

"Maybe," Chenille mumbled, but kept her eyes riveted on the text, reading the next highlighted portion.

"Your hands are like little white doves," Devlin said, stroking Vixen's knuckles.

"Goodness gracious!" Chenille said.

The woman gave her a sharp glance and made a big show of putting on her earphones.

Chenille couldn't believe it. Drake had stolen all of his poetic lines from Devlin Shaft!

She kept turning the pages in horror, now reading only the highlighted portions. It was confirmed. Every single thing Devlin had said to Vixen, Drake had said to her.

As she neared the end of the book, an entire paragraph was colored yellow:

> *Devlin, his dark eyelashes jeweled with tears, handed her a box.*
>
> *"For me?" Vixen asked. Her lovely forehead creased with lines. "Not more jewelry. You can't win me over with expensive baubles."*
>
> *"Just look, my darling."*
>
> *She opened the box and saw a cardboard heart with lace wings. "What's this?" she asked.*

Chenille slammed the book shut. Drake's gift to her of his paper heart had been the reason she'd decided to marry him. Now she'd discovered he'd stolen the idea from a cheesy romance novel. Who was Drake Dupree? And what did he really want from her? She didn't know, nor did she care to find out. She desperately wanted to escape from the plane, but the jet was already rumbling with movement. It was too late to leave.

As soon as the plane landed, she planned to catch a flight back to Augusta. Drake was several aisles behind her. She could deplane and disappear into the crowd long before he realized he'd been ditched.

She thought about Chiffon, whom she'd treated so harshly. Her sister's instincts about Drake had been accurate. He had manipulated her into accepting his proposal for some reason other than love.

Taking out a pocket mirror, she saw a pale, pinched face staring back at her. She snapped the mirror shut, and her mind momentarily flickered on Garnell, but she blinked the thought of him away. He'd already moved on to Jewel. Besides, who was to say he'd ever been interested in a dour old maid like herself? She'd probably just imagined his attraction to her.

She thought of Miss Beezle, who'd also never married. Was there a time when her former teacher had imagined herself as a bride? Had she dreamed of picket fences, baby booties, and tandem bicycles? And if she had, when did the moment come when she'd realized that her dreams had passed her by? That her narrow bed would never be replaced with a queen-size one; that the only "dear" in her future would be a cat or a dog; and that the years of her life would unfurl without being marked by christenings, children's birthday parties, and anniversaries? Chenille stared out the window at the froth of clouds that surrounded the plane. Her own such moment had arrived.

When someone gets you

hot and bothered, turn on

the prayer conditioner.

Sign outside the Rock of Ages Baptist Church

CHAPTER THIRTY-ONE

Garnell stood outside at the gate of the Augusta airport peering through a pair of binoculars.

"A jet is coming this way," he said. "How much do you want to bet Chenille's on that plane?"

Chiffon shifted Gabby from her right shoulder to her left. "I wish I had your optimism. I'm worried sick. Maybe we should have stayed home, where she can reach us if she needs to."

Garnell had tried to page Chenille at the Newark airport, but either she hadn't heard the page or they'd somehow missed her. After much pleading and wheedling with airport personnel, he discovered that she'd failed to board her flight to Rome. Clearly something had happened between Drake and Chenille en route to Newark.

"She'll know we're here at the airport if she calls, because you left a message on the machine. But I just know she's on her way back home to Augusta," Garnell said. "I feel it in my bones."

They'd checked with the airlines, and it was possible that Chenille had boarded a flight in Newark bound for Augusta at 4 P.M.

"Mama, there's a snack machine in the lobby," Emily said. "Can Dewitt and I get a treat?"

Chiffon foraged through her wallet for some coins. "You may, but come right back afterwards. I don't want y'all roaming around."

She shielded her eyes from the sun as she watched a jet drift down toward the runway. "The air's got that spring smell about it today. A fresh new scent that makes you feel like anything is possible."

"You know what happens to a young man's thoughts in spring?" Garnell said. His lips twisted into a sappy little smile.

"I know," Chiffon said with a laugh. The blue scarf she wore on her head flapped against her ears in the breeze. Despite Chenille's troubles, she'd never felt better. Tomorrow morning she was going to start work at the *Crier*, and when Elizabeth saw the proofs for the Bottom Dollar Girls calendar, she'd hired Chiffon to take some professional photographs of baby Glenda. "I'll recommend you to everyone in my Mommy and Me group," she'd said.

Chiffon had enough money left over from the sale of Lonnie's things to purchase some additional photography equipment she'd need to do freelance work. Things were definitely looking up on the career front. But perhaps best of all, she no longer found herself pining over her two-timing husband. The fever had finally broken, and she felt healthy and free.

And now that she'd renewed her passion for photography, she didn't have any urgency to run out and replace Lonnie with another fellow. Why, she was turning into a Jewel Turner, something she couldn't have imagined only weeks ago. Now, instead of pitying Jewel, she admired her, realizing that the diner owner was operating from a position of strength. It was so liberating not to need a man!

Once Chiffon earned a little money, she'd decorate her house in her own style. There'd be no trying to fit furniture around a pool table, no camouflage curtains, and no gun racks hanging on the wall. Then, as soon as she was able, she'd hire someone to paint her little house. Maybe a nice lemon color, or a barely-there blue. She'd kiss that horrible purple good-bye for good.

The kids returned with their animal crackers, and they chased each other around the grassy plot near the gate as a Continental plane landed. Chiffon wrinkled her nose at the smell of jet fuel, and Garnell plugged his ears with his fingers.

In moments, they watched as passengers filed into the baggage claim area. Chiffon scanned the tired-looking travelers for her sister, but didn't see any sign of her.

"There she is!" Garnell said after a few moments. Chiffon looked in the direction of his pointed finger and spotted her sister trudging toward the baggage carrel. Her face sagged as if it were weighted down with sandbags. But then Chenille glanced up and saw Garnell, waving furiously and calling her name. Almost instantly, her expression shrugged off its droopiness and she looked as hopeful as a teenager.

Garnell ran toward her and flung his arms around her. Her sister returned the hug, and Chiffon knew that any misunderstanding between the two had been resolved by their embrace.

When Chenille reached Chiffon and the kids—with Garnell holding her hand tightly lest she get away again—her cheeks were pink with excitement and her eyes jumped with questions. "Why are you here? How did you know?"

Her questions were tabled for the moment as the children crawled all over her.

"Aunt Chenille, Walter ate a bug," Dewitt said.

"He did not!" Emily said. "He only tasted it and then he spit it out."

"Come on, let's go get your bag," Chiffon said. "We'll sort it all out for you while we wait."

As they walked, Chenille told Chiffon and Garnell about how she'd discovered that Drake had borrowed all his best lines from a romance novel, and Chiffon told her sister about Drake's Canadian citizenship and his relationship with Veronique.

"So that's why his apartment was so empty," Chenille said with a knowing nod. "All of his things must have been in her apartment. I'm so sorry, Chiffon. You were right about him all along."

Emily tugged at Chenille's sleeve. "You sure got back quick, Aunt Chenille. Didn't you like Rome?"

"I didn't make it to Rome," Chenille said. A pained expression crossed her face. "Oh dear, I suppose I'll have to call

Mother at her hotel when I get home. I'm not looking forward to that."

"I'll call the old sweetie for you," Chiffon said, smiling. "It's always a joy to hear her screeching voice."

"Mama, I've lost Hulk," Dewitt said, patting his pockets. "I think I left him outside by the planes."

"You sure?" Chiffon peeked in her diaper bag to see if the toy had inadvertently been stuck inside. "All right, let's go outside, and you show me where you were playing. Em, stay here with Aunt Chenille and Garnell. See you in a jiff."

She and Dewitt walked back to where they'd met Chenille's plane. He crawled around in a grassy area, searching for his action figure while Chiffon walked up and down sidewalks outside the tarmac, Gabby babbling in her arms.

"Are you sure you had it with you?" she asked, watching the arriving passengers. The travelers, as a rule, appeared happy and relaxed, and Chiffon wondered where they'd flown in from. One day she, too, would get on a plane and go to some far-flung, glamorous destination.

"He's here!" Dewitt shouted. "He's finally here!"

Chiffon looked up, expecting to see her son with the Hulk in hand. Instead, Dewitt was in the arms of a man wearing a denim jacket. The stranger was covering her son with kisses and ruffling his hair.

Like a mama cheetah, Chiffon ran in the direction of the pair, wielding her pocketbook like a weapon. "What in the heck are you doing, mister?"

With a swish of his streaky red-brown hair, the man turned his head slowly in her direction, and Chiffon saw his face. She swiftly registered the high-planed cheekbones, the full, slightly parted lips, and the intense squint of copper-colored eyes.

"It's Daddy!" Dewitt shrieked. He buried his face in Lonnie's neck.

"So it is," Chiffon said, holding Gabby even closer. Her entire body shook from the jolt of his sudden appearance.

"It ought to be illegal to look that good," he said, eyeing her, his voice a mixture of honey and gravel.

"I was just thinking the same thing about you," she said with a husky voice. The words tumbled from her mouth without her say-so.

The two stood there, eyes locked, postures tensed, breathing heavily like wrestling opponents catching their breath. He made the first move by leaning in to her, his lips brushing up against her ear. "Sorry, Tweety Bird," he whispered.

Then he drew back to gauge her reaction. The sun was low behind him, and he glowed golden in its light. His odd penny-colored eyes sparkled with an unspoken plea.

She noticed a familiar set to his mouth. A smidgen of cockiness. Like he knew he was going to win her over regardless of what he did. Anger pinched at her like a chigger bite. She needed to feed it or she'd be forever lost.

"Lonnie—" she began. "You have no—"

"Daddy." Dewitt lifted his cheek from his father's shoulder. At five, his head was still too big for his body, a baby still. "Please don't go away again."

The bitter words stalled in her throat. Lonnie wiped away a tear on Dewitt's cheek. "Don't you worry none. I'm not going anywhere. Am I, Chiffon?"

No one will win the battle of the sexes. There's too much fraternizing with the enemy.

Message tacked up on the bulletin board at the Bottom Dollar Emporium

CHAPTER THIRTY-TWO

Chenille sat at a table in the Bottom Dollar Emporium, sipping on a cherry phosphate.

"It's been two days and I haven't heard a peep from her," she said to Mavis and Birdie, who were sitting at the table with her. "They aren't answering the phone, and there's a do-not-disturb sign taped to the door."

Attalee, who was polishing heavy, scallop-rimmed glasses behind the soda fountain, looked up from her work. "What do you reckon they're doing in there?"

"I don't think they're playing Parcheesi," Birdie said, lifting her chin.

"I know that," Attalee said. "But it can't be too X-rated. Their house is crawling with young 'uns."

"The kids are at school most of the day," Chenille said. "She's probably dropped Gabby at day care. She enrolled her again because she was going to start work at the *Crier*."

"Which she isn't doing," Birdie said, setting down her glass of cream soda. "Although she did leave a message on the machine at the office saying she wanted to delay her starting date."

Chenille toyed with the paper from her straw. "She's making the biggest mistake of her life, going back to Lonnie. Mavis, I do appreciate you putting Walter and me up in your spare room until we can find an apartment."

"It's been my pleasure. Not that I've seen much of you since you've left Chiffon's," Mavis said in a teasing voice. "I don't think I heard you come in until well after midnight last night."

"Do tell," Birdie said, leaning forward with interest. "Who's been filling up your dance card, Miss Grace?"

"It's interesting that you mentioned dancing," Chenille said. "Garnell took me to a place in Augusta called the Eagle Roost and led me around the floor like Fred Astaire. Thanks to his dancing lessons from Jewel."

"I'll be hacked," Attalee said. "Love's in the air for sure. Dooley from the Tuff Luck Tavern called me the other night, asking me did I want to come over and see his fish hook collection."

"Did you go?" Mavis asked.

"I did not," Attalee said, bristling. "I knew them fish hooks were just a trick to lure me over to his house for a lip-locking session. I did say I'd be open to dinner at the Pick-of-the-Chick. He says, 'Fine, so long as you order the dark-meat special; I'm a little short this month.'"

"Tell us, Chenille," Birdie said mischievously. "Have you seen Garnell's fish hooks?"

"I'll never tell," Chenille said with a giggle.

"By the way you're blushing, I'd guess you'd seen the whole tackle box," Attalee said.

"Certainly not," Chenille said. She cast her eyes down coyly. "But I've been thinking about it."

"My, my, my," Birdie said over her soda glass. "I think our little Chenille is in love."

Chenille's face flushed at the mention of "our little Chenille." Finally she'd managed to carve a place for herself in the community.

The bell over the door jingled, and Mrs. Tobias and Elizabeth strolled in. Elizabeth was holding a cooing Glenda, and Mrs. Tobias had a manila folder tucked under her arm.

"Sorry we're late," Elizabeth said as she walked back to the soda fountain. "We got delayed at the pediatrician's office."

Mrs. Tobias pulled off her leather driving gloves. "You should have seen that baby. She got a shot and barely whimpered. A true stoic, just like her great-grandfather Harris Tobias. Even the pediatrician was impressed."

Elizabeth sat down at the table. "Where's Chiffon? Is she running late?"

"I don't think she's coming," Chenille said.

"Is she still holed up in that house with Lonnie?" Elizabeth asked, her forehead forming faint lines of concern.

"I'm afraid so," Chenille said.

Elizabeth dejectedly shook her head. "She's always been a fool for that man."

"Let's get started then, shall we?" Mrs. Tobias said. She unfastened the clip on the manila envelope she'd brought and shook the contents out on the table. "Ladies, I have the calendar."

Everyone gasped at the finished product.

"It's gorgeous," Mavis said, running a hand over the glossy cover. They all crowded around as she slowly flipped through each month.

"My favorite is the one of Attalee sitting in the corner with the dunce cap captioned, 'Naughty by Nature,'" Mavis said. "It cracks me up every time I look at it."

"That's because Attalee *is* naughty by nature," Birdie said with a high cackle.

"The whole town's buzzing about your publicity campaign, Elizabeth," Mavis said. "Everyone's wondering what we're up to."

Chenille had helped Elizabeth post flyers all over town. The circulars featured a Betty Boop–looking cartoon with a finger over her lips. The caption read, "Can you keep a secret?" Beneath the cartoon the flyers said:

Come to the Senior Center, Friday night at 7 P.M., for refreshments. Friends of the Senior Center will be raising funds with a top-secret surprise. Please join us. We can "barely" contain ourselves.

"I also got a call from Reverend Hozey," Birdie said. "He's convinced that we're still doing the nudie calendar. I didn't tell him otherwise. I'm sure he and his minions will be there to protest."

"That's wonderful," Mrs. Tobias said, clapping her hands

together. "That means we'll attract both sinners and saints. I just hope they all bring their wallets."

"Chiffon was supposed to help serve refreshments," Elizabeth said. "Do you think she'll make it?"

Chenille pursed her lips into an unhappy pout. "Your guess is as good as mine."

The sex was so good even the

neighbors had a cigarette.

Graffiti in the men's room at the Tuff Luck Tavern

CHAPTER THIRTY-THREE

Chiffon ran a nail along Lonnie's spine, and he immediately flopped over in bed to face her.

"You know that gives me the shivers, girl," he said as he leaned down to nibble on her ear. Chiffon turned her head to glance at the glowing numbers of the digital clock on the lamp table.

"Twenty more minutes and I'll have to go fetch Gabby from the day care," she said. "We best not start anything."

Lonnie kicked off the sheets. "Man, these feel like sandpaper. I'm used to something softer. Jay-Li got her sheets all the way from Ethiopia or some darn place."

"Egyptian cotton sheets, I'd guess," Chiffon said. "And what have I said about mentioning her name?"

"'Don't say that bimbo's name in my house,'" Lonnie mimicked. "Just thought you might be curious how she lived. She was as crazy as a Betsy bug in some ways."

Chiffon sighed, knowing she should not be in bed with Lonnie. She'd tried to resist him, but most of her gumption had drained out of her when she saw how delighted Dewitt was to have his daddy back home. Things had snowballed from there.

Emily had been more standoffish than her brother. When she'd first seen her daddy at the airport, she'd flattened herself against Chiffon's slacks and sucked her thumb. But by the time they'd driven back to Cayboo Creek, she was happily chirping away with him, like a little bird. Lonnie had that effect on people. He shone so brightly that his past sins seemed soft and hazy, as if you were looking back at them through a lens smeared with Vaseline.

The night he came home, Chiffon had shut their bedroom door and stood over him as he sat on edge of their waterbed.

"Why?" she'd asked.

He'd patted the bed and grinned. "Don't you want to ride the waves first?"

"No," Chiffon said, standing firm. "I want to know why you left your home and family. Why you betrayed me to run off with that floozy. Why you got her name tattooed on your—" She stopped short and narrowed her eyes. "Where is that tattoo of yours, anyway?"

"I don't have it anymore."

"How can you not have it? Tattoos are permanent."

"You know I can't stand needles," he said, a forelock of hair covering his left eye. "I just got it painted on my bicep with some henna. I'd cover it up with tape when I showered, and Jay-Li was never the wiser."

"You didn't take the needle for her?" Chiffon said, sitting beside him.

Lonnie traced the letters "TWE," for Tweety Bird, on his bare chest. "You're the only woman I've ever endured that kind of pain for."

Later, after they'd made love so hard that the headboard chipped the paint on the bedroom wall, Lonnie tried to explain how he'd fallen under Jay-Li's spell.

"She picked me out from that crowd of extras, like I was a pair of shoes she wanted to try on. I was willing to oblige, thinking I'd never had a tumble with a real live movie star." He leaned back on the bed, his fingers laced behind his neck. "Shoot, I didn't even think you'd mind so much. After all, it was one of those once-in-a-lifetime opportunities. Wouldn't you do it with Tom Cruise if you had the chance?"

Chiffon ignored his question. "You went a lot further than just sleeping with her," she said darkly.

"Yeah, I did," he said, wearing the guilty look of a dog who's peed the carpet. "I thought it was going to be a one-night stand. But then we got caught on camera kissing. It was all over the TV, and I guessed you'd seen it. So when Jay-Li asked me to stick around awhile, I figured I'd stay on until you'd cooled off."

"You were gone over a month." Chiffon's voice grew shrill. "You sent me signed divorce papers."

"I know. She got clingy on me. Thought we were 'in love' and all. I told her she could send you them papers, but you wouldn't sign them. I said you were much too feisty. You looked so cute shooting those reporters with the Super Soaker." He grabbed a strand of her hair and wrapped it around his index finger.

"You could have knocked me over with a feather when you mailed those papers back," he continued. "It broke my heart in two. I didn't think you'd do that in a million years."

"What choice did I have?" Chiffon said tersely. "Janie-Lynn was going to make public my affair with Skeet. She went on television and implied that none of our children were yours. She wanted to test Gabby to see if she was really your daughter. I wasn't going to put Gabby through that. I just wanted all of it to stop, so I signed on the dotted line."

"Jay-Li's a wildcat, all right," he said, staring up at a pale gray water stain on the ceiling. "I should've never told her about Skeet, but she wheedled it out of me when I was tipsy on champagne. When I saw that TV interview where she badmouthed you, I said, 'Enough is enough, I'm going home.' Then she started bawling and making threats until I promised her I'd stay, but the whole time I was plotting to come home."

"Plotting? Why didn't you just get on a plane?"

He rubbed his thumb and index finger together. "Cash. I didn't have the green. Finally her manicurist, Sake, gave me the money after I'd granted her a favor or two." He hung his head. "Made me feel kind of cheap. But I did it for you, Tweety. So I could be back home with you and the kids again."

She dismissed the Sake confession. A hasty rendezvous with a manicurist seemed trivial compared to a full-blown affair with a movie star. Covering her face with her hands, she said, "I thought it was over between us. I thought you loved her."

"Hey, now," he said, nuzzling up to her cheek. "That's what she wanted you to believe. That chick is squirrelly. But Love Bear is in your arms again. He might stray a time or two, but he always comes back to the lair. I thought you knew that."

She tingled with pleasure and relief at his words, yet knowing at the same time she was falling back into an unhealthy abyss with him. How could something feel so wrong and so right at the very same time?

Since then they'd hunkered down in the house, ignoring phone calls and visitors. When the children were around, they often disappeared into the bedroom for "naps." When the kids were gone at school and day care, she and Lonnie scarcely got up from the waterbed.

She'd tried to forget the look of shock she'd seen on Chenille's face when she'd strolled into the baggage area with Lonnie at her side. There'd been little discussion on the way home from the airport in Garnell's van. When Lonnie went inside the house with his suitcase, Chenille hissed, "You're letting him stay?"

Chiffon shrugged, and Chenille stared at her as if she were a stranger. Then she packed up her stuff and drove away in her car, and Chiffon hadn't seen or talked to her since.

But what could she say? *I'm a fool and I know it, but sorry, I don't have what it takes to kick Lonnie to the curb*? Part of her defended her decision to stay with her husband because of the three children they shared. But in her heart, she knew she was making excuses. Truth was, she was as powerless around Lonnie as a wino with a bottle of Wild Irish Rose.

She'd have to face Chenille soon, as well as all of her friends. She couldn't spend the rest of her life burrowed under the covers with Lonnie. But right now she was just too ashamed.

Chiffon glanced at the clock again. She had to get up immediately if she wanted to have Gabby home and get to the grocery store before the other kids got off the school bus. Bounding off the mattress, she sorted through the pile of clothes on the floor for her blue jeans.

"Tomorrow's our last day to lay out, babe," Lonnie said, watching her dress as he reclined against the pillows. "I'm back on first shift at the plant on Friday. Gotta get some overtime so I can buy our stuff back."

Your stuff, she thought as she hooked her bra.

"What about you?" he asked. "When are you going back to your waitress job?"

"I'm not going back. Remember? I told you I was going to be photographer for *The Crier*?" *If Birdie hasn't already given up on me.*

"Oh, yeah. I forgot." He propped up on his elbows. "Is that such a good idea, babe? If you're being paid a straight salary, you're not going to make as much money at the newspaper as you did as a waitress."

"Maybe not right away. But I'll do some freelance photography on the side. Maybe I can have my own business one day."

Lonnie had gotten out of bed and was pulling his Levi's up over his slim hips. "Sounds mighty iffy to me. I don't how we're going to make it around here without your tips."

He stood behind her and wrapped his arms around her chest. His lips plowed through a tangle of her hair to reach her ear. "Maybe you oughta call around some. See if you can't scare yourself up a waitress job."

Her body betrayed her mind as she found her arm snaking around his back to pull him closer. No. Things had to be different between them this time. She dropped her arm and willed herself to face him. "I don't want to wait tables anymore."

Her tone of voice was all wrong. She sounded like a child reluctant to brush her teeth. He took her hand and passed it lightly over his cheekbone. "I know. I ain't looking forward to busting my chops over at the NutraSweet plant, either. It's not a fair world."

"But Lonnie—"

He placed a finger over her lips. "It won't be forever. Just until we get things back to normal. After all, you're the one who sold our stuff." He lifted her chin and searched her face. "Okay, Tweety Bird?"

"'Kay," she said, swallowing. An acrid taste rose in the back of her throat, but she choked it back. As she turned to go, Lonnie patted her bottom.

"Atta girl."

"I'll be back in a couple of hours," she said in a hoarse voice.

Tears blurred her vision as she drove down Chickasaw Drive to Gabby's day care. She'd been a complete weakling. Why hadn't she stood up to him?

Because he wouldn't like it. Because you'd lose him, only this time for good.

Although Lonnie claimed to admire her so-called feistiness when it was directed at a sloppy repairman or a short-changing pizza delivery person, he wanted her to be as meek as a geisha girl when dealing with him. He'd always been the one in charge of their relationship, and regarded any contrary behavior on her part as mannish or unattractive. Maybe that was the reason why he and Janie-Lynn Lauren had parted ways. Not because the movie star had "badmouthed" Chiffon on TV, but because she'd been too bossy with Lonnie.

Despite prancing around in pink and looking about as fierce as a Himalayan kitten, Janie-Lynn was a serious businesswoman who'd lent her name to three perfumes and a clothing line. She was used to calling the shots, and probably had discovered too late that it was Lonnie's way or the highway.

After Chiffon picked up Gabby from day care, she went to the Winn-Dixie and listlessly maneuvered her cart around the aisles. She hefted a ten-pound bag of charcoal into the buggy. Lonnie liked her to cook most meals on the grill even in cool weather. She stocked up on all the goodies he was fond of: peach Nehi, Cool Ranch Doritos, a case of Pabst Blue Ribbon, mint ice cream, and a package of black licorice. By the time she was done getting his favorite things, as well as the children's, she didn't have any money left over for what *she* liked.

With a flash of insight, she realized the buggy was a microcosm of her marriage to Lonnie. No room for her desires, plans, or hopes. Not even enough space for a package of gummy bears.

What was she going to do? The unfairness built into their relationship had never bothered her before, but now it throbbed like a rotten tooth. There was a side of her that wanted Lonnie so badly it made her bones ache, but another side burned to reclaim the freedom she'd gained while he'd been gone. She longed to talk with her sister, but she didn't even know where

Chenille was. She'd missed her terribly over the past couple of days.

After grocery shopping, Chiffon pulled up in the driveway and was disappointed to see Ferrell Haines's pickup truck in the yard. Ferrell and Lonnie were longtime hunting and drinking buddies, so there was no telling what they were up to. She parked her car around the side of the house to unload the groceries. Holding Gabby in one arm and a grocery bag in the other, Chiffon shouldered her way through the back door into the kitchen. She dumped her purchases on the counter and was about to go outside for another load when she heard a familiar clicking sound coming from the living room.

No, it can't be. She cocked her head and listened. *Christ on a crutch, it is.* After putting Gabby in her walker, she tore into the living room and saw Lonnie and Ferrell standing beside a brand-new pool table.

Lonnie was screwing his cue into a square of chalk, while Ferrell leaned over the side of the table, taking aim at a five ball.

"Baby, you're home. What d'ya think?" Lonnie said with a grin as wide as a gator's.

"Where . . . ? How did . . . ?" Chiffon stammered.

"It's a surprise. I had it delivered while you was gone," Lonnie said. "Look. Red felt instead of green. Your favorite color. And it's got a genuine cherry finish, none of that cheap vinyl coating like the last one."

"Hey there, Chiffon," Ferrell said, his wide brow shiny from lumbering around the table. "You sure do have a devoted husband, buying you a fancy pool table like this."

"Where did you get the money? I thought you were broke," Chiffon said, her hands shaking.

"There was plenty of money in the account, babe," Lonnie said, setting up his shot. "Heck, I even had enough left over for two top-of-the-line cues."

"The Predator," Ferrell said, running a beefy hand along the length of the cue. "The Tuff Luck Tavern don't have cues half this nice."

"Only the best for my wife," Lonnie said with a wink.

"Lonnie, that was *my* money," Chiffon said, her voice cracking. "I was going to buy some photography equipment."

"*Her money?*" Lonnie said with a chuckle and a sidelong glance at Ferrell. "Where'd you get the cash, sugar? By flying into a snit and selling all of my stuff?" He squashed his empty beer can. "Babe, will you get me and Ferrell a couple of cold ones?"

Chiffon stared at her husband, cheeks on fire. "I flew into a 'snit,' as you say, because I didn't have a dime to my name and you were off in California boffing that bim—"

"Whoa there, girl," Lonnie said. "Ferrell, you mind fetching us some beer? Get one for Chiffon, too. I think she could use a little cooling off. Take your time, now."

Ferrell nodded in understanding and ambled into the kitchen.

Lonnie put a hand on her arm and spoke in a low voice. "Enough of this. I'm not going to rag on you for selling all of my stuff, and you're not going to talk about Jay-Li anymore." He pulled his wallet out and handed her a couple of twenties. "Here. Why don't you scoot over to Augusta and get you one of those outfits you like at the Kmart?" He kissed her on the top of her head. "Ferrell's here, so make nice."

As if in a trance, Chiffon took the money and stuffed it in the pocket of her jeans. She walked on wooden legs into the bedroom and stared at her reflection in the mirror above the bureau. She wore the blank expression of a Stepford wife.

Something had to be done and it had to be done now, before she lost herself completely to Lonnie.

She just needed some courage, ASAP. Too bad they didn't package the stuff and sell it in bottles like soda pop. She'd need a six-pack to get up the nerve to exorcise Lonnie from her life.

Drumming her nails on the dresser, she remembered her tiara, stored in a shoe box on the top shelf of the closet. Had it really held some kind of magic that night she'd worn it for Chenille, or had she just imagined it?

Chiffon stood on tiptoe and reached for the box. Opening it, she spotted not only the tiara but also the satin sash she'd worn when she was crowned Miss Catfish Stomp.

Couldn't hurt to wear that, too, she thought as she slipped the sash over her chest. She picked up the tiara and placed it on top of her head. Almost instantly her neck elongated like a swan's and her shoulders pulled back, lending her a queenly carriage.

She raised her hand and tilted her chin upward. "Begone, peasant," she whispered into the mirror.

Leaving the bedroom, she regally glided into the living room. Neither of the men noticed her. Ferrell was absorbed in peeling the label from his beer bottle, and Lonnie was leaning over the pool table with a cue in hand.

From where she stood, Chiffon had an excellent view of her husband's backside, and what a fine round package it was, encased ever so fetchingly in a pair of faded jeans.

If you go through with this, you'll never see Lonnie's sweet little behind again.

Her hand touched her tiara, and strength surged through her. *If you back down now, you'll always be a prisoner to his whims.*

Ferrell looked up and noticed her. "Hey there, Chiffon. That's a sparkly little thing you're wearing on your head."

Lonnie turned around and grinned in that heartbreaking way of his. "Hello, princess. What are you doing? Playing dress-up?"

Chiffon felt the familiar blast of heat on her cheeks as he smiled at her. Over ten years of marriage and he could still turn her knees into noodles.

But was his sexy smile worth the damage he'd taken out on her heart and soul every single day of their marriage?

"No," Chiffon said in a near whisper.

"What's that?" Lonnie said.

"No," she said, this time in a much louder voice.

"No, what?" he asked, scratching his head in bewilderment.

"No to waiting tables. No to this pool table. No to Jay-Li, Jonelle, and all the other women you've strayed with, and most of all, *no* to you! Pack your bags. I want you out of here today."

"Are you crazy?" he asked.

Chiffon stood there, breathing heavily. Instead of feeling weighed down by loss, she was as light as a hot-air balloon.

"I'm not crazy," she said, drunk with the momentum of the moment. "This is the sanest I've felt since I met you." She swiped a bottle of beer from Ferrell's grip, took a swig, and wiped her mouth. She glanced at Lonnie, who stood there looking like he'd been hit in the face with a bag of nickels.

"Go on, now. You don't want me to have to get out the Super Soaker, do you?"

Much to Chiffon's surprise, Lonnie didn't blow up or get defensive. Instead, his bottom lip shook, his face turned purplish-red, and he started blubbering like a baby.

"Don't make me leave, Chiffon," he sobbed. "I love you."

Chiffon stared at his mottled, snotty face. She'd never seen him cry before, and Lord, was he ugly! His quivering mug looked like it had been tapped for turpentine.

Ferrell, embarrassed by his bawling buddy, slunk out the front door.

"Here," Chiffon said, shoving a box of Kleenex into Lonnie's chest. "Blow your nose. Don't know why you're crying. This is what you get when you treat a woman the way you've treated me."

"You ain't never complained before," Lonnie said timidly through his tears.

"I've never had the courage," she retorted. "I always thought I'd lose you if I stood up for myself. Now I could care less."

"You can't mean that, Chiffon," Lonnie said. "You and me belong together."

Chiffon touched the tiara to make certain it was still on her head.

"Not anymore."

Life would be easier if

everyone read the manual.

Sign outside the Senior Center

CHAPTER THIRTY-FOUR

Walter bounded across Garnell's yard, looking like an exuberant puppy. The breeze sifted through his wheat-colored fur as he propelled his short forelegs through the dewy grass.

"Born free," Chenille sang, blinking back tears. "As free as the wind blows."

"He does look happy," Garnell said. "I think the country suits him."

The pair swung in a glider on the porch. Chenille had her head pressed against Garnell's chest, and his hand dangled in her lap.

"He can't possibly be as happy as I am," Chenille said, brushing her lips against Garnell's cheek.

Walter trotted up the steps of the porch with something clamped between his teeth.

"What do you have, sweetie? Is that your Boo Bear?" Chenille asked.

A small gray object tumbled out of the dog's mouth. She squealed and jumped off the glider. "Oh my God, he's eaten a rat!"

Garnell examined the limp form of the animal Walter had deposited at their feet. "Looks more like a baby field mouse to me."

"This is dreadful." Chenille circled the porch in a tizzy. "He needs to see a vet. Mice carry all kinds of diseases!"

"Simmer down, sugar," Garnell said, putting a calming hand on her shoulder. "Walter's a Norwich terrier. They're bred to hunt vermin."

She stopped short. "My baby? Hardwired to hunt rats and mice? He's never done anything like this before."

"Maybe he feels more like himself running around out here. Maybe he's getting in touch with his inner canine."

Chenille looked at Walter, his tight black lips upturned in what looked like a grin.

"I guess he's okay," she said, reaching down to muss the fur on top of his head. "But no more kissy-kissy from Mama, now that I know where your mouth's been."

"How about me? Do I get a kiss?" Garnell asked.

"Haven't you had enough already?" Chenille said coquettishly.

"Nope," he said, his eyes crinkling in the corners. As she planted her lips on Garnell's, it was impossible to imagine a time when she didn't find him irresistible. He made Drake seem as sexy as a cold brisket of corned beef.

"I went by and observed Miss Beezle's classroom yesterday," Chenille said after they had kissed. "I'm going to enjoy teaching the gifted classes. I worked with some of the students, and there was a definite connection."

"I'm just glad that you're staying here in Cayboo Creek instead of going back to Bible Grove," Garnell said.

Chenille sighed contentedly. "I have a new job, a wonderful boyfriend, and that awful Drake Dupree is going back to Canada. Everything would be perfect, if only . . ." She stopped in mid-sentence.

"If only your sister wasn't back with Lonnie," Garnell said. "That's what you were going to say, wasn't it?"

She nodded sadly. "You already know me so well."

Turning her head, she saw a cloud of kicked-up dust on the dirt road leading up to Garnell's house. A car's engine roared in the distance.

"Are you expecting anyone?" Chenille asked.

Garnell shook his head and walked to the edge of the porch, squinting to see who was tearing up the drive.

"I'll be darned," he said. "It's your sister."

Moments later, Chiffon's Firebird came into view and screeched to a stop. She slammed the door of her car and strode toward them. She wore an askew tiara, and a smile so wide you could see the silver fillings of her molars.

"I did it!" she hollered. "I told that good-for-nothing, two-timing tomcat to hit the road. I'm a free woman." She galloped toward her sister and threw her arms around her.

"You told Lonnie to leave?" Chenille asked.

"I sure as heck did. Stood over him while he packed his things. When he walked out that door, I didn't feel a smidgen of regret. 'Course, I know the kids will be upset," she said, cutting her eyes toward the car, "but Lonnie won't win any father-of-the-year awards. He didn't call them once while he was gone away to California. Sometimes I think no father is better than a poor one. Plus, I'm a much better mama when Lonnie's not around."

Garnell extended his hand. "Congratulations, Chiffon. I know that took a lot of strength. All the time you were married to him, I never thought that fellow was good enough for you."

"It took me over ten years and a whole lot of tears to find that out for myself," Chiffon said. She squeezed her sister's shoulder. "Plus, I give Chenille a lot of credit for helping me."

"Me?" Chenille said.

"Yeah. You've said so many great things about me. I wanted to live up to the person I saw reflected in your eyes."

Chenille hugged her sister and whispered in her ear, "I'm so proud of you. Tiara or no tiara, I'll always see a queen."

· · ·

A few days after Chiffon had shown Lonnie the door, the two sisters went to pick up Wanda from the airport.

"I can't tell you how glad I am to land on American soil," Wanda said after she came out of the gate and air-kissed Chiffon's cheek. "Those Europeans are savages. The public toilets in France are black holes in the ground you're expected to squat over. And just try and find a restaurant in Europe serving bacon and scrambled eggs for breakfast. I did not see a single Cracker Barrel the whole time I was there."

"No Cracker Barrel," Chiffon said, suppressing a chortle. "Mama, how did you ever stand it?"

"Thankfully, there was a McDonald's on almost every street corner. Otherwise, I might have starved," Wanda said as she checked her appearance in a compact mirror. "Where's your sister? She didn't come with you?"

"She made a run to the powder room," Chiffon said, taking Wanda's carry-on bag. "She'll meet us in the baggage area."

"Chenille could have knocked me over with a feather when she told me she was getting married," Wanda said as she strode beside Chiffon. "Frankly, I'd convinced myself that she'd always be a spinster. Either that or I thought she might be funny."

"Funny?"

"Not ha-ha funny, but *funny*," Wanda said with a wrinkle of her nose. "Like Rosie O'Donnell and that Ellen person. If you recall, Chenille played an awful lot of field hockey when she was in high school."

"No, Mama. Chenille is definitely not funny."

"But then she calls me and tells me the wedding is off. My heart snapped in two. Now I have one daughter married to a rapscallion and another daughter who's more likely to be kidnapped by cannibals than find a husband."

"She's met someone else," Chiffon said, stopping at the baggage carrel. "And it's a match made in heaven. And as far as my rapscallion of a husband—"

"Chenille!" Wanda cried out as she spotted her elder daughter coming down the hall from the restroom. "There you are. Chiffon tells me you're tearing through men like they were tissue paper."

"I said no such thing—" Chiffon began.

"I'm on the ground for five minutes and already you're sassing me," Wanda snapped.

"You're looking well, Mama," Chenille said, pecking her cheek.

Wanda stood back and eyed her daughter. "There's something different about you. It looks like you've finally taken my advice and started using Mary Kay's signature blush line. What color are you wearing? Desert Bloom or Pink Meringue?"

"It's not blush, Mama," Chenille said with a shy smile. "It's love."

"Hummph. Love's never been *any* good for my skin," Wanda said.

"I can't wait for you to meet him," Chenille said. "His name's Garnell, and he's a foreman—"

"Enough," Wanda said, holding up a hand. "Last week you were marrying a veterinarian named Drake. I'm not interested in hearing about your latest fly-by-night fellow."

She turned away from Chenille and gave Chiffon an up-and-down glance. "I see you've been busy since I've been gone."

"Well, Mama, there have been some changes in my life—" Chiffon began, her chest swelling with pride.

"I'll say," Wanda said. "It looks like you've ballooned from a size ten to a size twelve. Honestly, Chiffon, do I need to get one of those oink-oink alarms to attach to your refrigerator?"

"Mama—" Chiffon started.

"Chiffon, I hear a whine in your voice, and I'm in no mood. My flight was bumpy, the movie was trash, and they served me a steak as tough as an old wallet." Wanda pointed to the turnstile. "There's my bag. The one with the yellow ribbon tied to it. Chenille, be a peach and fetch it for me. My sciatica's flaring up."

Chenille complied, and the three of them trudged to the car with Wanda's things.

"That husband of yours should be here to help with heavy lifting. I'm sure his little tryst with that movie star is over by now," Wanda remarked. "But I suppose he's too busy lifting beer mugs or hunting down defenseless animals."

"That's what I've been trying to tell you," Chiffon said. "I kicked Lonnie out of the house. We're going to get a divorce."

Wanda stopped in her tracks and dramatically flung her hand to her forehead. "God Almighty, Chiffon!" she said. "Would you not dump all of your problems at my feet the second I get back home?"

Chiffon shrunk back. "I don't understand. You've always complained about Lonnie. I thought you would be pleased that—"

"*Pleased?*" Wanda said in a dumbfounded voice. "What's pleasing about a daughter who's managed to lose a job *and* a husband in the course of a couple of months? Lonnie might have been a loser, but at least he kept a roof over your head."

"Mama, Chiffon has a job," Chenille interjected. "She's going to be a photographer for the *Crier.*"

"Photographer. Sounds more like a hobby than a job. Listen, girls, why don't the two of you just quit chattering. It's been a long day, and I need peace and quiet."

"Okay, Mama," Chiffon said. "You'll have all the peace and quiet you need." She dropped Wanda's carry-on bag on the sidewalk.

"What now?" Wanda snapped.

"Chenille, put down Mama's suitcase," Chiffon said. Chenille shot her sister a perplexed look but did as she was told.

"Mama, you can catch yourself a cab home," Chiffon said. "Cabbies are generally very quiet, 'specially the ones who don't speak English."

"You're just going to leave me here?" Wanda said in disbelief.

"Yes, Mama, I am," Chiffon said.

"What about you, Chenille? Surely you're not going to abandon your mama?" Wanda asked.

Chenille nodded. "I stick with my baby sister."

Wanda's face turned red with outrage. "I cannot believe this. What wicked daughters I've spawned! If you leave me here alone, I'll never speak to either of you again."

"That's fine," Chiffon said calmly. "Because we don't want to talk with you unless you can give us the respect we deserve. Right, Chenille?"

"That's right," Chenille said with a definitive nod.

Wanda stood in openmouthed shock. It was the first time Chiffon could ever remember her mother at a loss for words.

The two sisters hurried off to Chiffon's car before Wanda had the chance to recover her venom.

"You did it, Chiffon." Chenille grasped her sister's wrist. "You stood up to Mama."

"I know," Chiffon said with a smile. "She's had it coming for a long while." She put a hand to her mouth to suppress a snigger. "This time I didn't even need the tiara."

People in glass houses

shouldn't walk around naked.

Quote of the day in the *Cayboo Creek Crier*

CHAPTER THIRTY-FIVE

Birdie shuffled her index cards on the podium at
the Senior Center and looked out at the sea of people milling
about the room. Reverend Hozey was curiously absent, but
many of his congregation were among the crowd. It was standing room only for the unveiling of the calendar, and Attalee,
who was working the door, had to turn some folks away.

Birdie tapped the microphone with her index finger. "Test,
test," she said quietly, until it quit squealing.

Mavis, who was in charge of the P.A. system, gave her a
thumbs-up.

"Ladies and gentlemen, if I may have your attention,

please," Birdie said. The room gradually settled down into a soft murmur.

"Thank you," she said. "I hope you've enjoyed tonight's refreshments. I'd like to thank Boomer's Butcher Shop for providing the pigs-in-a-blanket and meatball appetizers, as well as Jewel Turner at the Chat 'N' Chew for the lemonade and cookies. Thanks also to Dun Woo of the House of Noodles for being our deejay for the evening's event."

Dun Woo, who was in the back of the room, bowed nattily at the waist. He'd been playing teaser songs for the last hour, such as "Ladies Night" and "Baby Got Back."

"And now the moment we've all been waiting for," Birdie said, pausing dramatically. "Tonight is a very special night in the history of the Senior Center. The fundraising committee has come up with an unusual and, some might say, daring—"

Darla Garvey, the Baptist choir leader, popped up from her chair and plucked a tuning fork. A low hum vibrated throughout the room.

"Darla, what in the world —?" Birdie began.

A chorus of voices interrupted her. They started softly and gradually gained momentum.

"Your calendar is scum. Your calendar is scum," the voices sang to the tune of "We Shall Overcome."

"Stop this singing at once," Birdie pleaded. "We need to get on with our program."

At that moment, Reverend Hozey, wearing his usual uniform of a dark pin-striped suit and a homburg hat, burst through the door. Attalee tried to stop him, but he barreled past her.

"Brothers and sisters," he bellowed as he planted himself in the front of the room. "A blight has infected our fair town. A moral turpitude of smut and filth. One that threatens our young, our old, and our sense of decency. This obscenity is masquerading as an act of charity, a way to raise money for the elderly members of our community. But do not be fooled, this so-called fundraiser has Satan's fingerprints all over it."

"Hold your tater, preacher," Attalee said as she took a step in his direction. "You got it all wrong. There ain't nothing—"

"Hush, harlot!" Reverend Hozey snapped. He continued to address the crowd. "Brothers and sisters, if you support this vileness, you'll be aligning yourself with Beelzebub. I urge you to turn your backs—"

"Listen here, smarty-pants, you're making a big mistake," Attalee said, standing nose-to-nose with him. "Our calendar is pure as freshly fallen snow."

Reverend Hozey leveled a finger at her. "Do not listen to this woman. She's in cahoots with the devil."

"All right, now," Attalee said. "You asked for it." She started unbuttoning the front of her dress.

Reverend Hozey stared at her in horror. "What are you doing?" he sputtered.

She undid the last button and held the dress together with her fingers.

"Are you ready for an eyeful, Preacher?" she challenged.

Reverend Hozey covered his face with his hands and shrank back from Attalee. "This is an abomination. Clothe yourself, sister, or face the wrath of God."

"I've been on God's bad side before," Attalee said. "Go on, take a gander."

The audience held its breath as Attalee flung open her dress for all to see.

A titter of nervous laughter filled the room, reaching a crescendo and exploding with full-force hilarity.

Reverend Hozey parted his fingers to peek at Attalee. She wore a bright red union suit.

His jaw dropped open. "What's the meaning of this?"

"I would have told you if you'd gotten your head out of Hades and listened for a minute," Attalee said. "This is what me and the other Bottom Dollar Girls are wearing in the calendar. We didn't have the gumption to strip to our birthday suits, so we all wore long johns instead. Mavis stocks a heap of them at the Bottom Dollar Emporium."

She twitched her hips through the room as if strutting down a catwalk. "For you fellows who are interested, I'm featured in January, May, and October. And, by gum, I still have some snap in my garter belt."

Dooley, who was sitting in the front row, let loose with an appreciative whistle. "I'm getting a calendar for every room in my house," he said with a flash of his dentures.

Attalee winked at him and continued, "The calendar is only ten bucks, so get your wallets out. The money goes to the Senior Center, so they can quit watering down the Metamucil."

"Actually, we have brochures outlining the proposed plans for the Senior Center," Birdie said over the microphone. "And there are people posted throughout the room with calendars and change boxes. We're pleased to take cash or a personal check."

Reverend Hozey picked up one of the calendars from the podium and leafed through it.

"I was wrong," he said, blushing deeply. "This calendar is

about as racy as the *Farmer's Almanac*." He pulled out his wallet and opened it. "I'll take two. One for me and one for the missus."

"Thank you, Reverend Hozey," Birdie said, clapping her hands.

. . .

An hour later, after everyone but the Bottom Dollar Girls had left, Mrs. Tobias counted the bills they'd received while Elizabeth added up the checks with a calculator.

"I think by the time we're done, we'll have taken in almost three thousand dollars," Elizabeth said triumphantly. "That's ten times the amount we would have gotten at a bake sale. And that's just the beginning. We're selling the calendar all around town."

"Beats the heck out of peddling brownies," Attalee said as she fanned herself with a twenty-dollar bill.

Chenille and Chiffon were clearing the tables of discarded cups and paper plates.

"I think that's the last of it," Chenille said as she dropped a stack of debris into a large plastic trash can.

"I saw Lonnie here this evening," Mavis said. "He bought a calendar."

"I know," Chiffon said, wearily parking her bottom into a chair. "He calls the house constantly and follows me all around town. Yesterday I photographed the mayor in front of City Hall, and who did I see but Lonnie, rustling in the bushes."

"Did you notice the photo in this morning's *Crier*?" Birdie asked. "Hizzonor looked like a true statesman."

"The mayor liked his picture so much, he wants me to take photos of his family," Chiffon said. "I bought some top-of-the-line photography equipment after I took back Lonnie's pool table, so I'm ready to start my sideline business."

"I'm so proud of you!" Chenille said, slipping an arm around her sister's waist. "You're doing work you love, and you've left behind that poor excuse of a husband."

"We're all proud of you, Chiffon," Elizabeth said, lifting her cup of lemonade in a toast. Those who still had drinks raised their cups and made murmurs of agreement.

"Thank you," Chiffon said gratefully. Although she was exhausted from the day's activities, it was a pleasant sort of fatigue, born from work that she'd truly enjoyed.

. . .

Later the two sisters drove back to Chiffon's house to relieve the babysitter.

"Everyone's asleep and I just took the dog out in the yard," said Brittany, a freckle-faced fourteen-year-old who lived two doors down from Chiffon. "Did you know the Oscars are on tonight? I was watching it on TV. Nicolas Cage just won for Best Supporting Actor. I'm going to rush home for the Best Actress award."

"I'd forgotten that," Chiffon said, counting out some bills in the girl's upturned palm. "Did you let the answering machine get the calls?"

"Sure did, Mrs. Butrell," Brittany said with a shake of her auburn ponytail. "I followed your instructions to the letter."

"I was afraid my ex-husband might call and make a nuisance of himself," Chiffon said. "Turned out he decided to do it in person. Thanks so much, Brittany. Oh, and by the way, from now on, instead of calling me Mrs. Butrell, call me Ms. Grace."

After Brittany left, Chenille grinned at her sister. "I am

woman, hear me roar," she said teasingly. "You're going back to your maiden name? Good for you!"

"I have always hated the name Butrell," Chiffon said as she dropped her car keys into a glass ashtray. "And I want a fresh start. I've even considered selling the house if I get it in the divorce settlement, which I'm sure I will, considering how public Lonnie's adultery was. Maybe you and I could rent a place together? That is, if you aren't going to run off and elope with Garnell."

"Oh, that Garnell!" Chenille said, sighing contentedly at the mention of his name. "He's such a sweetie. Did you know he bought ten calendars? That was more than anyone else. But I don't think we'll be running off to a wedding chapel anytime soon. I'm savoring our courtship. After all, I've never had one before. So, if you want, I'd love to share a place with you."

"Great!" Chiffon said happily. "And now that Lonnie's gone for good, why don't I move the baby into my room and you take the nursery?"

"Are you sure? It would save me looking for a place to stay in the meantime."

"It's settled. I'll start getting that room cleared out tomorrow." Chiffon walked to the end table and mashed the blinking red button on the answering machine.

"Girls, are you there?" It was Wanda's voice on the machine. "This is Mummy. Pick up the phone if you're home."

"Mummy?" Chiffon said in a puzzled voice. Chenille shrugged.

"Listen, girls," Wanda continued. "I thought it might be fun to drive to the Augusta Mall sometime next week. We could have lunch in the food court, throw change in the fountain, or maybe poke around in JCPenney. Call me and let me know."

"The olive branch has been extended," Chenille said. "Augusta Mall used to be our favorite destination when we were in high school."

"She's lonely," Chiffon said, deleting the message. "We're the only people who put up with her. But I promise, nothing's changed with her. As soon as we get to the mall, she'll be saying, 'Chiffon Amber, march right past Cinnabon. Do you know how many grams of saturated fat are in those rolls?'"

"True," Chenille said. "And when we get to Penney's she'll criticize all the clothes I try on."

The two sisters sat in silence.

"I suppose I should be grateful that she doesn't want me to blow up to the size of the Hindenburg," Chiffon said finally, rolling her eyes and looking at the ceiling. "Maybe that's just her way of loving us. Even if it *is* twisted."

"You'll never allow her to go too far again. That's the important thing." Chenille settled herself on the couch and pointed the remote at the television set.

"I'll call her tomorrow," Chiffon said, plopping down next to her sister.

Chenille channel-surfed through a Power Juicer infomercial, a rerun of *Bewitched*, and a weeping evangelist. She paused on Catherine Zeta-Jones flirting with Billy Crystal.

"Do you want to watch?" she said. "Jay-Li's up for the Oscar."

"What the heck," Chiffon said, leaning back into the cushions. "It could be kind of fun. You should hear some of the dirt Lonnie told me about her."

"Bring it on," Chenille said, leaning in closer.

"First of all, she has a person called a colon hydrotherapist on staff. She's paid to flush fifteen gallons of water through Jay-Li's insides."

Chenille grimaced. "You're kidding!"

"And once she threw a temper tantrum in her private jet just because her manicurist forgot to bring the cuticle cream. The pilot had to turn around."

"Oh my," Chenille breathed. "Speak of the devil. Here it comes, the award for Best Actress." Russell Crowe stepped up to make the presentation.

Before the winner was announced, the camera panned on the faces of the nominees. Janie-Lynn gripped the arm of her seat, her hand sheathed in a long white glove. Even in her nervousness, she sparkled like a jewel.

"And the winner is," said Russell Crowe, with a distinct Aussie accent, "Janie-Lynn Lauren for *The Winsome Whistleblower.*"

Janie-Lynn broke into a spontaneous grin. She glided to the stage in a strapless gold gown, looking like a sparkling flute of champagne. Once she was at the podium, her hands trembled as she gripped the statuette to her chest. The names of the people she wanted to thank came out in a babbling rush as if she were reciting a tongue twister. Then she paused for a moment, as a pearl-like tear skimmed her creamy cheek. In a sad little-girl voice, she said, "I'd also like to thank the dearest man in the world, Lonnie Butrell." She lifted the statuette with a long pale arm. "This one's for you, baby."

"Oh my Lord," Chenille said with a gasp. "Did you hear that?"

Chiffon stared at the television set, stupefied. "She's got the Lonnie bug, and she's got it bad."

An ALLTEL commercial quickly replaced Jay-Li's simpering visage.

"I almost feel sorry for her," Chiffon said, clicking off the TV. "I know what it's like to have your heart held hostage."

Moments later the phone rang, and Chiffon glanced at her watch. "How much do you want to bet it's Lonnie? Probably wants to gloat about having heard his name on national television."

"What do you want now?" Chiffon demanded as she answered the phone.

The line was silent. Then a barely audible voice said, "Is Lonnie there?"

"Jay-Li, is that you?" Chiffon asked.

"Yes." Her voice was a broken, jagged thing, lacking all the confidence of previous encounters. "I'm sorry to be calling so late, Chiffon, but I just wanted to talk to him. Just for a second. Did he see the show?"

"*I* saw it. You just won the Oscar. Congratulations."

"Yes, I'm backstage now. Would you please let me speak with him?"

"He's not here, Jay-Li," Chiffon said, cupping the mouthpiece close to her lips. "He doesn't live here anymore. We're getting a divorce."

"Because of me?"

Chiffon shook her head. "Nope. Not really. You were just one indignity among a heap of others."

"How did you do it? How could you leave him?" Her voice came out as a desperate squeak. "He's all I can think about. I've tried everything to forget him. I practically live at my analyst's office, a Scientologist has cleared me, and I've had my aura purified. Nothing works. Not even winning the Oscar has distracted me."

"You ever won any beauty pageants?" Chiffon asked.

"Beauty pageants? What does that have to do with—"

"Hear me out. A gorgeous woman like you is bound to have a pageant or two in her past."

There was a pause on the other end. "I was crowned Miss Mung Bean," Jay-Li said finally. "But that was years ago."

"Miss Mung Bean? What kind of title is that?"

"The kind they give to girls growing up in small towns in Southern California," Jay-Li said stridently.

"The title doesn't matter, so long as they gave you a tiara and you kept it," Chiffon said.

"Oh, hello, Harrison," Jay-Li said, addressing someone on her end. "Thank you so much. Yes. I *am* delighted. And give my love to Calista." She came back to the phone. "I'm sorry. You were saying?"

"Get the tiara, put it on your head, and remember what it was like to be a queen. A queen has no use for a man who treats her like mud on his shoes." Chiffon caught the eye of her sister, who was listening and winked.

"A queen knows she deserves better," she continued. "Try it yourself, and see if it doesn't work." She set down the phone and went to join Chenille on the couch.

"That was sweet of you," Chenille said. "Considering how horribly she treated you."

Chiffon yawned. "Lonnie's the kind of man who makes women behave badly. I ought to know." She patted her stomach. "I'm getting kind of hungry. Any of those carob cookies around? The yogurt-covered ones aren't half bad."

"No, I threw them out," Chenille said. "I've lost my taste for them." A guilty look crossed her face. "I do, however, know the location of a secret stash of gummy bears."

"*What?*"

"One night I couldn't find anything to eat, and there they were in the pantry, so cute, so pudgy." She hung her head. "I'm afraid I've grown somewhat dependent on them."

"What about elevated blood sugar, rotting teeth, and all that other stuff?"

Chenille shrugged. "*C'est la vie?*"

"Well, don't just sit there talking pig latin. Bring them on."

Chenille scurried off and returned, victorious. She handed the bag to her sister, who pried it open with her teeth.

"I guess I'll have to fight you for the red ones," Chiffon remarked.

"Actually, I prefer the green ones," Chenille said, holding out her hand.

"What?" Chiffon poured candy into her sister's palm. "Nobody likes the green ones. It's not even natural."

Chenille daintily nibbled on a bear. "I guess that makes me one of a kind."

Chiffon neatly severed a red bear in half with her teeth and smiled warmly at her sister. "Yes, it certainly does."

ACKNOWLEDGMENTS

Much gratitude goes to the following people: Edward Gillespie, webmaster, fan club, and fabulous father, all rolled into one; Magda Newland, mother extraordinaire; my husband, David Neches; the Red Room Writers, who include Gretchen Hummel, Renee Mackenzie, Kyle Steele, Rhonda Jones, Nancy Clements, and Steve Fox; my editor, the marvelous, inimitable Denise Roy, as well as her assistant, Christina Richardson; friend and road warrior Michele Childs; wonderful Simon & Schuster publicist Rebecca Davis and her assistant, Alexis Saarela, and my savvy agent, Jenny Bent. Thanks also to the devastating Dixie Divas: Julie Cannon, Jackie Miles, and Patricia Sprinkle.

Supportive friends and family include Judy Gillespie, Lynda and Stephen Brett, Brandon, Tracy, and Chris Skelton, Tim and Ken Gillespie, Harriet Speer, Sandra Gurley, David Vantrease, Melinda Murphy, and Collin White.